D1042235

Lu Wenfu

The Gourmet
and other stories of
Modern China

readers international

Published in English by Readers International Inc., and Readers International, London. Editorial inquiries to London office at 8 Strathray Gardens, London NW3 4NY England. US/Canadian inquiries to Subscriber Service Department, P.O. Box 959, Columbia LA 71418-0959 USA.

The editors gratefully acknowledge the advice, translation and editorial assistance of Judith Burrows, William Jenner and Beth McKillop.

Front cover: *Chrysanthemum and Wine* by Qi Baishi (1863-1957).
Back cover: *The Reader*, detail from letter paper by the Ten Bamboo Studio (mid-17th century).

Design by Jan Brychta
Typesetting by Grassroots Typeset, London N3
Printed and bound in Great Britain by Richard Clay Ltd, Bungay, Suffolk

ISBN 0-930523-38-5 Hardcover
ISBN 0-930523-39-3 Paperback

Contents

Introduction:
A Writer's Life

NO MATTER how you look at it, writing is a hard profession. Writers are forever torturing themselves. They constantly overrate their own abilities and toil away, burning their hearts' blood to emit a feeble light. Seldom content, seldom composed, they drive themselves relentlessly, anxieties outweighing consolations, experiencing extreme emotions that breed destruction.

I had many aspirations when I was young, but none of them was to become a writer. This isn't to say that I saw it as a bad profession. On the contrary, I admired people who could write books—if they weren't actually gods, then they inhabited the same terrain. When I was seven I began to study the works of Confucius, and even my teacher bowed before the sage's tablet.

Imagination needs inducement and mine was a great river—the Yangtse. I was born on March 23, 1928 in a small village on its north bank. The river was only two hundred metres from my house and every day I was awakened and lulled to sleep by the sound of its rolling waves. Every day I sat gazing out from the dyke, watching boats heave into view on the horizon and then disappear slowly again into the distance. This aroused a wonder about what the world was really like. But I couldn't quite imagine. Looking eastwards there was water and sky, to the west sky and water, a vast blank expanse which couldn't fully nurture my daydreams.

When literature came into my life, it gave my imagination food to grow. Here were monsters and fairies, then love and friendship, happiness and tears, dastardly deeds and noble acts, robbery and right-eousness. I was totally bewitched and wanted to experience everything myself. But none of these things happened in my village, nor in the small county town where I went to school. The most distant settings were faraway lands, the closest Shanghai, Nanjing and Suzhou. Suzhou I could get to—my aunt had a shop there.

In late spring of 1944, I arrived in Suzhou wear-ing a hat and long gown. This city, famed as a paradise on earth, was even more beautiful than I had imagined. In history and ancient poetry it was the source of all kinds of wonderful stories. In a way, I seemed to have been here before. The young man who had toured the world in his imagination had found his resting place. I spent three years there at secondary school and have loved the city ever since.

At the end of that three years I realized Suzhou was like a lake with a lot of dirt beneath its clear sur-face. A city of beautiful women, but too many were content to ride in rickshaws pulled by emaciated, gasp-ing old men. In those years of Kuomintang corruption, Suzhou's lovely exterior could no longer hide its peo-ple's sufferings. My interest and imagination turned to society, to fighting for a better social system so that its people could live in a real paradise.

After graduation, I didn't go to college and left instead to join the guerrilla forces. But before I had fought a single battle, the Kuomintang collapsed. I went back to Suzhou with the army and worked as a jour-nalist on the *Suzhou Daily* for eight years, during which time our country made great progress. I warmly praised the new order in reports, articles and commentaries. But this kind of journalism didn't satisfy me, for it was based purely on fact and made me feel as if I had something stuck in my throat. I decided to try my hand at writing stories. Though based on real life, they could still be fictitious. Imagination could bring an artistic perfection to fact. By this time I no longer considered writers sages, for a writer and a journalist were not that different. I was twenty-five then, and fairly quick off the mark. To be honest, I thought of writing fiction partly to praise the new society, partly for the fun of it and partly to gain the limelight. It certainly never occurred to me that writing could turn out to be a dangerous game.

I worked morning till night for over a month writing a story which I sent to the *Literary Monthly* in Shanghai. This first attempt wasn't accepted, but the kind editor wrote a three-page letter saying that my writing showed promise and encouraging me to continue. I liked compliments in those days (now I'm rather wary of them) and was spurred by this editor's opinion to make another attempt. My next story, "Honour", was indeed published in the *Literary Monthly* and was accompanied by a complimentary review. There weren't that many short-story writers then, and this piece turned me into a writer and a member of the East China branch of the Chinese Writers' Association. I went to its first national conference of young writers in Beijing and met a lot of the people who made their names in the fifties and are now quite distinguished. After that I couldn't stop. I published another story, "Deep Within a Lane", which caused a sensation because most stories then were about war production, model workers and heroism, while this was about the life and love of a prostitute, about humanism, and was written in fine language. In the contemporary jargon, it was full of petty bourgeois sentiment. In the spring of 1957, when a professional writers' group was established under the Jiangsu branch of the Federation of Literary and Art Circles, it recruited people who had made some headway in literature in the provinces. I was no longer a journalist and became a professional writer in Nanjing.

It had never really occurred to me that I would be a professional writer, but now I had to give the idea some consideration: what was it that a writer actually did, what were his responsibilities towards society, what should he write and how? With me were Gao Xiaosheng, the late Fang Zhi, Ai Xuan, Ye Zhicheng, Mei Rukai and Chen Chunnian. We put our heads together and decided that literature ought not only to praise, it should intrude on life in all its aspects and should use creative methods other than socialist realism. It should be about about people and should look at the course of human events rather than be about political policies and movements. We also felt that excessive class struggle had already destroyed normal human relationships and shattered the fabric of our social life. These views—acceptable now—were outrageous twenty-eight years ago. Yet we not only stated them verbally, we decided to publish a magazine called *Explorers* to realize our views through art. We wrote a foreword expounding our ideas, but before the magazine was published the 1957 anti-Rightist movement began. Calamity befell us. We became an "anti-Party clique" and were criticized, struggled against, asked to examine our thinking and sent out of Nanjing. Chen was sent to a labour farm; Gao, back to his village; Ai, to work in an orchard in the Western Hills; Fang and Ye, to a steel mill. I was ordered to return to Suzhou to be an apprentice in a machine plant. None of us came out to the good. This was the "Explorers Incident", notorious in Chinese cultural circles in the fifties. After less than half a year of the writer's life, I tumbled right down into the abyss.

I worked at a lathe for two years, during which time I genuinely learned a great deal from my fellow workers. Here were human beings whose hard but also creative work was unsung. There was a lot for intellectuals to learn from. In those days, life was not easy for a Rightist or an anti-Party element; if you saw a friend you didn't dare acknowledge one another. But workers didn't pay attention to that sort of thing, and provided you were honest and hardworking, they befriended you and secretly sympathized with you. They praised my work and I even won several prizes, including a track suit and a large enamel basin. Good fortune hadn't entirely forsaken me in my disaster. Yet this good fortune harboured misfortune too. Who could define what was good and what was bad...?

In the summer of 1960, after three years of natural disasters, an economic readjustment took place and the cultural world came back to life. A professional writing group was set up again in Jiangsu Province. Since my work at the factory had been outstanding enough to indicate that my reformation had been successful, I was transferred to Nanjing to be a professional writer again. My wits were sharper this time. I took care and knew my place. But it was hard to write when class struggle was everything. Heroes were robust giants, three or four times bigger than ordinary people. I couldn't really fall in with this; I was only 1.74 metres tall myself and had never seen such giants. Maybe they existed up in heaven, but I had never been up there, even on a plane. So I wrote about ordinary labourers, about their work and their outlook. Using my two years or more in the factory, I broke fresh ground in my writing and was quite prolific. This once again attracted attention and praise in the literary world. Wasn't that wonderful? Wait.

In 1964 when the economy picked up a bit, class

struggle began again. Writers and artists became more tense and writing was difficult. Being anxious, the heads of the Writers' Association convened a meeting in Beijing to discuss which approaches to literature were most suitable. The meeting was attended by Mao Dun and other famous writers and literary theoreticians. I was present too. Mao Dun expressed interest in my stories, saying that they indicated a promising future. But the review he then published in the *Literary Gazette* couldn't have come at a worse time, for literature and art were being hounded for their revisionist tendencies. And who was Lu Wenfu? On investigation I was discovered to be one of the 1957 "Explorers"—an anti-Party element. The re-appearance of such a person on the literary scene was itself a proof of class struggle. I had to be denounced.

This time I really got it. The attacks were much more severe than in 1957 and went on for six months. The newspapers carried condemnations. Two whole pages in a Jiangsu paper were devoted to long diatribes about me. I was totally bewildered. It seemed only the day before I had been praised for my writing and now I was suddenly accused of being anti-Party and anti-socialist. Was this reasonable? Of course, those who criticized me (they were only carrying out orders) gave their reasons, claiming that I depicted mediocre characters, that I talked about the dark side of society and about humanism instead of class struggle, and that I still clung to my views as an "explorer". My new errors as well as my old 1957 ones were jointly denounced. At first they couldn't convince me I was in the wrong but later, overcome by despair, I almost threw myself off the Linggu Temple. In the end I didn't, stopped by a desire to see what would happen. I couldn't write any more, nor did I want to. I only wanted to watch.

So in the summer of 1965 I was kicked out of the

literary world again, back to Suzhou where I became a mechanic in a cotton mill. I didn't read or write. I just drank half a bottle of wine a day and hummed the *Song of Lake Baikal*, written in the days when the Chinese Red Army had been forced to retreat across the Soviet border. My tearful, hoarse voice would drive my children out of the house.

During the Cultural Revolution I had an even harder time. I was "struggled against", forced to confess my crimes and paraded through the streets with a placard around my neck. I was already numb to the pain, and only worried about when this disaster for my country would end. Every step socialism made was difficult, while destruction was so easy. When would that happy society I had dreamt of as a boy be realized?

A worker could always make a living by working. But they wouldn't even let me be a worker for long and told me to go off and be a peasant. In late 1969 my whole family was sent to the countryside. We had to leave Suzhou with five days' notice. I who had dreamt of building up that paradise was once again banished from it.

My wife and I and our two daughters went to the Yellow Seacoast, the poorest part of Jiangsu, known to the banished as the Siberia of Jiangsu. Here I built a hut and farmed for nine years. During my spare time I drank and talked with old friends who'd also been sent there. We talked about current affairs, about what we had been through and about the Marxist texts we'd read, trying to analyse our own and our country's experience. Those nine years weren't entirely wasted; I had the chance to think a lot. We believed that the Gang of Four would one day fall from power, but would it be in our lifetime?

That day finally came. Like everyone else in the country, I was excited beyond words. After a three-day drinking spree with friends, I went to hunt for my fountain pen. I had to write, but I hadn't written anything for thirteen years. Like an invalid who'd been bedridden all that time, I made my way along by clinging to the walls. I started by writing a few practice essays and playscripts and then I put my energies into writing a short story. The former editors of the revived *People's Literature* were hunting everywhere for old writers, and when they located me I had already finished a story called "Dedication". This was later published in the magazine and won an award in 1980.

My family returned to Suzhou from the coast, and at fifty I became a professional writer again. It had taken me twenty-five years, three rises and two falls to enter this unenviable profession.

For, strictly speaking, fifty was the age at which I really began to write; the preceding twenty-five were just a rehearsal and a tempering period. In the eight years since the Gang's downfall I've published numerous novellas and short stories, won four literary awards and been elected a Jiangsu provincial People's Deputy. I've also been given the title of Model Worker by the Suzhou municipality. At the fourth congress of the Chinese Writer's Association, I was elected a vice-chairman. All this has made me extremely happy, happy because Chinese intellectuals have finally emerged from their suffering and are starting to receive attention and trust.

Whenever I travel to Beijing to receive an award, I feel sad that so many of my friends aren't there. Some lost their lives, others their talents during those painful years. Because of this, I always feel I have a historic responsibility, a duty to write about all of human life and its changes. My feeble light burns so that those moving through the dark night may be consoled when they see it in the distance, and feel that they will soon reach their destination.

1985

The Gourmet and Other Stories

Chinese folk art cut-paper pattern.

The Man from a Peddlers' Family

TO COUPLE peddlers and family heritage is a bit odd. Let's just say that there is a certain Zhu Yuanda whose people from generation to generation have been engaged in peddling. During which dynasty did his family begin to peddle? It has never been established. What things did they peddle? This too can't be said for certain. All I remember is that, thirty-two years ago, the day after I moved to this lane, just after dusk, I heard the sound of a bamboo clapper approaching from a distance. The rhythm was very marked, "Duo duo duo, duo duo, di di di duo, duo duo, di di duo." Although there were only two notes, there were many variations in modulation and in the strength of the tapping. Under the cover of night it seemed as though someone were calling or relating something.

I opened the long window facing the street, and looking down I spotted a light at the end of the alley. The light wavered on the white chalk walls, whizzing along like a spirit on night patrol. Gradually it became more distinct. It was a brightly lacquered *wonton* carrying-pole. Steam was rising above the pole, while sticks of firewood burned in the stove. The carrier was Zhu Yuanda. At the time he was perhaps seventeen or eighteen, tall and thin. Beside him shuffled an old grey-haired fellow—his father. His carrying days were over. He'd very recently passed the job on to his son. Now he went on ahead striking the bamboo clapper, leading his son along the bumpy road he'd followed throughout his life to keep on selling *wonton*.

In those days I was out of work. I relied entirely on helping several overworked Chinese language teachers, correcting students' composition exercise notebooks, getting a share of "classroom chalk dust" so as to make ends meet. This was not easy work and every night I was burning the midnight oil!

The "di di, duo duo" sound of that clapper passed nightly beneath my window. It would always depart at dusk and eventually return, most often just as the Beijing opera goers were leaving the theatre.

Whoever works as I did through the long winter nights, dressed in a thin shirt, becomes frozen stiff, only his shrunken heart continuing to beat. Inside the room there is no stove, while outside the north wind cuts through the window lattice like a knife. The swirling night rain turns into ice crystals which dance on the roof tiles. After midnight the whole world becomes an icehouse. At that hour, a steaming hot bowl of *wonton* dumplings for five *fen* with which you can have extra helpings of soup and hot sauce is a powerful temptation and a delight!

Almost from the first day I became Zhu Yuanda's main customer. Later it became my habit that at the last sound of the Beijing opera gong, I would lift my eyes from the students' exercise books and wait to hear the warming sound of the clapper.

Zhu Yuanda's clapping was better than his father's. It was livelier and seemed at once both joyful and mischievous. Before long the clapper would be sounding beneath my window. "Eat, eat, come quickly and eat," it seemed to be calling. If I was a little slow, Zhu Yuanda would put down his pole and call up to me, "Mr Gao, come down and warm yourself."

I would hurry downstairs to stand by his carrying-pole, watching him fan the fire in the small oven and put the *wonton* in the pot while I listened to Zhu talk of the evening's business. He was very talkative; the words would flow in a stream, so that while you waited for your *wonton* you didn't feel at all lonely or anxious.

"Tonight's business was very good," he would invariably begin, as though sales never went poorly. "When the opera ended at least twenty people gathered around my carrying-pole. And would you believe it, there wasn't enough meat stuffing. I'm not kidding you. The last few bowls had dumplings which were only half-stuffed.... Oh! Yours I set aside specially. They're stuffed with meat." He used a brass spoon to stir the *wonton* in the pot so as to prove this to me. "See, each one is bulging with meat."

I laughed as I said, "I don't care whether they're stuffed or not, just add a few more hot peppers!"

Zhu Yuanda didn't miss his chance to add, "It's so cold. Would you like another bowl?"

"Okay. But you're sold out of meat stuffing."

Zhu laughed heartily, his eyes winking slyly. "You'd be throwing away your money selling *wonton*! In business, always say there's a limited supply of your product. Then people will snap it up. If you tell them that there's no meat filling left, then the customers will want even the pastry sheets!" Saying this he withdrew from a little cupboard an earthenware bowl of meat which he thrust before me. "See if this isn't enough for you!" He laughed, thoroughly pleased with himself.

I began to laugh myself. It was just like watching a magician gaily and deliberately giving away the tricks of his trade.

At that time I didn't think that Zhu Yuanda was doing anything dishonest or that he was putting his profits ahead of everything else. I felt that the reason I wanted to correct more exercise books and he wanted to sell more *wonton* was because our lives were so difficult. Every night he brought me a little warmth. If I was able to buy for his sake one more bowl of *wonton*, we would be helping each other out—as two fish in a drying pool splash foam on one another.

After Liberation I got a job as a cadre in an educational department. Although I was still busy, I didn't have to stay up half the night. Although my salary wasn't much, I felt it was beneath me to be having *wonton* at five *fen* a bowl. If I was returning home late from a Beijing opera, I would rather have noodles and shredded pork at fifteen *fen*—to say nothing of sitting ostentatiously in a restaurant—than to be eating tiny *wonton*, standing with hunched shoulders by the seller's stall.

Although the sound of the clapper would still pass nightly beneath my window, it lost its sense of mischief and joy with the passage of time, though it still seemed to be calling, saying something. And I rarely ran into Zhu Yuanda. When he'd return home late at night striking his clapper, I would be deep in sleep. If I did by chance catch that "duo, duo" sound, it would still bring a feeling of warmth to my sleeping, though very faint and far away.

It was probably sometime after 1958 when, being obliged to wait in line at a noodle shop, I suddenly recalled what I hadn't heard for a long time—the sound of that clapper in the dead of night. It seemed a shame, as though I was missing something. But ever since the anti-Rightist campaign, I could hardly dare to keep such attachments. I had not only to convince myself of this, but others too. Socialism required a certain uniformity. It wasn't proper to have capitalist peddlers roaming the streets late at night. I was happy for Zhu Yuanda. He'd broken free of his shackles and leapt into the torrent of the Great Leap Forward.

But things turned out differently. Zhu was no

longer beating his clapper but carrying willow wicker baskets through the streets and lanes sneakily and in a flurry. In the spring he sold red bayberries; in the autumn water chestnuts and lotus roots; in the summer it was watermelon. In the winter he would set up his stall beneath the eaves of a house and sell roasted sweet potatoes. Sometimes he would sell cabbage, soybean sprouts, live chickens, fish or shrimp. You never knew for certain what he would be selling. If someone in the courtyard had an unexpected guest, you'd hear the housewife quietly ordering her husband to "run down to Zhu Yuanda and see what he's selling". I never bought anything from him and I wouldn't allow my wife or children to go. I believed that buying his things was aiding the spontaneous rise of capitalism.

I recall that during the mid-autumn festival one year the anti-Rightist inclination campaign became particularly heated in my department. I had just been engaged in a war of words with someone with a Rightist inclination. When I reached home, the moon had already passed its zenith. The scent of osmanthus flowers was floating everywhere in the city. The moonlight was like water. It felt very strange—the struggle was so intense while all around one everything was so delicately beautiful. The world seemed out of joint.

As I was crossing a little stone bridge, I suddenly noticed Zhu Yuanda at the other end of the bridge setting up shop. One basket contained cherry-red water chestnuts, the other tender white lotus roots. I stopped immediately. I wanted to buy a few to take back with me. These are the traditional delicacies of the mid-autumn festival. I hadn't seen them for years. But I hesitated because before me wasn't a state-run fruit store, but a black market stall.

Zhu Yuanda came forward. "Comrade Gao. Why don't you buy a few to take away with you? See, they're very fresh. You can't get these at the state-run stores. They've a few but they can't compare with mine. You could hardly call theirs red water chestnuts. They'd break your teeth. They're all shrivelled up and they stink!'' He gave his basket of chestnuts a shake to show that his merchandise was as good as his words. He was as talkative as ever, still looking for ways to get his customers to buy.

But the moment I began to listen, something seemed wrong. His patter was exactly like that of the Rightists in my department. It was slandering socialism! I didn't want to enter into a "struggle" with Zhu Yuanda. But I had to say a few words to help better the man.

"You really should watch what you say in the future. You'd be wise to get out of these little business activities as soon as possible. They're the roots of capitalism and they're all to be swept away very shortly!"

He was startled. "What! They even want to arrest us peddlers?"

"They won't arrest you, but sooner or later everything that smacks of capitalism will be abolished."

He began to laugh. "Relax. It can't be destroyed. There are people who want to buy and those who want to sell. If the state-run stores won't sell things, how can you say capitalism will be abolished?"

"How can it be abolished! Chiang Kai-shek's armies of millions were swept away. What are a few little shops and stalls?" I had often used this gambit at "struggle" meetings. No one could resist its logic.

Zhu Yuanda made a sweeping bow. "Of course, Comrade Gao. Pardon my ignorance. I know nothing of the ways of the world. I'll take you as my guide from now on." Saying this, he quickly shouldered his baskets and left as though he feared I would arrest him.

As I watched him stagger away from me, I felt a

little regret. There was a taste of ashes in my mouth. Those years ago standing by his carrying-pole eating *wonton*, how could I have thought that he would be swept away? We had formed a genuine affection. As Zhu Yuanda slowly disappeared, I simply couldn't understand how this great distance had come between us.

I longed to run into Zhu again, to smile and nod my head at him, to say a few pleasant words to him to show that our friendship was still alive. Unexpectedly, it was he who came to see me. He carefully seated himself in my rattan chair and eyed the furniture approvingly.

"Comrade Gao, you're doing all right now. I can remember that year when you were sick and you asked me to bring up a bowl of *wonton* for you. All you had then was a plank bed and a broken-down desk. It was pitiful!"

I remembered this, not without some grateful laughter. But I was thinking to myself, "Why has he come to see me?" To tell the truth, ever since the anti-Rightist movement, I had become afraid of keeping contact with almost everyone, lest I stir up trouble where I would have difficulty defending myself.

But Zhu was very good at guessing your meaning from your face, so he quickly explained his reason for coming.

"Comrade Gao, I had no other choice. You're the only one I know who has a way with words. I've come to ask you to write something for me."

"Write something!" I was even more afraid of putting anything in writing.

"A self-criticism."

That was better. I could do that for him. "What are you accused of?"

"Profiteering. What else could it be!" He said this very easily as though it meant nothing to him.

I sighed, "And selling at exorbitant prices too?"

"Actually you could hardly call them exorbitant, I buy my shrimps at forty *fen* a catty and sell them at sixty. Take into account I'm up half the night running around for sixty *li*, and all I earn is two or three yuan. I know you won't like to hear this, but you earn more than I do and all you do is sit around and shoot the breeze."

This made me very uncomfortable. "How can you make a comparison like that. We serve the people. You just earn money for yourself!"

He wasn't convinced. "I don't serve the people? If I don't serve them, how is it that they have shrimps to fry?"

My goodness! This strange reasoning had to be refuted. I stood up and, jabbing my finger at him, said—"You serve the people when you sell at the proper price. It's profiteering when you sell at high prices. This is a very serious matter!"

Zhu suddenly woke up to the situation he'd gotten himself into. He was like a balloon with all the air gone out of it.

"Sure, Comrade. But you don't understand business. You don't understand prices. If you're talking about quality goods at fair prices, well, the vegetable market doesn't have any. Those list prices they hang up there are just to fool you. They're lies!"

"How dare you!..." I had learned my lesson from our last encounter so I did my best to keep myself under control, but in spite of myself I lunged forward blustering.

Zhu Yuanda immediately clasped his hands in the traditional manner of submission.

"Okay, okay. I won't say another word. Just please write the self-criticism for me."

For a moment I had him. "If you've done nothing wrong, what's there to criticize? I refuse to do it!"

Zhu grasped my sleeve; then from a pocket he pulled out a wrinkled sheet of paper.

"Don't be angry. I was mistaken. I'm a capitalist! Write what you like; dress it up a little! I've known you, old friend, since I was in my teens."

This softened me. I sat down at my desk and took up my pen. But I couldn't help asking him, "Can you guarantee that you won't break the law again?"

"I...I promise. I promise you I'll be a little smarter next time." He winked at me as slyly as he had in his youth.

I was compelled to put down my pen and say to him earnestly, "Look, you're very intelligent. You're a very capable worker and you can put up with a lot. Why don't you become a labourer or a shop assistant? Isn't that respectable work? Why do you have to slither about like a rat?"

His face darkened. He sat dumbly in the rattan chair, his arms folded across his chest. It was a while before he spat out, "I...I can't."

"Why can't you?" I drew my chair over towards him and began my analysis.

"Selfish thinking is the main cause of our trouble. It's the root of all evil. Capitalism rests on that. You have to be determined to reform. Naturally, it isn't easy to switch from doing everything for your own profit to looking after the common good. It will be a painful transition. Take us intellectuals for example; our reform is particularly painful."

He was startled. "You suffer too?"

"Painfully."

"No, no. Don't be polite. You and your wife are both cadres. You draw a hundred yuan a month. You don't have to worry about the weather. You get your salary every tenth of the month. If I could only exchange your sufferings for mine I'd be in seventh heaven!"

"Why... Why... Why don't you get a job? Workers... Cadres..." I was unprepared for his attack. I was babbling like an idiot.

"Get a job? Without knowing any of the tricks of the trade, how much money do you think I would earn in a month?"

"You'd earn about...about...about thirty or forty yuan."

Zhu jumped to his feet. "Comrade Gao, I have four children. And then there's my father and mother. Eight mouths to feed in all. What could I do with thirty or forty yuan? I'm not a despicable man, shamelessly thinking only of money, am I? You don't see my children crying from hunger. The old woman, her eyes full of tears. It cuts into your heart more painfully than a knife. I'm ... I'm ashamed of myself...." He choked back a sob and wiped away the tears running down his cheeks.

I felt as though cold water had been thrown in my face. It was as though I had been standing at the top of a high building looking out at the wide and beautiful universe when suddenly I noticed beneath me a dark swamp, destroying my lofty feelings and dirtying my beautiful picture. I didn't dare say anything more. All I could do was to erect a barrier in my mind: this was an individual and temporary problem. There was no way I could help this individual and temporary Zhu Yuanda. Nothing I could add by way of consolation. I was obliged to write a hurried and confused self-criticism and thrust it into his hands.

From then on I released my wife and children from their ban, allowing them to buy things from Zhu Yuanda. I felt that Zhu couldn't become a capitalist. If I could be counted a member of the proletariat, then how could he, being poorer and more wretched than I, be considered a capitalist? During the difficult periods when the free markets were permitted, I rejoiced for Zhu Yuanda. At that moment I knew for certain that he couldn't be a capitalist. But right afterwards there was a movement to adhere to the principles of class struggle. Then I would be confused. He really was a capitalist! I was in a terrible muddle. And then a thunderclap split the earth. The bugles of the Cultural Revolution were sounded, announcing the end of all capitalism.

It was altogether unjust. Now it was my turn to be publicly criticised and denounced because I believed that one should work hard for one's monthly salary, not always be spouting jargon, and that each person must make up his own mind. This had become "pushing an extremely reactionary capitalist line". I was angry. Fine. From now on I would be indistinguishable from the masses. I would be like everyone else.

I mingled with the crowds. I read the wall posters, watched the searches and seizures, the public denunciations and parading the accused through the streets. The more I saw of this the more alarmed I grew.

This was no way to live. In the back lanes it was a little more peaceful. There life flowed on like a river. So every day I avoided the big streets and chose instead the byways.

Little by little the big-character wall posters began to appear there too. But they weren't very striking. The paper was rather small and the characters were all higgledy-piggledy. It cost so much effort to read these posters that one paid little attention to them. Later when I did look more closely I realized how odd their contents were. No mention of the usual "reactionary capitalist line" or "cruel suppression". They were quite down to earth. Who had beaten whom? Who had thrown dirty water into so-and-so's courtyard? Who had had a child out of wedlock and with whom? Who was having a love affair with whom? They employed the most spiteful language, larded with terms like "ruthless" and "shameful".... My heart sank as I read them. It was like watching people pulling at one another's hair and thrashing each other. And it was for nothing. Sooner or later there would be a verdict on the political questions, but how could all this feuding ever be settled? I had no appetite to continue reading. I turned and started east, passing in front of Zhu Yuanda's door.

It was wide open. There wasn't a rear window so the interior of the main room was dimly lit. I was suddenly given a terrible start. Standing on a bench in the poorly lit room was Zhu Yuanda, his arms hanging at his sides, his head lowered as though he were suspended there. His head was half shaved, his left cheek a dark purple, his eye above swollen to the size of a walnut. Next to the door had been stuck up a sheet of white paper on which was written, "Evil Den of Capitalism—Zhu Yuanda must bow his head and admit to his crimes! He has twenty-four hours to turn over the offending tools!"

He didn't notice me. I didn't dare watch him any longer because I didn't know to whom he was obliged to confess his crimes. Was it to me? Although I hadn't the skill to mend the heavens, I felt a twinge of conscience.

I skipped quickly passed Zhu's house. I looked about again and noticed the white sheets of paper next to the doorways of the flatbread seller, the hot water hawker, the itinerant barber and the cobbler. The contents of the texts were the same and they all bore the signature, "Combat Unit to Smash Dens of Evil". I felt that something terrible was in the air—that Zhu Yuanda had landed himself in a dreadful fix. If the Cultural Revolution was bent on digging away all the soil which nurtured capitalism, then Zhu Yuanda was rooted directly in its path.

My fears were confirmed. Twenty-four hours later along came the "evil den smashers". Some were carrying iron clubs. Others, like wandering knights of old, had at their waists great shining knives with pieces of red silk tied at the handles. The children of the lane followed closely at their heels shouting, "House search! Come and watch the house search!"

I hesitated a long while upstairs. Should I go and watch or not? According to the self-protective "principles" of the times, it was best not to get involved in questions of right and wrong. But I had to take a look. They were going to a poor peddler's house—what could they confiscate there?

By the time I arrived the combat unit had already gone into action. This wasn't like the search and seizure of a cadre's home or an intellectual's. When they searched those places the emphasis would be on the "four olds"—documents, letters, diaries, manuscripts. The work would be done under the guise of a solemn mission. And those whose homes were being searched would stand silently to one side, sadly and indignantly watching the work of a lifetime, precious keepsakes, the wisdom of mankind all go up in smoke.

But the search and seizure at Zhu Yuanda's house was altogether different. It was absolutely terrifying. Even from a distance you could hear the cries and the wailing, the sound of things being smashed and torn, and the shouting of morale-boosting slogans.

Zhu's house had become a battleground. Inside, the din was deafening. Outside clouds of dust were blowing. The willow wicker basket was tossed and hacked to pieces by the great knives. This was because it had been an instrument of crime. It had been used to sell chestnuts and lotus roots. Neither did the vegetable basket escape. It had been used to carry fish and shrimps. One after another, pots and basins flew out the door and were smashed to smithereens on the stone street. These things had all been used in making bean sprouts. For some unknown crime a tin bucket was battered by an iron club. Zhu's wife and children would shriek every time an item was snatched away. The wicker basket that the children clung to so desperately had kept them alive. Zhu's wife hugged the earthenware bowl. Inside were green beans she had been keeping to sell. There was a great cacophony as they fought, bleeding and rolling around on the ground. I couldn't believe my eyes. How could a noble theory produce such piracy as this!

Finally the *wonton* carrying-pole was dragged out. Zhu Yuanda was pursuing it like a madman. ''Help! Spare that!''

How well I knew that *wonton* carrying-pole. It had always provided warmth and a full stomach. It had never committed a single crime. On the contrary, it was a thing of exquisite workmanship. It was a miniature portable kitchen complete with cupboards, water tanks, wood shed, water canisters kept hot by surplus heat and storage compartments for salt, oil and spices. One could profitably study it in designing a galley for an airplane. I actually thought of walking straight over there and rescuing the priceless artifact. But I didn't have the courage. All I could do was stand and watch as the bamboo splinters flew under the blows of the great knives and the iron clubs.

Once the capitalist den was no more, it was all over. No one came and pestered Zhu Yuanda about a self-criticism. The storm passed quickly. But no one knew how he would make a living.

After dusk about three days later, I saw Zhu's wife leading along their four children. There was a length of string in each of their hands. At dawn the five of them returned one after the other. Each had a great bundle of waste paper tied to his or her back. Those accusing posters that had been posted up everywhere had been quickly blown to the four winds and were being trampled into waste paper. By picking up enough of it, you could earn four or five yuan a day. So it's true—Heaven does allow a way out! Who would have thought that those same posters that had driven men insane and others to suicide could rescue Zhu Yuanda? Life is truly a mystery!

While Zhu was nursing his wounds at home, I went to see him. He was as talkative as ever. He spoke a lot about the past. "Comrade Gao, I'm truly sorry. I should have listened to you in those days. During the Great Leap Forward my wife and I should have managed to get into factory work. You wouldn't have to worry about looking after the little ones, you just drag them to the union office and beg for help. The Communist Party isn't going to let you starve to death. Hell no! Why should I care about losing a little face? The skin off this face can hardly compare with money. Ai! I believed in myself too much. I always believed in bringing up my children by my own efforts. Things are fine now! My old woman and the children are out picking up garbage in the streets...." Zhu's words poured out of him. It was as though he wanted to sum up his entire life for me.

There was nothing I could do but give him encouragement. "Calm down. First look after yourself. Later...oh yes, the *wonton* carrying-pole was destroyed. What a shame."

At that time the newspapers were filled with the slogan, "We have two good hands. Let's not loaf about in the city!" The rumour was that this was thought up by some city dweller. So why pay heed to it? Nevertheless I watched carefully to know if cadres might be sent with their families down to the countryside. I didn't want my name to be found on such lists. So I went scurrying about, looking for army representatives and workers' propaganda teams. This silent struggle was terrifying!

Fortunately, I wasn't sent down. But Zhu Yuanda came to say goodbye, his eyes filled with tears. His entire family had been sent down to the most wretched place. It was then that I understood the meaning of "We have two good hands. Let's not loaf about in the city!" Who was it that was loafing about in the city? Of course those with no jobs. Zhu Yuanda could not be counted as having a job; he must then be in the loafing category. It was useless to try to appeal. The two of us sat in silence. He regarded me with envy, I him with shame. I could avoid disturbance. But for him there was no escape. Even if I couldn't avoid being sent down, my salary would remain the same.

Just before we parted, Zhu took something out of his bag and gave it to me. "Yesterday when I was cleaning up the mess I found this in a corner. It would be a shame if it were chopped up for firewood. I want to give it to you as a memento." As he said this he placed the bamboo clapper before me.

I received it in both hands. I studied it carefully. It was a semi-circular bamboo clapper about eight inches long. It held no secrets. But in Zhu Yuanda's palms what wonderful sounds it produced. It had been caressed by generations of hands. The sweat and oil had penetrated the wood so that it now had a deep black sheen like a bronze mirror. Zhu gave it to me perhaps because he wanted me to remember that he had lived here and that he had done a little something for others.

Zhu and his family disappeared from the lane. Their departure was noisy. There was a great beating of gongs as the banner "Glorious Household" was pasted up at their door. How could an "Evil Den" be transformed into a "Glorious Household"? So, in the twinkling of an eye, an old chicken was turned into a duck.

Four other families in the lane disappeared at the same time. One was a cadre's, while the others were the hot water hawker's, the itinerant barber's and the cobbler's. All of them loafers. From then on you had to walk a mile to get hot water; it took twenty days to get your shoes mended. The old men had to wait in the streets for a haircut. The old women would curse, "Damn those who said they were loafing in the city. Now they've gone off to the countryside to loaf. You can forget about getting hot water to drink. Old man, don't bother about getting your haircut; just keep it in a pigtail!"

I heard no news of Zhu Yuanda for eight years. It wasn't until this spring that I heard that his two sons had been called back for work and had both been assigned to a nearby factory. Later I heard that Zhu had returned. He sent a message through someone explaining he wanted to ask something from me. The moment I heard this I knew it had to be the clapper he wanted. After all, at this time everyone was talking about "social service" and the "commercial network", "hot water vendors", "*wonton* carrying-poles" and what have you. Zhu Yuanda had returned, so of course he'd be returning to his old line of work. I got the clapper out and wiped it clean. I held it in my hands. In the deep gleam of the wood it was as though I could see the kindling burning in the red earthenware stove. I thought I could hear the "duo duo" sound reverberating at the end of the alley in the dead of night. Then it seemed to pause before a lamp-lit window. Inside perhaps there was a university student, or a young worker devoted to his studies, or perhaps a weather-beaten old man. They all feel keenly how much time they've lost and how little knowledge they have stored up in them. Their efforts are not for themselves alone. Their lives, too, demand that there be others bringing them warmth and convenience. It had taken me more than twenty years to learn this elementary lesson.

It was dusk once again when Zhu Yuanda knocked at my door. My wife and he talked spiritedly as they climbed the stairs. The sound of their voices and of their footsteps was as joyful and as playful as the sound of his clapper in his younger days. Youth itself cannot last for ever, but its spirit can be recovered.

"*Aiya*! Comrade Gao. I've been back now for over a month. I've been busy finding a home and applying for a residence permit so I haven't had any time to come by and see you. And we couldn't be enjoying this day if we hadn't gotten rid of the Gang of Four!" His resounding voice and exuberant facial expression were completely out of keeping with his former self.

I was very happy. I felt that he really had managed to free himself from his awful burdens. "Sit down," I said quickly.

He took a seat in the rattan chair and took out a pack of good cigarettes. Each of us lit one up. He inhaled deeply. Then out poured the story of his eight years in the countryside. I knew too well. It had been no picnic. But as Zhu told it, it all came off sounding like a victory for him. Even though he'd sold off even the broken furniture, he'd got a good price for it. When he was finished he cast an appraising eye over my place. He shook his head disapprovingly. "It's all the same here. Why don't you make some changes?" There was a tone of contempt in his voice as he eyed my shabby furnishings.

I laughed. "Things haven't changed but the man has."

"That's obvious! If you don't change, then how can life go on?" Zhu straightened his new clothes. "Look. Haven't things really turned out well for me? My two sons are back. They're in state-run outfits. The two girls are in the country now. In collectively-owned units. Then there's my youngest—the fifth; I want to see him go to university. Four iron rice bowls and a golden one. Everything's just right. And that iron club can't smash them!'' Zhu laughed heartily. He was thoroughly at ease and pleased with himself.

I quickly put the bamboo clapper in front of him. ''You'll be taking up your pole again. Congratulations on the reopening of your business!''

Zhu rolled his eyes as though he didn't get my meaning. Then his face reddened a little. He put the clapper I'd given him aside. ''You ... you... you're kidding me!'' He was very embarrassed as if he were a new-made millionaire whose shady origins had just been exposed.

I added brightly, ''No, not at all. It's permitted to go into business for yourself, now. You're needed. The people in the lane have been asking after you.''

Zhu raised his head. ''They still expect me to work my carrying-pole?''

I thought to myself: Of course that precious work of art had been destroyed long ago. You couldn't fashion a new one overnight. ''Okay, then sell sweet potatoes. The old folk love that sort of thing. You can't get them nowadays.''

Zhu Yuanda grinned and gave me a sly wink. ''To tell the truth, the labour unit also approached me about going back to my old line. I humoured them a little. I'm working in a factory although I'm a bit unhappy with the job. Originally I'd thought of being the doorman. But they sent me to the workshop to sweep iron filings. I do a little sweeping and I get by. It's far less trouble and worry than baking sweet potatoes.'' Telling me his little joke was just like the time he thrust that earthenware bowl of meat in my face.

I didn't feel the least amused. I just sighed. ''Why? If you don't take up your carrying-pole then your son won't either. That would be a shame.''

"A shame? Where's the shame in that?" He got up and straightened himself up. "From now on I'm not taking a backseat to anyone."

"But you never did. You were serving the people."

"Still 'Serving the People'? That was petty capitalism—it was to be abolished. I nearly gave my life for that 'den of evil'!" He'd become very excited all of a sudden. His voice was trembling. He shook as he took out the pack of cigarettes. "Come, let's have another smoke. Let's not talk about all those awful things. I came here today to ask you for some review materials to help my son, the fifth one, to prepare for the university entrance exams."

I was certainly not opposed to someone going to university. I got together some mimeographed materials and put them in Zhu Yuanda's hands.

He thanked me effusively, and then said he had to be going. He asked me over to his place sometime. "Come on. Don't worry that you'll eat us out of house and home. The five iron rice bowls are refilled every month!"

The door below creaked as it closed. Distractedly I opened the large window facing the street. Was I looking for some *wonton* peddler coming with his steaming wares? Did I want to hear that "duo duo duo" sound sweeping along?... There was nothing. Just Zhu Yuanda with the mimeographs tucked under his arm, slowly disappearing into the night. I had felt disappointed, but I hadn't dared say so in front of him. In these past years I and others had hurt him. We had stifled so much spirit. In the end all anyone wants is to hold an iron rice bowl in his hands, safe from trouble and worry. Each month that rice bowl may not be all that full. And there will certainly never be enough in the pot to go around.

1979

Tang Qiaodi

ELDERLY female workers in the Tailong Cotton Mill often have the syllable *di*—an ancient term for the wife of a younger brother—in their names. Names like Qiaodi, Jindi, Fudi, Gendi, Mingdi, Zhaodi and Laidi. When first syllables ran out, some just ended up being called Adi. The original meaning of *di* was lost long ago—and these names arose from *glyphomancy*, the attempt to influence fortune through manipulating Chinese characters. *Di*, composed of the character "female" next to that representing a younger brother, has strong implications of male superiority. When your child is female but you wanted a male and cannot turn her into one, all you can do is place the character for female to the left of "brother". With names like Zhaodi and Laidi the aim is even more apparent—next time you will not bear another daughter because you have wished for (*zhao*) a little brother (*di*) or will let a little brother come (*laidi*).

These women with *di* in their names did not come from distinguished families, nor were they born into the educated elite. Their fates were all sad ones, for they came into a world of poverty and hardship, and silently went into the next world, still in poverty and hardship.

Some of them came to work in the cotton mill as "foreign mill girls" or what are now referred to as female textile workers. As far as their work is concerned the "foreign mill girls" and female textile workers do exactly the same job but there is a world of difference in their status. I used to live in a dilapidated wooden house opposite the Tailong Cotton Mill and knew how "foreign mill girls" were treated.

Whenever the market price of cotton was expected to rise suddenly, every spindle had to be put to work and Tailong Cotton Mill would put up a sign advertising for workers. Then women with *di* in their names and without connections or the wherewithal to buy "presents" would come crowding in from the surrounding countryside to stand before the mill gates. Those awaiting work would arrive quietly in the small hours. Some squatted, some stood, some coughed and some sighed. There were also some who cried; perhaps they were newly-widowed or had run away after quarrelling with their mothers-in-law. As the sky began to brighten they started getting restless, the atmosphere becoming increasingly tense as the sky grew lighter, with shouting, weeping, cursing, pushing, moving bricks around and crowding tightly together before the iron gates of the mill. Some stood on bricks, some on others' toes, any method at all to make themselves taller, because the mill would not take short workers who found it hard to reach the raw yarn at the top of the machines.

When the sun finally climbed as far as my small wooden building, the iron gates of the mill were pulled open to a roar of shouting ... and then a sudden silence fell, and no one dared move. The mill was heavily guarded from within by men armed with staves or hoses ready to thrash anyone daring to rush in. Finally someone who looked like an overseer would look around and drag in a few tall ones with good bodies and pretty faces, one by one.

Tang Qiaodi was very tall and by no means ugly, so she went to work in the mill as a child of fourteen and was twenty-three in 1949, the year China was liberated. Thus, while you could say she was still young, she was in fact already a mature worker with ten years' experience.

I am the same age as Tang Qiaodi. After graduating from a secondary teachers' school I was sent to work as a night school teacher at Tailong Cotton Mill. Although I was new as a teacher there, when I had lived opposite the mill the women working there used to shelter from the rain in my home or leave things there that they could not take into the mill, including children. So I was quite familiar with many of those called *di* and we would smile and nod on meeting each other. Naturally this included Tang Qiaodi.

Although Tang Qiaodi had been working since childhood she was not afraid of speaking in public. She had a hoarse voice, but spoke in a well-organized and lively manner. In the early years of the People's Republic there were numerous political campaigns in which the oral description of past suffering played a major role. Tang Qiaodi used to represent other old workers by speaking in public about their past hardships, reducing both those beside her on the platform and those in the audience to tears. I also wept when I heard her—those women with *di* in their names had gone from poverty and hardship into hell! Thus moved, I sought out Tang Qiaodi for an interview and wrote a long report for a newspaper. It did not occur to me that because of this Tang Qiaodi would become a celebrity, a "model" wanted everywhere to give speeches and attend meetings. Because of this I too was promoted to cultural and educational committee member, sports committee member and special reporter.

The newspaper office told me there was a need for more articles on such "models", describing not only their hardship but also covering more positive aspects, for example how they went through the process of liberation and threw themselves into the production struggle as mistresses of their own fate. I took note of this and kept a close eye on Tang Qiaodi's every action, often seeking her out for a talk or participating in her small group meetings.

Tang Qiaodi certainly had an extraordinary capacity for hard work. She was young, strong and skilful, constantly increased her production output, formed small advanced groups of workers and initiated work competitions, all with great enthusiasm and zeal. Whatever she did I wrote about and was able to publish every piece. Some people said I was making a fortune off Tang Qiaodi's back, but that was an injustice, because the money was barely enough to buy peanuts, and what's more, most of them were eaten by other people. It was not money which drove me to write, but thoughts of the time before Liberation when I used to lie reading while Tang Qiaodi and the others were sweating. So now I wanted to do whatever I could to help the working class.

Tang Qiaodi often came looking for me too. She could not read or write and often wanted me to write a reply for her to an admiring child's letter or help her compose group pledges or conditions for competitions. It was no fault of hers that she was illiterate, but a result of the old, bad days. And so, no matter how busy I was, I stopped to help her, urging as I did so, "You should come along to evening class, Qiaodi. Workers are standing up now and must have education; so if you come to the classes I promise to teach you to the best of my ability. It will take someone as intelligent as you less than two years!"

"Truly?"

"Truly!"

"Good! I'll come for sure!"

And Tang Qiaodi did indeed come, bringing with

her a new notebook and a new fountain pen, and sitting, very well-behaved, in the last row. When I saw her I was extremely pleased and taught with greater enthusiasm, projecting every word clearly and distinctly towards her.

Yet, only a few days later, when Tang Qiaodi sat down in the classroom she yawned and eventually dropped her head down on the desk and slept, needing to be shaken awake by her colleagues at the end of class.

I kept Tang Qiaodi behind and asked if I had been teaching badly, whether she had not understood something or was not interested in a particular topic.

Vaguely she replied, "No, I just wanted to sleep...."

"But that's no good! You should remember that not only did the exploiting classes squeeze you dry but they also deprived you of your right to an education. A deprivation of this nature is extremely serious because it causes ignorance among the working class and thus hinders you from ever becoming completely emancipated! You should think of...."

"I don't have the strength to think. I'm too tired." I was stunned! It was true that ever since Tang Qiaodi had increased her output she had been walking back and forth non-stop while working, covering over thirty *li* in one day's shift. And that was not like walking in the countryside, where all you need to do is to swing your arms and go forward in the fresh air, with the blue sky and white clouds above and perhaps, if you are lucky, the sound of birdsong, the fragrance of flowers and a murmuring stream. Working on shift is different, for there is no walking pure and simple but constant, noisy work, when every second of every action counts and your mind can never rest. A factory is definitely not like the countryside, with machines thundering so loudly you cannot hear the person in front of you speak. What is more, it is also stuffy and hot. After a shift is over a worker looks like a wilted vegetable. But then if she still has to go on to a small group meeting and then on to class, what strength does she have left for thinking? And I... all I could do was encourage her:

"Try to perk up a little, Qiaodi. After all, it is much better now than before Liberation when you had to work like dogs from dawn to dusk twelve hours a day!"

"You don't understand. No one was willing to work hard before Liberation. Half of those twelve hours were spent loafing."

"This...." What could be done? Suddenly I had an idea and asked her loudly, "Are you awake now?"

"Eh? Yes, I feel better after that nap."

"Alright then, open your textbook and I'll go over the lesson with you."

"From that time on I used to let Tang Qiaodi take a nap first and then keep her behind afterwards for a private lesson. She was very intelligent and made fast progress so that I was filled with hope for her, hope that she, who had been through so much, would be able to open her eyes to the brightly-coloured realm of education.

Unfortunately there were times when Tang Qiaodi was not even able to take a nap. There were many political campaigns at that time when even production would halt and evening classes hardly counted! I became a sort of general factotum at the Party committee's propaganda department, working every day on preparing meetings, arranging rooms, composing slogans and writing summaries. As a "model" Tang Qiaodi was even more actively involved in meetings and the little she had learned was soon forgotten. Nor was she the only one—all my students were reverting to their original levels. Whenever they heard there would be no class that evening it was as if they had been relieved of a heavy burden: "Oh good! Tonight we can rest!" Only a few were willing to come to the classroom. I was perturbed and went to the Party committee to object. The Party secretary was impatient with me, yet could not say my objections were invalid. "Alright then, there aren't any meetings arranged on Saturdays. You can have them for your classes."

How could I possibly put up with giving only one class a week on Saturdays? Tell me how I could possibly teach this way!

There was nothing else the Party secretary could do. "You tell *me* what to do! There will always be meetings, so you'll have to think of a solution yourself!"

The workers themselves objected to so many meetings, complaining that while the Kuomintang had been famous for too many taxes the Communists had too many meetings. Attendance fell off, and the Party secretary wanted to correct the general attitude towards meetings. Since it was difficult to criticize the working class, he picked on me instead, before a large gathering.

"There are some people who do not take meetings seriously enough, even to the extent of opposing them and stressing the importance of their own work instead and asserting their independence from the Party! Culture, culture! Can you eat culture? Were the eight million troops of the Kuomintang defeated by culture? Tang Qiaodi cannot read, but that means she can't work or give speeches? Of course, it is better to be able to read."

Everyone turned to look at me. I kept my head lowered, my brain in confusion, desperately hoping the ground would open up and swallow me.

Tang Qiaodi did not return to the evening school and thereafter always hurried past me looking rather awkward. Since I was still assigned to report on her progress I was often right behind her, listening to speeches she gave at meetings both at the mill and elsewhere. Whenever she spoke there were always people praising her, saying, "Well! It can't be easy for someone who's illiterate to speak so well. That's the working class for you!"

Tang Qiaodi also lumped illiteracy and the working class together, always starting her speeches with the words, "I am a worker and cannot read. Please forgive me if I make mistakes when I speak."

Whenever I heard these words they always made me feel uncomfortable—why was she unable to read? If she were able to read she could speak with even more depth and not just touch the surface, which also meant that at the moment my series of reports had nothing new to say and were being sent back to me.

I could not restrain myself from saying to Tang Qiaodi when someone was praising her, "Qiaodi, don't listen to this—you'd be better off finding some time for studying."

Tang Qiaodi shot me a surprised glance. "Didn't you get your fingers burned enough at that meeting?"

I blushed from head to toe and stuttered, "The Party secretary's in favour of literacy too—it's just that he doesn't want education to supplant meetings. Wait a minute...." I had thought of a solution. "How about this—if you can spare half a day on Sundays I'll give you private lessons!" I knew that she now had a boyfriend so I only suggested a half-day, leaving her the rest to spend as she wished.

Tang Qiaodi chuckled. "What a man you are! What's the point? I can't read a thing but I'm still earning eighty yuan a month!"

Perhaps she meant nothing by this but it was nonetheless a considerable blow to me. It was true. In terms of wages Tang Qiaodi was earning the same as a shift foreman, the highest level for women workers, and with extras she could receive over eighty yuan a month. I was just a trainee, on the same level as a probationary technician, earning less than half Tang Qiaodi's wages. I dared not take away half a day from her—let her spend the time with her boyfriend, for those who had suffered so greatly needed a satisfactory marriage, a happy family and people's respect, for did not these combined add up to true emancipation?

At that time the female workers at the Tailong Cotton Mill were, as they say, doing very nicely. Their wages were all up in the sixty to eighty range, nothing very startling these days, but back then things were cheap. Female workers neither drank nor smoked. They did not eat very much either—a small three-cent meal was enough. But just wait until they went into a big department store or fabric shop, their gestures and expressions caught everyone's eyes. A group of four or five, parcels under their arms, would walk down the street and everyone would know from their manner that they were from the Tailong Cotton Mill. The saying went around: "Marrying a Tailong Mill girl is like opening your own bank." These women's feeling of emancipation, their sense of glory and their enthusiasm for work were all so strong that you could almost feel the heat!

Tang Qiaodi's future husband was an experienced worker in an electricity plant. He earned more than she did and was several years older. He was a very open man but apparently had no ideas of his own and was content to follow Tang Qiaodi's lead in everything. The day they got married I bought them a small gift and went over to offer my congratulations. Their new home made my eyes bulge. An embroidered quilt, a big red wood bed, even a radio—an unusual sight in those days. They had a fourteen piece set of furniture which was far more impressive than today's suites of "forty-eight legs", and less expensive. In those days, speculators and families who had gone down in the world relied on selling their possessions to support themselves and there were loads of old furniture for sale. Who would want it? Capitalists were pretending to be poor, landlords and officials needed to sell too, and as yet cadres had not reached the stage of buying furniture.

Tang Qiaodi's marriage caused quite a stir at a time when another "model" was needed. Photographers came from the papers, the chairman of the Trade Union came to offer his congratulations and I wrote a long article entitled *Tang Qiaodi Stands Up*. This gave a detailed description of Tang Qiaodi's house and furniture and enumerated the woollen garments and lengths of cloth stored in their camphorwood chests. The inventory was to indicate Tang Qiaodi's emancipation, a symbol more attractive to women workers than any evening class.

I did not raise the issue of evening classes again and when there were no classes to teach I did odd jobs for the Party committee's propaganda department. The Party committee was pleased with me and was preparing to bring me into the Party.

But then came the early summer of 1957 when I was stupidly over-zealous. There was a slogan at that time which said, "Care for others." It had come out in the early stage of the movement to help the Party to rectify itself. The mill's way of caring for others was to make lots of cool, refreshing lentil soup and set it up outside the main entrance of the workshop so that everyone could drink some when they came off shift. When I saw the women coming off shift with clothes so damp with sweat they looked as if they had just crawled out of a river, I believed the provision of this soup marked a genuine desire to help and revealed a respect for hard work, so I suggested that the matter be publicized. It did not occur to me that the Party propaganda department would make a big fuss by moving out all the evening class desks and setting large buckets of lentil soup behind the desks and enamel mugs filled with soup on top. There was a long poster fixed along the desktops which read, "Be thankful for the generous gift of lentil soup! Give thanks to Chairman Mao and the Communist Party!" The Party secretary, the mill head, the chairman of the Trade Union and other leaders were all there, tightly gripping ladles while a group of gongbeaters and drummers banged loudly and enthusiastically off to one side.

When the women workers came off the mill floor they were stunned and dared not move forward. Furthermore, they felt embarrassed about eating in public. The Party secretary, looking stern, called out some names, "Mingdi, Laidi, come and have some soup—you'll work much better afterwards!" Mingdi and Laidi were so frightened by this attention that they hid behind the others. Only the young maintenance workers were unafraid, lifting up the enamel mugs, drinking and listening to the Party secretary as he talked; and when they had done they stretched out their arms and said, "Can I have another mug, Secretary?"

I could see things were not going well, so when I caught sight of Tang Qiaodi standing at the back of the crowd I turned and went back there to tug at her, saying, "Go and drink some, Qiaodi. You should take the lead."

Tang Qiaodi pulled her hand away and said, "Go away! Do we have to bow and scrape just for a bowl of lentil soup?"

Later I informed the Party propaganda department of these general sentiments, believing its action to have been too extreme. Giving the workers lentil soup should have been to help them, not to gain their gratitude, and the way it was done had only caused bad feeling.

Fortunately the leaders doled out soup for one day only and by the next day all the fuss and pomp had gone and it became very casual, with everyone happily drinking and hoping it would be repeated in summers to come.

In principle the matter was over and not even the head of the Party propaganda department had taken offence. Who would have guessed that disaster would strike? "The working class speaks up!" (As far as I knew, Tang Qiaodi and the others had certainly not said anything.) And I was involved too; my crime rested on that mug of lentil soup.

I was "struggled against".

"And why shouldn't you bow and scrape? Chairman Mao's generosity is higher than Heaven itself and you wouldn't be able to finish thanking him in a lifetime. You are in opposition to the Communist Party and to Chairman Mao."

I said, "I am not in opposition, it's just because Tang Qiaodi said it that I felt it was overdoing things."

"Lies! You're slandering the working class!"

Tang Qiaodi did not feel that I had slandered her in any way so she stood up and ran over to where I was being "struggled" to try and clear things up. "Don't wrong him! I did say that!"

The members of the leading anti-Rightists' group pushed Tang Qiaodi away. "Be off with you now, go back to work. You don't have any education and don't know what goes on in intellectuals' heads. You didn't mean what you said but he's got hidden motives—he's against the Party and socialism and has been all along. He wants to be independent of the Party!"

Tang Qiaodi rolled her eyes in despair and tried to clear things up but she had no real notion of all the undercurrents involved.

Now I knew the advantage of no education—

without education you cannot have any underlying motives, you cannot overrate the importance of your own job, nor would you want independence from the Party—so nothing can happen to you!

I was made a Rightist and sent to the workshop to do supervised labour. However, I still had a bone to pick with the head of the propaganda department. All these years I have worked hard for you, composing slogans, writing summaries, working late into the night whenever you wanted something the next day and then you do this to me—consign me to hell! Well, since the worst had already been done I could let off steam and say something.

I bumped into the propaganda department head in the street and tapped him on the shoulder. "People aren't made of stone you know, old friend. What did I ever do to you?"

The head blushed vividly, looked around to see if anyone else was there and then said, "You don't understand—there is a fixed quota for Rightists, and while there are lots of people working in our mill, workers can't be made Rightists. The majority of cadres come from the workers' ranks and the old staff members just eat and don't open their mouths, so we only had you intellectuals to fall back on. Anyway, you wouldn't have escaped. But to be frank with you, I didn't want to make you a Rightist. It was really hard to find someone who could use the pen for me."

When I heard this I sighed heavily. No one could be blamed but myself. When Tang Qiaodi and the others trooped into the mill before Liberation, why did you stand and watch? Why did you not follow them in?

The head saw how stunned I looked and patted me on the shoulder. "Don't be depressed. Work hard, and if there's a chance in the future I won't forget you!"

Perhaps the head did not forget me, but the chance

he spoke of did not materialize. I worked on Tang Qiaodi's shift as an auxiliary labourer until my sons had left primary school and had gone on into high school. They no longer remembered that I had once been a teacher, but only that I was a Rightist, because they had to fill in forms saying so each year. The people in the workshop certainly did not think of me as a Rightist, simply considering me a very competent auxiliary labourer, for they always saw how hard I worked—I worked like mad! Was it because there were people supervising me? No, I wanted to work hard to transform myself, to get onto the right road. I fantasized that the blood and sweat of my labour would accumulate every day, build up day by day and increase in pressure until it would suddenly shoot upwards with tremendous force and knock the hat labelling me a Rightist off my head, so that I would no longer be considered either that or an intellectual. I also dreamed of acting heroically in a fire (cotton mills catch fire easily) and being severely burned. And as I struggled to breathe, the Party secretary would come to see me and say, "Comrade, you are a true son of the working class!" I would be so moved that I would weep and not even regret dying! I used to have such fantasies before going to sleep and my tears would wet my pillow.

I always came to work early and left late, falling headlong into the fray the moment I arrived at the workshop.

Tang Qiaodi used to tell me discreetly to rest a bit and gave me all kinds of hints on how to ease up a little or save my energy. "Don't be stupid—there's no point in killing yourself!"

I was very grateful to Tang Qiaodi and admired her greatly, for while she had no education, nor did she think too hard, she always saw straight to the heart of any issue. And although I knew all this, I still continued dreaming—I could not live if I did not dream!

Tang Qiaodi did not have a fixed place of work, but in a corner of the workshop she had a small office where the women workers who found it hard going after three a.m. on the night shift would come to sit for a while. They were all so-called "little sisters", but their children were already in middle school. Tang Qiaodi often used to call me in to have a cup of tea and a chat. All those with *di* in their names always used to like talking about their youth, how full of energy they had been, how actively they had worked, how doing the night shift had been as easy as blinking, no effort at all, and how the next day they used only to need sleep in the morning and still be able to go off in the afternoon to see a Shaoxing opera! And all the while they talked they would rub their arms and yawn.

Tang Qiaodi would talk about her youth too and sometimes mention me: "Hey! Do you still want to help me study?"

"Huh! If I'd known then that you'd be sitting here chatting I'd never have let you off like that!"

Tang laughed out loud. "Luckily I was never taken in by you! There was one of us girls who went off to study at the Worker-Peasant Crash Middle School. Oh brother! My brain's no use.... What was her name ? Something *di*...."

"Gendi," prompted someone beside her.

"Right! Tong Gendi! Well, Tong Gendi became some kind of technician, but she had a hard time of it in '57. It's best just to quietly get on with your job, do a bit more if you can and if you can't, ease off a while. My two sons don't want to study and my old man's angry about it. What's he got to be angry about? Let them stay at home, do some cooking and look after their little sister. They can go out to work later and we'll have saved on their tuition fees!"

Several other "sisters" agreed. "That's right? Just

look at those people's kids who have graduated from university—their wages are nowhere!''

Tang Qiaodi swept me a glance. "Yes, just ask him sitting here!''

"Qiaodi, you earn a lot; can you spare me some?''

"Not at the moment—we've got some old debts we still haven't cleared.''

"You've got old debts?'' asked someone, disbelieving.

The person beside her affirmed this. "Yes, that's right. She bought a large house last spring with a front and a back part, two side wings and a courtyard in the middle. And even though it's so big it only cost 1,200 yuan!''

"You must have stolen it!''

"No I didn't! The owner was afraid of a reform movement against private ownership, so he wanted it off his hands, but most people didn't dare buy it for fear of stirring up trouble. I'm not scared—they won't dare reform me!'' She looked at her watch and pursed her lips at me. "Hey, Mr Literacy! Time's up! Get back to work now. Ah! It's all very well being literate, but it's the seed of disaster.''

Tang Qiaodi was absolutely correct—the disaster of education was worse than any car crash, for not only was it arbitrary but also prolonged. I shall not mention all the events of the Cultural Revolution—it was hard enough to bear dealing with investigations into reactionary slogans or a certain business of lentil soup! The suspects were always those with an education above middle school level, about forty years of age and with a presumed hatred for the Party and socialism. The last I couldn't believe of anyone but the first two marks of shame were easy to see, like lice on a scabbed head. I was put through the grinder like everyone else and could not go home because I had to confirm times, have my handwriting checked, supply an alibi and attend meetings. Tang Qiaodi did not go to meetings. When she picked up her small bag in preparation to leave, an unthinking official once cried out, "Hey, Tang Qiaodi! Why aren't you coming to the meeting!"

Tang Qiaodi tossed her head. "You're crazy! I can't read a single word and you want me to attend a meeting? Huh! Was that reactionary pamphlet written by an illiterate?"

"Oh! Yes, you go home! Go on home!"

Thus the word "illiteracy" became protective covering—a bullet-proof vest!

By contrast I was defenceless, vulnerable however I turned. In the winter of 1969 I was once more the victim of a movement to "clean up the rubbish of the city", and this time my wife and children were affected too—the whole family was sent off to the countryside.

Just before we left, Tang Qiaodi and the others came to see me, their eyes filled with tears. When they saw how miserably shabby the family was, several of them talked together and then bought my two sons a padded overcoat each and me a woollen hat, the kind old men wore. They knew how strong the winds could be in the countryside.

The propaganda department head did not come to see me, but that did not mean that he had forgotten me, just that the time for that future chance had not yet arrived. Not long after the fall of the Gang of Four he came to the village to find me, expended a great deal of effort in getting me transferred back to the mill, helped me be rehabilitated and gave me the rank of director of a vocational part-time school.

I was very moved and grateful, but was not at all enthusiastic about teaching. I felt that workers should just get on with their jobs and that not everyone needed to be an engineer or technician or whatever. There was something else that made me very sad—most of the *di* had retired, some of them having reached retirement age and others leaving early to let their children take over their jobs. Tang Qiaodi had also retired to allow her youngest daughter to take her place. Her daughter's name was Jin Yunyi, a slim and beautiful girl who also worked in the fine yarn workshop.

My teaching work was comparatively straightforward. As soon as it was evening the classroom would be filled with lights and a mass of heads, all of them young. I never saw Tang Qiaodi and the others back there again—a generation had quietly slipped by. As a teacher I felt I had not been able to do anything for them, and my heart felt rather empty. Fortunately their sons and daughters now sat before me, and thus I felt a sense of new life emerging.

Jin Yunyi studied diligently and never missed a class. When I saw her I asked after Tang Qiaodi: "Is your mother well?"

Jin Yunyi nodded.

"She doesn't object to you studying?"

Jin Yunyi was extremely startled. "Object? She'd object if I didn't come! If I didn't show up one day she'd never stop nagging me."

What! What was up with Tang Qiaodi? Had she caught this new fever for studying and told her daughter to jump on the bandwagon?

"Do you intend to be a technician or an engineer?"

"Neither. I just want to improve myself a bit."

I rarely heard a reply like this and was very interested because I wanted to understand each person's motivation for studying. Yes indeed, I should go and visit Tang Qiaodi—it had been ten years since I last saw her!

"Please take a note for me to your mother. I'd like to know when I can go to see her."

Jin Yunyi immediately waved her hand. "Oh no, please don't come—our house is much too small."

I laughed to hear such pleasantries from this child,

for I had been to her home, which had a large room at the front, three main rooms at the rear, two side wings with a purple magnolia growing in the courtyard. I did not have any classes on Saturday evening so I strolled over to Tang Qiaodi's house. It was an evening in early autumn and there was a hazy night mist in the streets. I had been along this road many times, but now I felt at a loss, out of my element.

Tang Qiaodi's main gate was ajar and in the otherwise empty main hall there were seven or eight bicycles. In the centre hung a very dim 15-watt bulb. The main rooms at the back were brightly lit and a radio-cassette recorder gave out a tune that sounded like a frog croaking. I heard the sound of people's laughter, the frog croaking and someone beating time. I called out, "Tang Qiaodi!"

There was no reaction from the main rooms but I heard Jin Yunyi's voice coming from the east side of the main hall. "Oh Mother! It's Mr Zhu, the teacher. He's here!"

I turned around to look—when I had entered I had not noticed a structure resembling an earthquake shelter to the east of the main hall. When Tang Qiaodi came out from inside, I was astonished at her appearance. Her hair had turned white, her back was bent and her face wrinkled. Around her waist was an apron—it was really hard to imagine that she had once been a distinguished and famous shift leader!

Tang Qiaodi took off her apron and dusted herself down. "Oh, Mr Zhu, you came after all. I was thinking of going with Yunyi to see you! Please, please come inside ... oh dear, there's nowhere to sit. Yunyi, go to the back and borrow a chair so that Mr Zhu can sit outside." The way she spoke was still the same, her voice hoarse and lively.

I felt rather embarrassed and did not know what had happened to her. "Your ... your husband?"

"Retired and gone off in a huff back to his old village, and if Yunyi weren't here I'd be gone too!"

"What's wrong?"

"Ah, I shouldn't bring it up. My two sons are no good—uncivilized and disobedient. When they got married they fought over dividing the house and came to blows, each of them determined to get his share. It was terrible. So in the end we let them have it all. As you see, now I live in this shed like a refugee!"

An argument suddenly erupted from the main rooms at the back—the thin voice belonged to Jin Yunyi. "Just let us borrow it for a while, we're not stealing it!"

"Borrow! You're always borrowing from us, but you won't touch Younger Brother's stuff!"

A woman retorted, "Younger Brother is a shark! Who knows where all that stuff in his home came from anyhow?"

"How rude can you get!"

"Crash!" Some glass broke.

Several people shouted out, "Okay, okay, don't argue; you should stick together. Come on, let's have some music!"

The volume of the recorder increased. Perhaps it had four speakers because the "wah-wah" noise even made the paper in the door-screens tremble!

Tang Qiaodi stamped her foot. "Come back here, Yunyi, you can't deal with people like that!"

Jin Yunyi, her face flushed, returned and spat out, "Riff-raff!"

Tang Qiaodi said impatiently, "Alright, alright! Mr Zhu isn't a stranger, please come in ... sit on the bed."

Inside the shelter there were two small beds tightly crowded together and piles of things everywhere. The only things I recognized were two camphorwood chests I had described in my article *Tang Qiaodi Stands Up.*

Tang Qiaodi saw how my glance fell on the chests and sighed, "They divided or sold everything I had but it still wasn't enough for them, so we old folk have to give them each thirty yuan a month on top of that!"

"A son doesn't support his father. His children live off their grandfather too." I quoted a saying common among old workers.

Tang Qiaodi shook her head. "No, I don't agree. I should help them out if they can't get by—I don't want to take the money into the grave with me. But they're just squandering it. Today they want to buy some kind of recorder, tomorrow they'll sell it to buy a scooter—and that's nothing more than a bike with an engine attached!"

"Then don't give them the money!"

"Don't give them money? You just try it! Without money they get up to all kinds of tricks—my eldest's been detained twice and one of these days he'll end up in prison! What a disgrace! A disgrace to the working class!" As she said all this Tang Qiaodi was scrabbling through a drawer looking for cigarettes. She passed me a crushed-looking pack. "Well, you're better off—have both your sons gone to university?"

"No, one's at university and the other's in a factory. Both of them often talk about their Aunty Tang who gave them overcoats when we got sent to the countryside."

Tang Qiaodi smiled and said to Jin Yunyi, "You see how polite other people's children are. Kids from an educated home are different!" I shook my head. "Not necessarily. Some are just as bad."

"Well of course, the fingers on a hand are all different sizes, but I do know that the parents of the kids who mix with those two precious lads of mine are all workers."

Jin Yunyi objected, "I don't want to be lumped in with them!"

"Of course you're not the same—you've had some education and go around with a book in your hand all the time; your head's always in a book."

"Education!" flared Jin Yunyi. "It's all your fault! You told them not to study, saying that an illiterate earns eighty yuan a month!"

Tang Qiaodi looked as if she had been scalded and flung out her hand. "Alright, alright, it's all my fault, completely my fault! And yet perhaps I'm not to be blamed totally. Who wouldn't have been wary, the way intellectuals were treated?"

My heart went cold, for I had never thought that Tang Qiaodi's problems could be connected to the troubles that had faced "stinking" intellectuals. Now times were changing and I had already been rehabilitated, but what of Tang Qiaodi? The propaganda department head could not help her and neither could I. All I could do was look towards the next generation and ask them to forgive and understand what we went through.

"Yunyi, you mustn't blame your mother! That's not right! Today you see me lecturing and I'm somebody, but you didn't see me in the days when I was like a lost soul."

Tang Qiaodi was not comforted by this and shook her head. "No, I was wrong. You wanted to help me study back then, but I ran away. Mr Zhu, my time's past, so please do what you can to help Yunyi—that's all I hope for!" Tang Qiaodi was crying.

I left. Tang Qiaodi escorted me to the main gate and stood under the streetlamp there, waving and wiping her tears on the edge of her apron. After walking on a bit, I turned to see the white-haired Tang Qiaodi still standing there in the hazy lamplight. Go home, Tang Qiaodi. I know you have faith in me; let me take it with me on the road before me and I will be able to go on for ever.

1980

The Boundary Wall

IN THE STORM last night something unfortunate happened: the boundary wall round the Architectural Design Institute collapsed.

This was not entirely unexpected, seeing how old it was. From the look of it, it was more than a hundred years old, and it had already fallen and been repaired a number of times. But since that wall had never been repaired properly, the result was that its thirty-odd metres bulged and buckled, here higher, there lower. It might well have collapsed at any time, let alone in last night's storm.

Once the wall was down it seemed as though the Design Institute had suddenly changed, like an old man who has had all his front teeth pulled out. When he opens his mouth there is simply a cavern with nothing at the entrance, or like a beautiful young woman suddenly transformed into a shrunken-lipped, ugly old hag. But it wasn't just that it was an eyesore; the problem was that now that the wall had come down, this peaceful office suddenly found itself directly linked to the street outside. Hordes of pedestrians and the surging tide of traffic seemed to be rushing in on the office. It was like sitting in a 3-D film feeling that those cars might actually come rolling in right over you! And with no wall to keep it out, all the uproar from the streets poured straight in through the windows, which had to be kept open in summer. People were obliged to speak much louder than before simply to make themselves heard, serious conferences were disrupted by unusual sights on the street, and study sessions got diverted to idle chat about some traffic accident. People were unsettled and lost concentration; work efficiency was low and everyone tired easily. The demand was unanimous: get the wall rebuilt fast!

Needless to say, that morning at the daily meeting which the director of the Institute always held for progress reports and exchange of ideas, the moment everyone sat down they started to talk about the boundary wall. Things didn't seem quite right since it had gone, they said: coming to work each morning they had the feeling that something was wrong, like the year there had been that earthquake. Someone put it even more ingeniously: when he had come to work that morning, he said, he had actually walked straight past the gate. Seeing the heaps of bricks lying all over the ground, he had mistaken it for the construction site next-door....

Director Wu rapped the table with his ball-point pen: "All right now, let's discuss the problem of the boundary wall. Frankly, I've known for some time that it was going to come down. It's only been lack of funds that has stopped us pulling it down and rebuilding it long ago. But it's just as well now that it's finally happened. If the old doesn't go, there's no room for the new!... So, we'll build a new one..." Director Wu took a sip of water. "But what kind of wall? That is the question. I'm no expert on construction, but I always felt that the old one was out of keeping with the character of this establishment; like a master tailor wearing a tattered gown. On principle the new wall must be original and unique, attractive and tasteful, and it must unify form and substance...I'm throwing it open for your ideas."

As far as the importance of repairing the wall went, Director Wu's introductory remarks were both overly solemn and somewhat loquacious. In fact all he'd needed to say was one sentence: "Everyone think about it—how are we going to fix the wall?" But that would never do. Work at the Design Institute could not be oversimplified.

The mention of construction invariably evoked a division into three factions: the modernists, whose special interest lay in research on modern multi-storey construction; the conservatives, who found it difficult to think of anything but classical architecture; and a vaguer grouping who would accept a *fait accompli*, but were opposed to all changes and frequently displayed tendencies of nihilism.

Although Director Wu claimed he was a mere layman when it came to construction, he did, in fact, consider himself to be far from an amateur, for he understood a great many things: for example, practical economics, what was attractive and tasteful, what was advantageous to production, convenient for everyday life, etc. How to convert ideas into blueprints was not his problem, but he couldn't neglect his role as leader and so had to rouse the two factions to a debate in which both would bring forth their construction plans. Director Wu could then select the best according to his principles and pass it on to the nihilists to unify. For the nihilists had one notable virtue: when they couldn't downright reject something, they had a great flair for effecting compromises that would leave everyone happy.

The style of leadership that could convert hostility into friendship was really very profound. Although to begin with Director Wu might seem dilatory and hesitant, equivocal and wordy, in the end he would make one feel it was a case of a wise man appearing slow-witted, and one would appreciate his prudence and reliability. Rebuilding the wall seemed a small matter, but it was nonetheless construction work, and in addition it was going to be built right across the front door, so it had to be treated seriously in order to avoid possible repercussions.

But perhaps Director Wu's opening remarks had sealed people's mouths, for the factions who should have begun skirmishing were temporarily silent, unwilling to reveal their firepower too early.

Director Wu was not worried. He turned to a young man seated in the corner and asked with a nod, "Logistics Department Head, what do you think?"

The so-called Logistics Department Head was in fact Ma Erli of the administration section. According to the principles of literature, in depicting a character, one does not necessarily have to describe his face, but in the case of Ma Erli it is essential, for he had come to grief several times in recent years precisely because of this face.

Ma Erli's face was certainly not ugly or sinister; on the contrary it was good-looking. It was a plump oval with clear white skin, rosy cheeks and dimples when he smiled. His bright black eyes were particularly lively. Not bad, eh? If he'd been a woman he could have enjoyed its benefits for a lifetime. But unfortunately his face had got its sexes mixed and found its way onto to the shoulders of a man, and the thirty-seven-year-old Ma Erli, an extremely capable and efficient administrator, had found himself with a baby face that did nothing to inspire people's confidence in his abilities. It was said he was a victor in the field of romance, but when it came to other matters, he invariably lost out. The sight of him filled his higher-ups with misgivings, they doubted that he could stand up to hardship and were afraid that he wouldn't be reliable in his work. And neither fear was completely groundless.

Ma Erli was always immaculately dressed. Even when he was going to the suburbs to plant trees, you wouldn't see him in sneakers or cloth shoes. He did as much work as anyone else, but there was never a speck of dust on his clothing. This roused the suspicion that he'd been dawdling. If he'd worn overalls and leather working shoes, army boots or straw sandals all day and paraded up and down in them, the results would have been quite different: "This man is prudent and experienced, hard-working and plain living." Even if his work had been mediocre, they would have commented: "One's ability may be limited, but what counts is the attitude to work."

There were also grounds for believing that Ma Erli was not a steady worker. Reliability is often a synonym for slowness, but Ma Erli seemed unduly agile. He was like the wheel of a bicycle—once set in motion it goes flying.

"Xiao Ma (literally, '*little horse*'), two window panes have been broken; what shall we do about it?"

"Don't worry, I'll fix it right away."

Word was given in the morning and that same afternoon the new glass was fitted in place. People couldn't resist going and poking it with their fingers to see whether it was just cellophane, for though it was easy enough to go and buy ginseng, buying a pane of glass was another story. Even if he had been lucky enough to find some glass to buy, how could he have got the glazier to come and put it in straight away? Yet there it was, all nicely nailed in with the cracks puttied over.... Oh no! They were just putting up a building next door. Don't say this slick operator had waited till they'd gone to lunch and then seized the chance to....

People's misgivings vanish in time. But it does take time. Ma Erli had worked previously in the Housing Administration Bureau. There, in his first year, everyone had been wary of him, afraid that this sharp-eyed, quick young man was going to slip up. The second year they had discovered that he was extremely capable, if only one kept a tight rein on him. Then by the third year he had been lauded from above and below, and all kinds of work got piled on his head. And by the fourth year his leaders had all declared that Ma Erli should long since have been promoted to deputy section head and have risen a grade on the pay scale. Unfortunately, the post of deputy had already been filled, and pay increases had been granted two years ago.

So the head of the Housing Administration Bureau, a kind-hearted old man who didn't like to treat his subordinates unjustly, seeing that Ma Erli would have difficulty getting promoted in his own office, had overcome his reluctance about letting go someone so valuable and recommended him to Director Wu, impressing on him how extraordinarily capable Ma Erli was, and saying that there wasn't a shadow of doubt that he had the makings of an administration section head.

Director Wu had agreed to take Ma Erli on, but as soon as he saw him his doubts were raised. Could a person like this stand up to hard work? And would he be reliable? The unfortunate Ma Erli was faced once again with the slow process of having to prove himself...

Director Wu invited Ma Erli to speak first, partly as a means of getting the others talking, partly with the intention of testing Ma Erli's abilities and his knowledge of the way things were done. So he gave a slight nod in Ma Erli's direction: "Well, Logistics Department Head, and what do you think?"

As expected, Ma Erli didn't know how far he should go. On the basis of his experience and personal connections at the Housing Administration Bureau, he briefly considered the bricks, mortar and labour required and said, "No problem. I can guarantee that wall will be up within a week!''

Director Wu gave a grunt of understanding. He felt he knew what was going on in Ma Erli's head.

''You can't just consider the bricks and mortar; you have to think of the significance of the style of the wall to the character of our establishment.''

That word ''significance'' opened the floodgates, and everyone started to discuss the significance of the wall, though what was at stake for each of them went far beyond the wall itself.

As expected, the erudite scholar of classical architecture, Huang Daquan, took up the question. He was a rather naive old fellow, and what he had to say could easily have been predicted:

''I first raised this matter a long time ago, and more than once, but unfortunately I failed to attract the attention of certain people...Now that the wall has collapsed, this is a serious lesson to us all. In our planning in the past we have never given due consideration to boundary walls. We never appreciated that a mere wall could actually make the difference between motion and stillness, and create a sense of security and unity. But now it has become clear to us that a boundary wall not only has functional, it also has decorative value. And what's more it is of tremendous significance in giving a particular character to a group of buildings. Director Wu was right: this is a question of how to unite form and content.''

This speech, which seemed to have grasped the motives of the leader, was in fact a call to battle. And no sooner were the words out of his mouth than everybody quietly turned their gaze eastward.

There on a long sofa sat Zhu Zhou of the modernist faction, a mug of tea cupped in his hands as he listened to the speaker with rapt and respectful attention.

The flow of Huang Daquan's eloquence continued

unabated: "...As far as traditional architecture is concerned, our ancestors fully understood the miracles that can be worked with a boundary wall. There were more than a dozen different kinds of boundary wall: flowery walls, white-washed walls, high and low walls, grey-brick and dragon walls, cloud walls and hundred-pace walls, wind and fire walls, open-window walls and screen walls. And each had its own particular functional and aesthetic value. Most ingenious of all was the dragon wall with open windows: that could not only create a division between motion and stillness, it could also create stillness within motion, or motion within stillness. It could encompass people, while giving them boundless scope for the eye. It would be true to say that without a boundary wall, there can be no such thing as a coherent group of buildings. A deep courtyard must have a high boundary wall, or where's your deep courtyard? Think of the Daguan Garden in *The Dream of the Red Chamber*..." As Huang Daquan had got more and more excited he had stumbled into the garden of the classical novel.

Zhu Zhou, from the sofa, put down his tea and launched straight in: "Excuse me, we are not confronted with the task of building a Daguan Garden now, may I remind you. If some day we have to restore the Old Summer Palace, your ideas might be worth our consideration. But even then, only some of them, because the styles of the Old Summer Palace and the Daguan Garden are not the same. You have to consider a problem from the practical point of view. Although classical architecture appeals to our feelings and can encourage people to respect and cherish our ancient culture, it won't do for our present purposes. The urgent task before us now is to build five and six-storey blocks. I fail to see what significance a wall even ten metres high could have for a six-storey block."

"It has significance!" Having mistakenly wandered

into the Daguan Garden, Huang Daquan turned hurriedly back. He was not totally ignorant of modern architecture: "Even a six-storey apartment block should have a surrounding wall, because apart from floors four, five and six there are also floors one, two and three. The boundary wall is chiefly for the benefit of the first two floors. The fourth, fifth and sixth floors make use of space to create the difference between motion and stillness, but the first and second floors must depend on the wall to create an impression of distance."

The battle array of the adversaries was drawn up and the rest of the debate continued in phrases and sentences without more lengthy exposition. It had become hand-to-hand combat.

"Let's get this clear: what's the distance between a boundary wall and its buildings. Can we afford so much space in a city?"

"If the wall is built right next to the windows, how will you get any fresh air and sunlight?"

"Build a wall with open windows."

"Open-windowed walls are 'motion within stillness'. Aren't you contradicting yourself?"

"They are also 'stillness within motion'. You didn't hear that part of it!"

"Hold on. Let's just calculate the cost of this open-windowed wall of yours." The speaker pulled a calculator out of his back pocket.

Immediately Director Wu rapped the table with his ball-point pen:

"Don't get too far off the subject! The important question is how we are going to rebuild our boundary wall."

But Zhu Zhou would not let the matter drop. As he saw it the conservatives had been fought into a corner, and victory must be followed by hot pursuit:

"We haven't got off the subject. This relates to

the kind of wall we should build—whether we want it open-windowed or not.''

Director Wu had considerable experience in controlling meetings, and he never allowed anyone unbridled freedom, so he swiftly parried: ''Then in your opinion, what kind of wall should we build? Be more specific.''

''More specifically...'' Zhu Zhou was somewhat caught off his guard, because he hadn't actually formulated any specific ideas, and had only got involved for the sake of the argument. ''More specifically...Looking at things as they stand, the wall fulfils two main functions: one is to cut us off from the noise of the city and the other is to provide protection. There's nobody in the building at night, only Old Hong who sleeps in the reception room, and he's getting on in years...''

Zhu Zhou beat about the bush for all he was worth. He knew that the more specific his proposals were, the more easily he could be attacked, with no room left for manoeuvre or escape.

Huang Daquan saw his predicament and, looking at his watch, he moved step by step in on him. ''Time's almost up. So where are the brilliant suggestions then?''

''To be more specifič, the wall must be high and must offer security.'' Zhu Zhou had no choice but to voice his ideas. But even now they weren't exactly specific—How big? How tall? Made of what materials? He hadn't addressed himself to any of this.

Huang Daquan couldn't restrain himself and immediately cut in, ''So according to you we need a steel-reinforced, eight-metre high concrete wall with an electric fence on top, to give everyone a taste of what a concentration camp's like!''

''That would ruin our image for ever. One look and people would beat a retreat, imagining the Institute was an army munitions store,'' someone chimed in.

"I never said we had to build a concentration camp wall," Zhu Zhou flared. "The steel-reinforced concrete and electric fence on top were your ideas. Honestly, how can we discuss the issue like this!" Zhu Zhou raised his eyes in search of moral support, then continued:

"High and secure is right; if it's style you're talking about, then we should have a tall, solid wall with sharp-edge glass or iron spikes on top to deter undesirable intruders."

"There lies the stupidity of your country landowners. Sharp-edged glass! It's as good as telling burglars: you can climb over the wall, but just mind you don't cut your hands on the glass!" Huang Daquan retorted sarcastically.

Everyone laughed, and the atmosphere in the meeting room relaxed a bit.

He Rujin, who wasn't a member of either faction, had sat there all this while and hadn't uttered a word. When the debate was at its most heated he had taken no part, but now that things had quietened down, he ventured, "As far as I can see, this argument is completely unnecessary. Supposing the boundary wall had never come down, nobody would have thought that it needed open windows or broken glass. Everyone found it perfectly adequate just as it was. All right, so it's come down now, but there isn't a single brick or tile missing, so the most sensible thing to do would be to rebuild what was there originally. Why embark on a major construction project? A pure waste of money! Our funds for administration are limited; we ought to put economy first. And as far as the wall goes, we can easily follow the example of the past."

Had this been said at the start of the meeting it would certainly have created an uproar, but its timing was just right. Everyone had argued until they were dizzy, and no one could come up with a concrete suggestion that was acceptable to them all. Hearing what He Rujin said, it was as though they suddenly saw the light: it was true, if the boundary wall had never collapsed there wouldn't have been any problem. Now it had fallen, it was plain common sense to shore it up again. What was there to argue about? The two factions noded their heads and smiled, as if what had just passed had all been a needless misunderstanding.

Director Wu shot He Rujin a look of disdain. He didn't agree with this kind of negativism. His idea was to build a new, original and unconventional wall that would add lustre to the Institute. But time was already up, and it would be hard to reach any definite conclusion now. There was nothing for it but temporarily to postpone things: "All right, that's as far as we can take it today. Now everybody go away and think about it. Our boundary wall is the face we present to the outside world. Things shouldn't be judged by appearances, but it doesn't do to be too ugly either. I want you all to use your imaginations. We want to build something a bit different. Now, meeting's over!"

Director Wu's words brought the warring factions back to their senses. What He Rujin had said was tantamount to zero; he might just as well have said nothing. They couldn't let him off lightly for this, and chasing him into the corridor they launched at him,

"What you said sounded all very smart, old friend, but it's a complete evasion of the issue."

"According to your logic, we can disband the Design Institute. Everything we've got already is fine. What are we farting about with design for?"

As he listened to the voices fading into the distance, Director Wu smiled and shook his head. Then turning, he discovered that Ma Erli fellow still seated in the corner by the door.

Director Wu was surprised: "What? You still have problems?"

"No...nothing else. I just wanted to ask...How *are* we going to rebuild the wall?" Ma Erli stood there, his large eyes wide open.

Director Wu smiled. He had been just the same as a lively and enthusiastic youth. Once he had something on his mind, he would itch all over as if he had lice, and he longed to tear all his clothes off at once. But actually it didn't do to go to extremes. Getting over-excited, you simply lost grip of your common sense. If, to avoid the lice, you rushed to take your clothes off, then a snake might bite you instead. Or at the very least you might catch cold. That was experience for you! But Director Wu didn't see fit to tell Ma Erli all this. One had to encourage the positive side of young people.

"How we finally rebuild the wall will be up to you. I have already indicated the principles, and our comrades have offered several good suggestions. You can make a plan on the basis of these. Rebuilding the boundary wall is the responsibility of the administration section, so I'm putting you in charge!" Director Wu patted Ma Erli on the shoulder: "Do your best. You're in the prime of life and capable of doing a good job!"

Ma Erli wasn't very familiar with the procedure of making plans, and he didn't know how much difference there was between plans and actual practice. But when he heard that he was in charge, he was highly delighted: that seemed to show that Director Wu had confidence in him, and hadn't been misled by his baby face. A man will give of his best to those who understand him. From now on he would work with even more enthusiasm.

Even when Ma Erli wasn't enthusiastic he got things done pretty fast; and once he was, his speed was really phenomenal. But this time he felt the weight of responsibility too, so first he sat down in the office, lit a cigarette and thought through what he must do.

Before he had finished the cigarette he was on to his bicycle and pedalling furiously towards the Building Repair Centre at his old Bureau.

The Building Repair Centre was in a dilapidated old edifice, the very sight of which made you feel that there certainly were lots of buildings in urgent need of repair. Form and content really were unified here.

Ma Erli had been pedalling fast, and he arrived just as the daily meeting was breaking up, and the director, a technician and several work group leaders were walking together past the lime-pit. Without dismounting as he rode in, he started to wave at them, shouting: "Hi, comrades, wait!" And by the time they had turned to look, there he was beside them.

"Oh! It's you!"

Ma Erli had worked at the Housing Administration Bureau for five years and was familiar with all the people in the Building Repair Centre. For some reason his baby face was always welcome at this basic level unit. Everyone looked on him as a lively, capable younger brother.

Ma Erli jumped off his bicycle still puffing. "Thank heavens I caught you, or it would have had to wait till tomorrow."

"Congratulations, Xiao Ma, we hear you've got a promotion!"

Ma Erli wiped the sweat from his forehead: "Never mind all that, but if you're willing there's something you can do to help me..." He pulled some cigarettes out and handed them around: "Let's sit down and have a chat. This isn't a simple matter." To get them all settled he took the lead and sat down on a pile of old bricks—despite his excitement, remembering his clean clothes, and spreading a handkerchief down first.

The technician sat down, the director squatted in front of Ma Erli, and the group leaders stood to one side smoking.

The director looked at Ma Erli and laughed: "Well, so what's all the excitement about?"

"Nothing serious, but the wall outside the Design Institute collapsed."

"Is that all! You go back and we'll get it fixed for you—it's as simple as that." The director stood up. He didn't see anything remarkable in rebuilding a wall.

Ma Erli grabbed the leg of his trousers with one hand, "I asked you to sit down, so sit down. Listen to me. Fixing the wall is not so simple. The leadership has passed the job on to me. They want me to come up with some good suggestions. I'm hopeless by myself. I have to rely on you people to back me up!" He went on to explain all the details of the argument about the wall.

The director scratched his head: "This isn't going to be easy. Here all we take responsibility for is laying the bricks."

The technician smiled: "It's true, the Design Institute can't put up any old sort of a wall. It's a question of window-dressing."

Immediately Ma Erli leapt on him and wouldn't let the technician go. He knew that this man had a lot of good ideas tucked away, and was soon to be promoted assistant engineer: "You've got it, old friend! Come what may I'm going to ask for your help in this. Next time something crops up that needs a lot of running about, you just give me a ring, and I guarantee I'll be around in fifteen minutes." Ma Erli's words were pointed: last year when the technician's wife had suddenly been taken ill, it was he who had rushed around and got hold of the car to take her to hospital.

The technician threw Ma Erli a playful punch— "Get along with you! Pity the poor sod who sends *you* running for him! Not to mention the fact that this business is quite a different ball game. It's hard to take those Lofty Ones over at your place seriously. They discuss something for hours, and still they can't get to grips with it.''

Ma Erli blinked rapidly: "No, you can't say that." His brain really was quick, and without any problem he could pick the main threads out of a complex argument: "Altogether they had several ideas. Firstly, that it has to be solid."

"Of course. It would never do to build it today and have it fall down again tomorrow." The technician picked up a piece of tile and began to draw on the ground. He was a man who liked to see things in bricks and mortar, and was adept at incorporating all kinds of demands into a workable blueprint: thickness, length, a buttress every five metres—that ought to be solid enough.

"Secondly, it must be high, but it mustn't look like a concentration camp."

"Boundary walls are usually the height of a person with arms raised plus a quarter of a metre or so. There's no need for it to be any higher than that." The technician wrote "2" for two metres high.

"Thirdly, it must have open windows or something—something attractive that will also let air through."

Still grasping the piece of tile, the technician shook his head, unable to go on: "That makes things difficult. Open windows on top of a two-metre wall will make it too tall, and it wouldn't look good bottom-heavy. But if the windows are less than two metres high, you won't cut out the noise from the street. And what's more, it's just asking for passers-by to poke in their heads and have a look. Difficult!"

Ma Erli waved a hand: "All right, let's put that one aside for the moment. Fourthly, the wall must be burglar-proof, but it mustn't have broken glass on top."

"Another problem!"

"All right, we'll shelve that one too. The fifth

requirement is economy: it's got to be cheap." Ma Erli patted the old bricks on which he was sitting: "Hey! There's a problem I can solve. You can sell me the old bricks from your demolition jobs. Charge me a nominal sum and you save yourselves having to pay to get rid of this rubble!"

The director shook his head: "You're a sharp one all right. You don't miss a trick, do you?"

The technician was still puzzling over the problems: "Well, anything else?"

"Everyone was agreed: it's got to be original and unconventional."

"Yes, of course..." The technician tapped the ground with his piece of tile. "The biggest problem is these open windows and where they should go..."

One of the group leaders spoke up: "Why not put hollow glazed bricks in? We pulled a great pile of them down from old houses last year. They've been stacked over there ever since." He pointed. "If we don't get rid of them soon they'll be completely smashed to pieces!"

The technician clapped a hand to his head: "Brilliant! Lay hollow glazed bricks above one metre seventy-five—you've got your open windows and they're not too high. And they're a nice bright colour too. Old Wang, go and fetch one for Ma here to take a look. See what he thinks."

Old Wang brought one over. It was a foot and a half square with hollows cut in the centre and was glazed a deep sapphire blue. You could make open windows of any shape or size you liked with them. In older buildings they had mostly been used in the walls of inner courtyards.

Needless to say Ma Erli liked what he saw. Where could you find anything like it nowadays? But still he had to ask: "First down to the nitty-gritty; we'll be more refined later. How much are these things each?

If they're too expensive we can't afford it!''

"Eighty cents each. How about that: it's as good as giving them to you!''

Ma Erli slapped his thigh, "Terrific! Here, have another cigarette.''

The technician waved his hand: "No, put them away. Your problems have already been solved.''

Ma Erli stuffed a cigarette into his hand: "What, thinking of slipping away? You haven't solved how to keep the thieves out!''

The technician started to laugh, "That's one for the gatekeeper to solve.''

But Ma Erli wasn't letting him go: "We human beings aren't just brick walls, you know. Stop playing around with me.''

"All right, all right, I'll be serious. But Director, it's your turn. Your place was burgled last year.''

The director had in fact done quite a bit of research into crime prevention: "Well now, do you know what a thief is most afraid of when he climbs over a wall?''

"How should I? I'm not a thief.''

"What he's most afraid of is noise. If you build a small roof on top of the wall, with sloping sides and an overhang, then as soon as your thief climbs on to it, the tiles will go crashing down to the ground with a noise that'll have him shitting himself!''

"Great! Far more effective than broken glass: these days thieves all wear gloves!''

The technician took it up from the aesthetic point of view: "Yes and flat-topped walls look ugly. It needs something—like a bamboo hat.'' With a foot he scrubbed out the rough draft he had drawn on the ground, and taking his piece of tile completely redrew it, adding a little roof with a curved ridge to it. Finishing his drawing, he tossed the piece of tile away: "There, if that isn't a roaring success all round, you can write my name upside-down on it with a cross through it.''

Everyone stood around, looking it up and down. The verdict was unanimous approval.

And Ma Erli too was thoroughly pleased with it, but not to the point of complacency. Whatever he did he liked to get settled all in one go. If he was fitting some glass, then he would never forget to buy putty; and when it came to building a wall, how could he leave it at that? ''Hey, stop preening yourselves! Let's get it built first, then see what it's like. When can you start?''

The director did some lengthy calculations, then consulted the group leaders on the situation at various work-sites. ''This is what we can do: We'll rush things along a bit and fit you in in fifteen days' time.''

Ma Erli leapt to his feet, retrieving his handkerchief and giving his hands a wipe: ''That's no good! I've already promised them at the meeting that I'll have it up in a week!''

The director uttered a sigh: ''It's no wonder people say that you're unreliable! It's not as if you didn't know how it is: we're up to our ears in work here. How could you have made such a commitment?''

''I know! I know it only too well! And to be frank with you, if I didn't I would never have dared to make such a commitment. Can you find a way of fixing it for me?'' Ma Erli took a stride forward as if he were about to force the director into the lime-pit.

The director still shook his head: ''There's no way. There isn't enough time.''

''All right, if you can't fix it, I'll do it. I'll give you three days' grace and you can start on Saturday evening. Send the materials over in a truck that can take the rubble away, and send a dozen labourers to clear the foundations. Then on Sunday send a good crowd of skilled bricklayers over, all you old hands included, and we'll work nonstop till it's done. You'll get over-time, an evening meal allowance, cigarettes... It's nothing: I can afford four or five packets of cigarettes!''

"Well, you certainly are asking us to do a bit of overtime!''

"So what? Never done overtime before? You don't expect me to lay on a banquet, do you!''

"No, what you...that's fair enough—half official, half out of your own pocket,'' the director had to admit.

"We're doing this all in the public interest. I'm just asking you to help me save face.'' Ma Erli sighed, "I've moved to a new post. If the first guarantee I make turns out to be so much hot air, who's going to trust me in future? Help me out, friends.'' Ma Erli had begun to plead.

It was one of the work group leaders who was first to slap himself on the chest: "No problem, just leave it to us!''

"Yes, smooth sailing, Ma Erli!''

The trivial but teasing problem of the wall was thus decided. From start to finish it had taken roughly half an hour.

By Saturday evening, the staff of the Design Institute had long since finished work and gone. An electric cable was temporarily wired up outside the gate and four 200-watt light bulbs flooded the road-way in brilliant light. People arrived, trucks arrived, bricks, tiles, lime and glazed blocks were brought in and the rubble was cleared out. In four hours all the pre-construction preparations had been completed.

Then early on Sunday morning, the work began with the centre director and group leaders all lending a hand. The technician took meticulous care to super-vise every step of the way. He scrutinized it from left and right, near and far, and even climbed up to the top of the office building to get a view of it from there.

He checked from every angle to make sure the height was right and to decide where the glazed blocks should be laid so that the wall harmonized with the original building and was aesthetically pleasing from any angle.

The office was empty on Sundays, so Ma Erli flew around in a whirl of activity, even requisitioning the services of Hong, the old gatekeeper, to give him a hand. He made tea, proffered cigarettes and hunted out odds and ends of nails, aluminium wire and cotton thread, when necessary making flying trips to the hardware store. Here they shouted for Xiao Ma, there they shouted for Xiao Ma and true to his nickname, Xiao Ma would spring like a young colt over to whoever was calling him.

The boundary wall went up at an amazing pace. People chased around shouting and calling in a bustle of activity that evoked the astonishment of passers-by.

"They must be putting up a private house!"

"No, they're having a technical examination. It's a test of expertise to decide their grade and level."

Laying the wall was pretty easy and if they'd had new bricks it would have gone up even faster. But the glazed blocks and little roof were not so easy, particularly the roof. It was delicate work and you couldn't get everyone up there working on it either. The tiles had to be arranged carefully ridge by ridge. After every foot or so, the tiles were placed to form decorative tops, and allowances also had to be made for the dripping of rain water. They'd originally planned to finish work and then eat dinner, but in the end the lights were burning until eleven at night.

Ma Erli bowed and scraped and thanked them a thousand times. He saw everyone on to the truck and then took down the electric cable, tidied up the odds and ends lying about and swept the ground. He didn't feel tired and was so pleased with himself that he couldn't resist running over to the other side of the road to admire every detail of the masterpiece.

Seen dimly through the moonlight, the boundary wall looked enchanting. It was full of poetry with its white wall, black tiles and sapphire blue windows suffused with a sparkling brilliance. The light that shone out through the patterned blocks was transformed to a shining emerald green. A light breeze blew, swaying the tree branches and making the rays of light glimmer and dance as if there were a fairytale world hidden deep within. Above the wall one could see the black roof of the building inside jutting into the night air and the wall suddenly seemed to change, melting into one with the main building, whose style it matched to perfection. The nearby road had changed too; it seemed to be the entrance to a scenic area or cultural palace. The more Ma Erli looked, the more beautiful it seemed. He felt it was the most perfectly handled job he had ever undertaken. He didn't feel like going home, so he stretched himself out on a long sofa in the upstairs meeting room. He hadn't slept properly for two days, but this time he slept very deeply and very sweetly....

The sun rose high in the sky and a ray of sunshine crept in through the eastern window and shone on Ma Erli's baby face. He was smiling peacefully, and the faintly visible dimples gave him a most attractive, naive, childish air. But he slept too deeply, for he didn't hear the exclamations of wonder and general hubbub that filled the courtyard below.

On Monday morning, people arriving at work were stunned by the sudden appearance of the boundary wall. Although everyone had hoped the wall could be speedily rebuilt, they hadn't been in the least prepared to see it up by today. If construction had been carried out under one's very eyes—adding a foot today and six inches tomorrow, with people coming and going and the ground littered with bricks and plaster, when it was finally finished everyone would have felt a great sense of relief that the chaos was over. Then regardless of the style of the wall, it would have seemed fresh and new to look at. Today, in the blink of an eye, old mother hen had turned into a duck, and it was as if the new wall had been stolen from somewhere and brought here in the night. They weren't used to it; it was too dazzling. But the vast majority of people blinked their eyes a few times and became accustomed to it. Everyone could see clearly that this wall was better than the old one, and far better than no wall at all. But there were also some people who looked it up and down and from side to side and couldn't set their minds at rest. Despite the fact that they couldn't specify anything particularly wrong with it, they still felt that it was a bit too "uhh...." What "uhh" was, they hadn't really thought about and were even less capable of stating clearly. That judgement would have to await the arrival of someone in authority. Should Director Wu say "good!" most of the "uhh's" would disappear and the small number remaining, quick to grasp the situation, would praise the wall to the heavens!

Director Wu stood in the midst of the crowd looking at the wall, offering no comment. He felt the boundary wall was what he'd imagined, and yet not what he'd imagined. It was what he'd imagined because it was very unconventional, but not what he'd imagined because he hadn't envisaged *this* kind of unconventional. When he was asked to comment on the wall he just said softly, "Hmm, I never thought Ma Erli could move so fast!"

"That's just it, he's gone about this like a harum-scarum, didn't even bother to consult general opinion," someone immediately chimed in. This person primarily felt that his opinion hadn't been sought on the question of the wall; it was really a bit too "uhhh"....

The three factions whose opinions had been solicited were also highly dissatisfied. Each felt that the wall had assimilated too few of their proposals. Their wonderful ideas had been messed up by unorthodox and wrong notions. They all stood beneath the wall explaining how it should have been done amidst much discussion and appraisal. Their ideas were concrete, penetrating and rich in humour.

"Call this a good-looking wall? Neither Chinese nor western. Wearing a western suit topped by a skull cap and with a green scarf wound round its neck. Which dynasty does that getup belong to? Does it have the slightest flavour of the modern age?" Zhu Zhou finished his appraisal and perused the crowd in search of support.

"That's right, a perimeter wall is after all a wall, what do you want to give it a great roof for?" The people who found the wall a bit too "uhh" began to express themselves more explicitly. All that offended their eyesight lay in that small roof. But in fact it could hardly be called a roof; it was just shaped like a roof, that was all.

Zhu Zhou was thoroughly pleased with himself. He went over to the wall to measure its height and rub his hand over its buttresses. He felt the height and solidity of construction were just what he'd had in mind. It was those windows and that little roof that seemed too preposterous. It was the conservatives they had to thank for that. He turned his head and called to Huang Daquan:

"Old Huang! You should be satisfied this time— the flavour is entirely classical!"

Huang Daquan shook his head, "What are you talking about? He hasn't completely grasped the spirit of my conception. The roof ridge shouldn't be a flat line, it's too monotonous. He could have built two decorative squares in the centre to symbolize good luck; that would have been different without being too flowery. Why did it have to be so tall? Old Zhu, go stand over there and don't move, I want to take a picture. I'll call it, 'Even with wings you couldn't fly away'.''

"You're right. It's too tall.''

"There should have been corner eaves sticking up at either end.''

"They didn't lay quite enough glazed blocks.''

Everyone who had felt the boundary wall was a bit "uhh" helped to pick fault with it. Their critical faculties had always been more highly developed than their creative abilities.

He Rujin didn't have any specific comments to make, but he approached it from a different angle and raised a question likely to have the masses rising in anger:

"Let's ignore for the moment whether this wall is good or not. What I'd like to know is does it conform with our principles of economy? How much labour was required for that little roof, and how much did each of those glazed bricks cost! I'm afraid this will have taken every penny of our administration budget. Our thrift bonus this quarter will only be twenty cents each!''

He Rujin's words provoked a storm of excitement: "That's right! He should have just built the wall and had done with it; there was no need to add icing to the cake!''

"This is just....'' The speaker glanced around and saw there was no sign of Ma Erli, "This is just Ma Erli's work style. The man is wasteful and extravagant. By the look of it he's a spoilt young rich boy, spending money as if it were water out of the tap!''

"Director Wu, did you tell him to build it like this?''

Director Wu hastily waved a hand: "No, no. I

just told him to think about it. I never imagined he would go and anticipate us all like this. Ma Erli!... " Director Wu shouted, but Ma Erli was still asleep on the sofa and didn't hear.

"Old Hong," someone took up the search, "have you seen Ma Erli arrive this morning?" He wanted the chief offender brought to book right there on the spot.

But the old gatekeeper was furious. "Stop your screaming and shouting! Young Ma hasn't rested two days and two nights. Not like some I could name!" Old Hong was disgusted by all the clever talk. He sided with Ma Erli because he had seen him while it was going on: running backwards and forwards without a break, and his shirt soaked through with sweat. Not everyone could do that. And sitting there at the gate he had also heard the comments of passersby: they had all said how attractive the wall was. As for him, he had an added reason to take the wall to his heart, for from now on he could rest in peace. If any burglar tried to climb in, those tiles on the eaves would come crashing down!

With a frown Director Wu waved a hand and told everyone to go and get on with their work, and at the same time he called Zhu Zhou, Huang Daquan, He Rujin and one or two others to attend a brief meeting upstairs.

Zhu Zhou pushed the door of the meeting room open to find Ma Erli peacefully asleep on the sofa.

"Heavens! We've been looking everywhere for you and couldn't find you. And all the while here you were snoring away. Get up!"

Rubbing his eyes, Ma Erli got to his feet, and then half asleep he blearily attended to their criticisms.

But it wasn't so bad. Although there was a lot of talk, no one suggested demolishing the wall and rebuilding it. The boundary wall passed the summer and autumn unscathed. Delicate grasses began to grow around the foot and wisteria began to climb across its sides.

That winter the Design Institute played host to the annual architectural conference to which several scholars and specialists from different parts of the country were invited. Because there weren't a great many participants, the conference was held in the meeting room on the ground floor. No sooner had the experts entered the room than their attention was drawn to the boundary wall. They looked it up and down, brimming over with admiration. And when the conference got under way it was the wall that they chose to talk about, saying that it solved one of the major problems of modern-day city design! City architecture today was too monotonous. Everywhere it was the same old matchbox design, never varying, completely unadorned and totally lacking our own unique traditional flavour. Yet there were also places which blindly followed the ways of the ancients, erecting buildings with curving eaves and upswept corners, carved rafters and painted cross-beams, that made a hotel look more like a temple. The good thing about this wall was that it preserved the traditional style, while not blindly going back to the ways of the ancients. It was economical and what's more it harmonised with the style of the original buildings. They hoped that comrades of the Design Institute would ponder it well, and produce a scholarly report on the subject.

Those members of the Institute who were present at the meeting were pleasantly surprised. They had never imagined that a golden phoenix would rise from their hen's nest!

Director Wu pondered: ''This is chiefly thanks to the guiding thought being clear and unequivocal. Right from the start I made clear and explicit demands, at the same time rousing the masses to comprehensive discussion...''

And Zhu Zhou also pondered, "That's right, the functional value of the wall cannot be over-looked. Right from the start I maintained that we must build it higher and more secure..."

Huang Daquan was downright delighted with himself. "If it hadn't been for me holding out for what I knew to be right, who knows how this might have turned out? Architects just cannot afford to forget their origins in a welter of conflicting styles. Our ancestors long ago understood the virtue of a boundary wall. Look for a start at the scores of different names they had..." Huang Daquan opined that these thoughts should stand as the opening paragraph of the report, perhaps as its forword.

For a moment He Rujin felt miserable, then immediately it occurred to him that he too had made a considerable contribution. If he hadn't insisted on economy, Ma Erli would never have gone looking for old bricks and tiles, and then he would never have discovered those hollow glazed bricks, without which there would be nothing so special about the wall; it would be nothing at all.

Ma Erli didn't take part in the conference. Instead he busied himself rushing in and out, arranging tables and chairs and fetching tea and water. He pondered the fact that the room was so cold, and from somewhere or other managed to produce four charcoal burners, which were placed in each of the corners. Immediately the room became as warm as springtime. Everybody felt cosy and relaxed....

1983

The Doorbell

ELEVEN doorways lie at the east end of the lane. Behind some live one or two families, behind others four or five. The entries conceal smaller doors and anyone wishing to come in must first knock at the outer one. That is why the sound of knocking can be heard day and night at the eastern end of the lane. A knock late at night echoes widely and, while rather poetic, also disturbs everyone's sleep. Happily, progress has come in the last year or so, as many people have installed electric bells. The doorframes now have rows of buttons, neatly marked with names like Zhang, Wang, Li and Zhao. So if someone forgets his key or has visitors, the appropriate household can be roused without disturbing others.

The eleventh door has no electric button, but instead an unusual doorbell which for twenty-six years has distinguished the household of Xu Jinghai. It is a small bronze bell, once part of the trappings of a Buddhist monk, which Xu Jinghai riveted to a sheet of spring steel and nailed to the street door. The effectiveness of this bell lay not in its role of calling people to the door, but as a warning to those inside that someone was coming. When the door opened, the spring jumped and the bell sounded, those within could swiftly conceal whatever an outsider should not know.

Xu Jinghai had put up the bell at that time of the anti-Rightist campaign. During that time which decided the fate of millions, Xu Jinghai was neither singled out for criticism, nor did he point the finger at others, but he learned to play clever. He learned that you should not stick your neck out or have any particular views of your own, and certainly no reckless ideas about anything, just study a bit in your spare time. Xu Jinghai never had much to stick his neck out about in the first place, so that was not a great concern, but judging from what happened at that time, he felt you couldn't be too careful, especially at home, where words and actions were quite unguarded. For example, he might read comics instead of studying Marxism-Leninism— dangerous. He might joke with his wife—even more dangerous. Many Rightist tendencies were perceived in jokes. Moreover in those days Xu Jinghai's wife was still lively and pretty, enjoying calling on others and having company pop in unexpectedly. Xu Jinghai found this impossible to guard against. Thus he adopted the ingenious warning bell. As soon as it sounded, everything would be tidied up, and a book or a newspaper grabbed up for study.

Xu Jinghai trained in a hard school, and over twenty-six years his self-protective instinct became so refined, he became a shadow. You could say he did not exist, though he was all there. You could say he existed, yet there was no sign of any substance. What he said meant as much as saying nothing. What he did he could stop doing, and it would hardly matter.

When a person changes from being someone to being no one, the aim is usually to get something for nothing. This might seem a little obscure, but in fact there is no deep mystery. For years we have treated cadres as successful simply if they made no mistakes. Qualifications and seniority are based on the accumulation of years. Thus every time there is a universal wage increase or a move up the ranks, there has been no reason not to promote Xu Jinghai—let alone the fact that he still continues his studies with dedication.

Nowadays he is the head of a locality, and after one more promotion he will merit an office to himself and first-class travel. How many Chinese are able to sit quietly in a first-class compartment on those long, crowded, noisy train rides back and forth each day?

Some say Xu Jinghai is a lucky man, surviving by being passive. He would disagree if he heard this. "What the hell do you know? It's much harder to do nothing than to do something. You have to be circumspect, to be patient, to use your brains all the time. You can't be the slightest bit careless—put one foot wrong and everything will be lost!" To be fair, there is some merit in Xu Jinghai's argument, for he has been surrounded by dangers for over twenty years. The reputation of a lifetime is not easily attained, and to preserve it, apart from his own skills, Xu Jinghai can only depend on that bell.

The doorbell rings and now the small drama begins. The time is seven a.m. on a Sunday at the beginning of June, 1984.

When Xu Jinghai heard the bell ring, he sat up straight in the armchair and took up a newspaper. The point of this action was to show callers that he was busy studying at all hours of the day. However, the time for such enthusiasm was past and it was no longer necessary—it was merely a conditioned reflex.

"Dad, there's someone to see you!" Xu Jinghai's youngest daughter, twenty-eight-year-old Xu Dongya called from the main entrance hall, her voice at once reticent and excited.

Xu Jinghai looked at his watch—who could it be this early in the morning? It must be Party Secretary Chen, who has retired and lives at the western end of the lane. Secretary Chen goes off to the market every day with a basket on his arm, buys a couple of fish cheap and then comes knocking on the door to boast about it for half the day. He no longer worries about the political meaning of each action, but specializes instead in calculating the price of fish, prawns and vegetables. Of course he has not entirely forsworn politics—he always wants to hear a bit of news: who has fallen from power and who has been promoted.

Xu Jinghai lives in an old-style small courtyard house. The courtyard lies between the entrance hall and the living-room. But in the middle is a clump of bamboo like a green screen shielding the living-room, so that even if a guest comes through the main entrance people inside still have time to retreat. Xu Jinghai stood up hurriedly from the armchair, thinking that he would go into the courtyard to stop Secretary Chen's advance. They would talk outside for a while, so that the Secretary would not sit down in the armchair and be reluctant to get up again, all the while the stench of fish seeping from his small shopping basket.

Just as Xu Jinghai stepped over the threshold, something unexpectedly colourful appeared: Xu Dongya was escorting a brightly dressed man and woman through the green screen. While the man was not young, his face was glowing with health and his hair gleamed. He was wearing a trim brown western-style suit, a cream shirt and a blue tie with white stripes. A pin flashed brightly on the tie. The woman was younger and very beautiful, with high-heeled white shoes, flesh-coloured stockings, a dark blue skirt, a light blue blouse and a crocheted top which resembled white clouds in a blue sky or blue sky within white clouds. She was pulling a large suitcase on wheels. The way she pulled the case was very attractive, like a beautiful woman with a dog on a lead.

As soon as Xu Jinghai saw this modern pair, his thoughts began to gallop: ''Who can they be? ... Ah yes! Some people at work are right in the middle of negotiations with foreign businessmen, but I've never had anything to do with business negotiations, so why should this boss-type turn up here in my house with that woman?'' The wary Xu Jinghai became even warier, "I must watch out—there's a sugar-coated bullet in that case—maybe even a cassette recorder with six speakers!''

Even though Xu Jinghai was on the alert, he was still able to greet the strangers with a smile. Foreign connections were involved and one must be polite; at the same time, because the woman was very beautiful and beauty demands admiration, his smile was not necessarily false. He went forward a couple of steps. "And whom do I have the honour of...?''

The gentleman said delightedly, "Old Xu, it's Meng Deyi!'' As he said this he flapped the lapels of his suit a couple of times. "Ah! The problem's this foreign suit. So you don't recognize me, eh? We used to work together just after Liberation, and then I was sent down during the anti-Rightist movement.''

"Oh, it's you!'' Xu Jinghai remembered immediately. He had developed the habit of remembering people and events through political movements. As soon as "anti-Rightist'' was mentioned the thick account book in his head flipped back several hundred pages and there he found Meng Deyi: named a Rightist in 1957, he had been taken back to his ancestral home to be reformed through labour. The two men had previously been quite close, but after that there had been a complete break and they had had nothing more to do with each other. "Oh! Please, please come in and sit down. Let the woman comrade have the sofa—you can spread out a bit. Go and make some tea, Dongya. Do you smoke? You don't? That's good, it's not good for you....'' Xu Jinghai brought out a stream of polite nothings as all the while his brain, like a computer, was sifting his thoughts on Meng Deyi. He no longer regarded Meng Deyi as a class enemy and even felt some sympathy and gratitude, grateful that he and others like him had acted as a warning so that he himself had come to understand life's secrets and become successful. Those who fell by the wayside had had a tough time, and even if they had righted themselves and got back onto the road, time had been wasted and their health often undermined. Life is like a hundred metre race—when you trip and fall and get up again, you come in last. Merely from the point of view of wages you are two to three ranks behind your contemporaries. What a shame! "Well! And what wind blew you here today?" Xu Jinghai was still marking time—he had not yet finished his private calculations.

"A lucky wind. I had to pass this lane on the way to the station and when I saw your doorway I was reminded of old times, so I knocked to ask if you still lived here. I never thought I'd actually see you!" Meng Deyi leaned back in the armchair, his hands crossed over his chest, measuring up the furnishings of the living-room. He was like someone who had travelled far across the oceans and returned to his original port, feeling that it was particularly peaceful and comfortable and that to live happily here in this small place for many years was indeed fortunate. "Not bad, old Xu. I heard you've done all right for yourself over the years—your children all grown, an important job; your 'historical task' is almost completed!"

"Not at all—much less than other people! What important job? I'm just a middle-level cadre, that's all. As for the kids—I'll never be finished with their problems. Just look, all these years and I'm still living in this old place." Behind every word Xu Jinghai spoke there was another layer of meaning: "Of course, compared to you I'm in heaven! My job's not so unimportant either—with one more promotion I'll be in the ranks of senior cadres. My children are all doing well. And as for the house—well, just wait awhile. As soon as this wind's blown over the problem will be solved. But I don't want to move—it's more relaxed living here in this small courtyard.''

But Xu Jinghai did not say this out loud. He could not say his situation was good, he must avoid the envy and jealousy of those who had suffered. Nor could he say his position was important because then it would be difficult to refuse someone a favour. There are not many coincidences in this world, and Meng Deyi's knocking at the door so early in the morning had to be because he wanted something. Even if he were not offering a sugar-coated bullet he could still raise a difficult problem which it would be best to try and avoid. Xu Jinghai's computer went into operation again: in order to deal with possible problems he must continue looking through the background material.

He recalled that all those labelled Rightists had some kind of fault—they thought too highly of themselves, liked the limelight, couldn't keep their mouths shut, or were pigheaded. But Meng Deyi's faults were even greater. When he was young he did not know his place, had an exaggerated opinion of himself and was always doing unexpected things. One year he was sent off to a factory on business and he wanted to meet the Party secretary there right away. The secretary refused to meet him and a security man kept him outside. So finally he colluded with the driver of a leading cadre, so that he was driven into the factory sitting in an official car. He went straight up to the Party committee's office. The Party secretary was uncertain whether or not he was an important official and so chatted politely with him for an hour. If in the fifties he pretended to be an important official, who knew what game he was playing nowadays in his Hong Kong businessman's suit!

Xu Jinghai looked at Meng Deyi and uttered some more platitudes: ''How long have you been here? Five days, eh? Quite some time!'' Five days and doing what? With his hair all smooth and slickly combed, wearing a trim western suit and bringing a beautiful woman along with him! Their relationship appears close—the matter bears some looking into. Xu Jinghai did not understand why he should be interested, but he still asked, "... Er, I forgot to ask who this lady comrade might be...."

"And I forgot to introduce you. This is my wife, Dong Bei.'' Meng Deyi spoke with confidence, but discovered right away the glint in Xu Jinghai's eyes and the astonishment on his face, and the way the other man's smile became forced. Meng Deyi had seen this phenomenon many times and he knew that if he had brought along an old wife much the worse for wear, everyone would treat it as normal. It was not normal to have Dong Bei: those astonished glances were always prying after some glimpse of immorality. While Meng Deyi could not care less about this, Dong Bei felt embarrassed, so he had to say something in explanation. "Perhaps you remember that my first wife flew the roost after I'd been made a Rightist. I was single for over twenty years and only remarried three years ago. Don't be fooled by her looks—she'll be fifty very soon!''

Dong Bei smiled and nodded her head. Apparently she liked to get herself up to look younger than she was, yet also liked people saying she was older.

Xu Jinghai was a little disappointed. Even though Meng Deyi had been through tough times it seemed as if he had come off lightly—he looked as though he had been in a deep freeze for twenty years and had come out as fresh as before, with a lovely wife and himself dressed in western clothes and leather shoes.

Wearing western clothes certainly makes a man look younger and more vigorous. Xu Jinghai had once thought of having a western suit made but on reflection did not quite have the courage, for wearing a western suit brought one a bit too much into the limelight. Besides, his once lively and attractive wife was now old and fat with no interest in getting herself up nicely, so if they went out together they would not match.

A couple like Meng Deyi and his wife were unique among their contempories. Too bad Meng Deyi could not hold a very high rank: a beautiful wife like that would need money to spend. She certainly would not worry over how much a catty of fish or prawns might cost; when she went out she would want to use a car, not squeeze onto a public bus. Xu Jinghai could not help glancing at Dong Bei. "You must be tired from travelling. Trains are very crowded these days." He tried to imagine this well-dressed woman with her large suitcase pressed on all sides in the train carriage.

Dong Bei smiled but did not reply.

Meng Deyi, however, replied casually, "It's all right. We go first class." "Ah...," said Xu Jinghai, forgetting to close his open mouth as he said to himself—even I can't go first class; how does he manage it? There was an announcement recently about claiming expenses for going first class—you have to follow the regulations and there are stricter controls.

"Ah!" Xu Jinghai took advantage of his mouth being open to say it again. "Where have you been staying?" This was by no means a superfluous question, but indeed central to the matter.

"At the Tianran Guesthouse, seventh floor, Room 7021."

Xu Jinghai closed his mouth and opened his eyes wide. What! The seventh floor of the Tianran Guesthouse was like seventh heaven, and 7021 the same suite in which he had once been received—by a minister! Even if you have money you cannot stay in a suite like that, and if you do stay there you cannot afford to pay for it. Xu Jinghai was extemely familiar with the treatment cadres receive: for most of his life he had been quietly and circumspectly climbing those well-known stairs. He knew a cadre's rank was not signified by clothes or food but by accommodation and means of travel. Clothes and food do not clarify matters—a worker of the second lowest rank can wear western clothes, a layabout can hold a banquet. But accommodation and means of travel are something else entirely. There are rules saying what kind of cadre lives in which house, rides in which car, enters which hospital and even where his ashes rest, because all this comes under the category of accommodation. All you need to know is a cadre's standard of accommodation and means of travel, and you have a fair notion of everything else.

Xu Jinghai was confused, and immediately his private computer began whizzing. There had to be a mistake! When Meng Deyi was made a Rightist he was the same rank as himself, eighteenth administrative grade. This he remembered distinctly and in this there certainly could be no mistake. He might be able to forget someone's age, but he could not forget their rank. He had also not forgotten that when Meng Deyi became a Rightist, he had been demoted three ranks, going from the eighteenth to the twenty-first grade. It was just that point which had scared him into rigging up the doorbell. Meng had been rehabilitated now, but he would still only be able to return to the eighteenth grade; there were fixed regulations on that. There had been two pay adjustments in recent years, but at best Meng Deyi would only get to be fifteenth grade and would not be able to stay in a suite or go first class. Yet despite this, one could not be sure that Meng Deyi was simply boasting—everything was topsy-turvy these days, high-class limousines could be hired and peasants could stay in fancy hotels, just as long as they could bear to part with the money. Meng Deyi had once enjoyed pretending to be a leading cadre and it was natural that he would pretend to be wealthy before a beautiful woman.

Xu Jinghai looked at Dong Bei again and noted how her hands rested on her knees. A smile was on her lips and her head at an angle, like the statue of a goddess. But a goddess is no god of wealth—and what mortal would be able to consider money in front of her? How could anyone bear to stuff her into a hard-seated train carriage or a shared hostel bed? Still, there was something that must be clarified: was this trip paid for privately or was it at public expense? If he was paying for himself then he was just pretending to be rich to ingratiate himself with a goddess. If it was at public expense, then it was most unusual and revealed that the smart chassis of Meng Deyi which had once fallen by the wayside had somehow changed motors and suddenly overtaken his own cart, which had never fallen at all.

"Did you come here on business or are you travelling for pleasure?" Xu Jinghai's question was apposite—business meant at public expense while travelling for pleasure meant paying one's own way. Of course, there were trips for pleasure taken at public expense, but they really came under the category of business too.

Meng Deyi laughed bitterly. "What time do I have for pleasure trips? We came here to participate in a meeting inviting tenders in construction engineering. What a struggle that was! It was only last night that we managed to get the contract into our hands." Meng Deyi could not suppress a yawn—he suddenly felt exhausted, not only because of the tension of the preceding days but also because Xu Jinghai was constantly bringing up boring topics. To meet an old colleague by happy accident and yet not hear a single warm word....

Xu Dongya at last brought the tea, saying as she walked in, "Oh dear, I really had to boil water for company! Every thermos was empty when we got up this morning so I put the small kettle on to make the tea—I've brewed it strong with boiling water the way my father likes it—Aunty, there are fewer tea leaves in this cup so you should have it because women don't like strong tea—it turns your skin as brown as an earthenware teapot if you drink too much." There was no punctuation in Xu Dongya's speech—it all came out in one lively stream.

Meng Deyi became livelier too and stood up to exchange cups with Dong Bei. "Let her have the strong cup. These days the most fashionable skin colour in the world is brown. European women spend a fortune to go to the beach and turn brown all over."

Xu Dongya burst into giggles, "What a tease you are!"

"What's all this about 'a tease'? You must say 'Uncle Meng' and 'Aunty Dong'. A girl your age and you still don't have any respect for your elders!" Xu Jinghai had some respect for Meng Deyi: he had keyed the western suit, first-class travel, hotel suite, contract, etc., into his computer and the terminal had reported—Meng Deyi was in foreign trade. A group had recently come to the fore—people with know-how and a knowledge of foreign languages who could do business with foreigners. In order to encourage them to earn more foreign currency, their treatment did not adhere strictly to their grade. Although Meng Deyi was not a high cadre, perhaps his chassis, which had once turned upside down, was now fitted with an imported motor so that it could travel faster.

Xu Dongya felt a little aggrieved at getting a lecture despite her good intentions towards the guests. "Next time guests come and you tell me to make tea

I'll ignore you!'' She turned and went to sit on the sofa, impatiently uttering a greeting to "Aunty Dong".

Dong Bei smiled and took Xu Dongya's hand. Although she said nothing her expression was very warm.

Meng Deyi made a gesture with his hand. "Don't bother calling us that—standing on ceremony's too cold. How old are you, young lady?"

"Twenty-eight."

"Married yet?"

"Not yet."

"That's right—these days it's not so easy for older young ladies to find a husband. Lower your sights a bit, young lady!"

Xu Dongya livened up. "Huh! Who'd have thought that someone like you, Uncle, with your sense of humour, wouldn't understand social problems. You must know it's easy to find a husband—but hard to find somewhere to live."

Dong Bei smiled, swept a glance at Meng Deyi and leaned closer to Xu Dongya to show that she concurred with the young woman's opinion. The beautiful woman seemed to prefer smiles and small movements to words.

Meng Deyi raised both hands. "Good! You've made a good point. You've shown the other side of the problem, but it isn't a problem the daughter of Xu Jinghai should be raising. Old Xu, it seems as if your 'historical task' is not yet over after all. If I had such a lovely young daughter I'd be going all out for her!"

Xu Jinghai sighed. "There's no way. I can't compete with you. You must be in foreign trade these days or the manager of some joint venture!"

Meng Deyi smiled. "Well, I'm certainly a manager, but not of any joint enterprise. Our company's rather different: at the most it could be considered a large collective. I'll tell you—when I was rehabilitated they told me to go and be a teacher, but that didn't suit me at all so I didn't comply. That meant automatic abandonment. Fine! Abandon me if you want; I'd already been abandoned all those years, and this time I couldn't turn my back on my speciality any longer. I had studied civil engineering at university in order to devote myself to building homes for the people. So I went and persuaded the commune secretary to let me first organize a contractor's team with a few people who used to go secretly into the city to be construction workers. We borrowed an account number and went into business. In less than a year we'd earned over 200,000 and after turning over a share to the commune some people got as much as two to three thousand each!''

Xu Dongya was fascinated by this tale, feeling that here was a man prepared to get on with things. She was just thinking of saying something when she was prevented by pressure from Dong Bei's hand telling her not to talk but to let Meng Deyi continue. Dong Bei was very familiar with the story of her husband's pioneering undertaking and was both sympathetic and admiring. She knew that the story which followed was one of harsh experience, enough to make one weep or even write a novel!

Luckily Meng Deyi had never thought of writing a novel and this time, moreover, he did not mention the weepy parts.

''We're no longer just a contractor's team but are called the Hongda Construction Company, enlisting people from three counties, our staff numbering four to five thousand. Our teams can be found as far north as Xinjiang and as far south as Shenzhen, and we've got over a dozen vehicles of all sizes!''

''Uncle Meng, let me work with you!'' cried Xu Dongya.

''Fine! Welcome! But if you joined us...what could you do?''

"At the factory I work with technical data and I know some English."

"That's excellent! We are planning to establish a technical data centre but unfortunately don't have the people. Really, first take our company test and then apply to leave your job. It's possible to change jobs these days, so move on over to us and go up a grade with extra bonuses." As if offering a sweet, Meng Deyi said into Xu Dongya's ear, "Let me tell you, the bonuses won't be far off your wages! How about that!"

Xu Dongya giggled. "I don't want a bonus, just an apartment!"

"An apartment...." Meng Deyi scratched his head. "Fine. You can stay with us temporarily and next year I'll guarantee you an apartment—not too big, one big room, one small, a good size hallway, a kitchen and a washroom."

"Is there room in your house?" It seemed as if Xu Dongya really wanted to go.

"No problem. My home's bigger than this and I'm often not at home, so it's lonely for your Aunty Dong to stay there by herself. In fact, if you wanted to get married this year, you could set up home in our place first and get Aunty Dong to help you—don't think all she can do is smile; she's great at choosing clothes and furnishings for a home!" Dong Bei smiled and nodded, holding Xu Dongya lightly as if she had already got a companion or found a daughter.

Xu Dongya burst into peals of laughter and half leaned back into Dong Bei's embrace.

"Dongya! Behave yourself!" Xu Jinghai was angry, but it was really Meng Deyi with whom he had a bone to pick: You so-and-so, you're not in foreign trade at all, nor do you have what it takes to earn foreigners' money. You've just reverted to your old ways. It's hard to change your nature. You don't obey when you're allocated a job, you borrow an account number, you trickster, and now you want to drag my daughter into it too!

"…. You! When will you learn to behave yourself better?" Xu Jinghai suppressed his anger, transforming it into resentment. There was nothing to be done. These days the more tricks you played, the better off you became, as well as earning yourself a good reputation as a reformist! Everything was topsy-turvy. The long line of cadres no longer advanced in a queue; some were now coming who could turn somersaults. One somersaulting 108,000 *li*, changing in a blink of an eye from the tail of the line to the top. Not increasing his wages made no difference, for people like him could call their own shots. What's more, you knew how limitless his bonus must be—it had to be enough for that beautiful woman to spend. Otherwise why would she simply smile and say nothing? Not like his own wife, always grumbling, one minute complaining that there is not enough money, the next saying the house is too crowded?

Dong Bei smiled once again, raised her white arm and glanced at her small gold wrist watch.

Meng Deyi stood up immediately. "Old Xu, we have to get going. Our train leaves at 8:40."

"What!" Xu Jinghai was rather disappointed. Originally he had thought Meng Deyi must want something, calling so early, but he had not wanted anything after all. He really had just popped in while passing by. "Oh dear, can't you stay a bit longer? Let Dongya ride over to get the tickets and you can have something to eat before you go. We haven't seen each other for twenty years, and who knows when we'll get another chance?" Xu Jinghai genuinely did want his guest to stay on, especially since there was no longer any need to remain on the alert and it would be very interesting to talk about old times.

Meng Deyi felt regretful too, having sat for an hour

and only now hearing words with a semblance of humanity in them. "Can't do it—someone's waiting for us at the station and there's a whole pile of family matters too. Frankly, I'd really like to stay here quietly in your little courtyard. No telephone ringing, no urgent telegrams and no one sitting outside waiting to discuss things. Sometimes you must come to our place and see all the hustle and bustle for yourself." Meng Deyi took out a card from his suit pocket.

"This is my address. Give me a call before you come and I'll send a car to the station to meet you. Ring this number during the day and the second number in the evenings—the second one is my home number." So saying he turned to Xu Dongya to bid her goodbye: "Young lady, if you really want to come you can count on your Uncle Meng."

As he held the card in his hand Xu Jinghai felt as if he had suffered a final blow. Not only did this so-and-so have a house, a car and a beautiful wife but also a home phone! Even if he were to be promoted one grade it was still not certain that he would get a phone....

After the guests had gone, Xu Jinghai paced back and forth in the small courtyard, feeling for the first time how cramped was the space, how stale the air. His whole body felt uncomfortable.

When Xu Jinghai heard the doorbell ring again he thought that Meng Deyi had come back—perhaps that beautiful woman had left her handkerchief on the sofa? He rushed to see but no, he was wrong. Xu Dongya was there with her hand against the main door, while outside stood retired Secretary Chen.

Secretary Chen, his face covered with sweat and carrying his shopping basket, did not wait to enter before producing a large Mandarin fish. "Old Xu, guess how much this fish cost!"

Xu Jinghai was not in a good mood. "Okay, okay, better go home quickly and cook it. It'll go off if you leave it too long." Both hands grasping the doorjamb, he blocked Secretary Chen on the outside.

"Hey, hey, what's all this? Had another squabble with your wife? This fish...."

"You've saved thirty cents on it, right? Some people think nothing of spending three thousand!" Thus flared Xu Jinghai, shutting the door with a bang. This was too much for the doorbell, which fell to the ground with a clang. The bell had been up too many years, the screws were rusty and the door panels had rotted a little. It could not take a shock of this kind.

Xu Dongya picked up the bell. "What shall we do with it?"

Xu Jinghai waved his hand. "Forget it—take it to the scrap heap. I'm not going to watch my every move from now on."

Xu Dongya gave a joyous skip. "Right! The stupid thing should have fallen off long ago. Let's install an electric bell, one that will play a tune." As she said this she made as if to throw the old one into a corner.

"Hold on!" Xu Jinghai had had over twenty years of training and would do nothing rash. "It... it'd be better to put it back up again."

Xu Dongya gave a flounce. "I'm not going to do it!"

Xu Jinghai shouted, "Put it back up! Those who don't follow the normal road will always trip up one day!"

So the Xu family's doorbell is safely in place, the old monk's trapping just nodding its head a little....

1984

The Gourmet

A Word About Eating

THE WORD *gourmet* is pleasing to the ear, perhaps also to the eye. If you explain it in simple everyday language, however, it's not so appealing: A gourmet is a person who is totally devoted to eating.

That a person who devotes himself solely to eating should be given a special name was something I'd never expected. But then the things you expect never happen and the unexpected often takes place right in front of your nose. It so happened a certain person who liked eating more than anything else haunted me like a spectre for forty years. I despised, I loathed and I opposed him, but in the end I turned out to have no special capacities while the gourmet succeeded precisely because of his obsession.

I should first and foremost make it clear that I am not opposed to eating. If I had been, I would have died soon after I was born. No, that's not what I mean. But hard work and frugality are a national tradition, and gluttony has always been frowned on. As a child, my mother taught me that greediness was bad. She would scold me, "You greedy gut, you're a little good-for-nothing." Children would tease by poking fingers in your cheek and saying, "Shame on you, Greedy, shame." Bashful girls would never dare eat fritters or buns on the street and young ladies drinking wine on stage always hid it with their sleeve. Growing up in this kind of environment, I always looked down on people who were too fond of good food, even more so after meeting Zhu Ziye, who'd been a glutton since childhood. After that, people who indulged themselves made my stomach turn even more.

Zhu was a capitalist, a property owner who owned almost all the houses in my lane. He didn't need much skill to exploit anyone; all he had to do was say three words, "Collect the rent." He didn't need to say it in fact, since his agent would do it for him. He didn't even know how many houses he had and where they were. His father was a shrewd property dealer who'd opened an agency in Shanghai and bought a lot of houses in Suzhou. A bomb had fallen on his Shanghai home at the start of the War of Resistance Against Japan and there had been only one survivor in the whole family—Zhu, who'd been in Suzhou attending a wedding banquet at his grandmother's. His liking for food saved his life.

He was almost thirty when I met him. Don't think that all gluttons are fat; that's not so, he was as thin as a willow twig. Perhaps thinking he was too thin led him to feel he'd never quite had enough. A truly tubby type wouldn't dare to eat so much. Gluttons take care of their mouths, not their appearance. Though Zhu had enough money to look after both his mouth and his looks, he had no interest in clothes at all. All year round he'd wear long gowns bought in secondhand stores. He put them on as soon as he bought them and left the dirty ones in public bathhouses. People said he was married, but he had neither children nor a woman. He'd been seen once riding a pedicab with a pretty woman at Huqiu Hill, but people later learned that she'd been unable to get a cab, had shared one with him and he'd boorishly made her pay half the fare.

His home in Shanghai bombed, he lived by himself in Suzhou in a western-style house. It had been built in the twenties and had screen doors and windows, carpeted floors and a proper bathroom. On one balcony were two large tanks for storing water pumped up from a well. This two-storeyed building sat behind a big courtyard, in the front of which was a row of six rooms used as a gatehouse, kitchen, storage room, pantry and servants' quarters.

My maternal aunt and Zhu's paternal aunt were cousins, so when my father died a few years after the war broke out, my mother and I moved into one of the six rooms. We lived rent free but had two duties: one was to be Zhu's gatekeeper and the other was to help with the housework. They were both pretty light tasks since Zhu went out early every morning and came back late every night. He had a house but not much housework and never asked my mother to do anything. He found it a nuisance when she offered to wash his sheets or dust and air the rooms for him. He thought this entirely unnecessary. To him a home was merely a bed after overindulgence, and the minute his head touched the pillow he'd start snoring.

Zhu got up very early and never overslept because his stomach worked like an alarm clock. As soon as he opened his eyes, the first thing that occurred to him was to go to Zhu Hongxing's to eat the first batch of noodles.

Zhu Hongxing's was famous for its noodles. You'd sit at a table and call out, "Hey (you didn't say comrade then), give me a bowl of such-and-such noodles!" The waiter would pause a minute and then sing, "One bowl of noodles coming up." The reason he waited was to see what other specifications you had for the noodles—how they were to be cooked, how much broth, how much leek, oil, or vegetables and pork were to go on top, whether you wanted to "cross the bridge", meaning that the vegetables and pork were to be served as a side dish instead of in the same bowl as the noodles. If it was Zhu at the table, the waiter would warble, "Yes sir, one bowl of lightly cooked shrimp noodles, a lot of broth and leeks, a large portion of vegetable and pork crossing the bridge."

This concoction, complicated enough in itself, was less important to Zhu than that the noodles should be from the first batch. All the noodles were boiled in the same pot and since the water gradually thickened, the later noodles were never so good as the first. If he got those, Zhu would be unhappy all day, feeling that something was wrong. Consequently, unlike Oblomov he couldn't sleep late but had to get up before daybreak, hurriedly wash his face and then get there in time for the very first batch. As with other art forms, the art of eating depended on how well one was in command of time and place.

As Zhu emerged rubbing his eyes, his rickshaw puller, A'er, would be waiting for him at the gate. Zhu would climb in ostentatiously, ring the bell with his foot and go off to Zhu Hongxing's. After that, he'd go on to a teahouse in Changmenshi Road.

There were teahouses everywhere in Suzhou and Zhu patronized this particular one because of its high standards. It was a large establishment with a few private rooms furnished with rosewood tables and rattan chairs. They made their tea with leaves straight from the Dongting Hills and rainwater boiled in an earthenware pot over a pine branch fire. Eating and drinking are an integral whole, and all gourmets like good tea.

After Zhu had settled himself in the teahouse, his dining companions would drift in. Gourmets eat alone only at breakfast. Thereafter, they must have between four and eight others, since Suzhou cuisine comprises a whole set of dishes: cold ones first, hot stir-fried ones next, then sweet dishes, then further specialities, then pastries and dumplings and finally a big bowl of soup. One person cannot manage the whole array and one

Old Man of Apricot·Valley by Qi Baishi.

dish does not provide an adequate sense of Suzhou cuisine. Therefore gourmets must move in groups. Zhu and his friends would first meet at a teahouse to reflect on the delicious food they'd consumed the previous day. The conversation would then turn to the venue of the next meal. If they were fed up with the restaurants nearby, they would go to a distant one by rickshaw or carriage.... Unfortunately I cannot describe in detail all the delicacies of Suzhou and its environs. I'm afraid it would make even more people hold their conferences here. It's hard to gauge the consequences of a story.

What Concerned Me

I wouldn't have loathed Zhu quite so much if he'd had nothing to do with me. He could have been a gourmet, I could have been a poor student, and we could have co-existed in peace. But so far I've described only his breakfast and lunch. He hasn't had his supper yet.

When Zhu had finished lunch, he would go to the bathhouse. This wasn't so much to take a bath as to find a comfortable place to digest his rich meal. As they say, you get listless when you're hungry, and lazy when full. His stomach full, Zhu would dazedly make his way to his rickshaw, basking in contentment, in a comfortable, languorous dreamland. He would sway back and forth in A'er's rickshaw, speeding to the bathhouse as if making an emergency visit to the hospital.

All he had to do at the bathhouse was reach out and lift the door curtain and the counter attendant would shout, "Manager Zhu is here." God knows how he'd become "manager", since property owners were usually addressed as "master". But that old title was no longer fashionable. What's more, small shop owners could be called master too. But managers were different; they worked in foreign enterprises or big companies, did big business and were never stingy with tips. As soon as his arrival was announced, two attendants would rush over. One on either side, they'd conduct him to a first-class room, similar to the ones you get in hotels today. It had two beds, an enamel bathtub, a wash basin and a shower. The only difference was that it was smaller and had no air conditioning. In winter it was heated by steam from the bathhouse and in summer cooled by a fan which rotated incessantly overhead.

Like an invalid, Zhu let everything be done for him. Tea was served, his bath water run, even his shoes were removed for him. He didn't want to do anything but concentrate on his stomach. Eating was a pleasure but digestion had its appeal too; you had to experience the thing fully and mustn't be distracted by externals. The best method of concentration was to soak in warm water and think about nothing, just experience the slow movements of the stomach, thereby producing an indescribable sense of well-being. This had as much beauty as tasting exquisite food, although one could not replace the other. Inert, his eyes half-closed, he soaked drowsily for half an hour until the masseur arrived with a large board. He drew Zhu out of the tub, placed the board on top and made Zhu lie on it face downwards. Massage is passive exercise. Strolling after lunch is also healthy but those who do it must move their legs. All anyone being massaged has to do is relax and allow their limbs to be rubbed, their body turned over, and then be helped to sit up and lie down again. The same results are arrived at without using a single ounce of energy. A true gourmet must know how to digest his food, otherwise his stomach might threaten to stop working and this would be very dangerous.

This period of exercise wasn't that long, usually not more than half an hour. Afterwards he moved over to a couch to have his limbs kneaded and pounded.

This was the final stage and possibly had a soporific effect, for he soon dozed off to the light, rhythmic pounding. During his minimum three hours' sleep his stomach would empty, making room for the next meal.

I would return from school before he woke up. As soon as I put down my satchel, my mother would say, "It's still Yuan Dachang Inn today; go quickly."

This made sense only to me, since I knew that Zhu still had one more meal to devour.

Zhu's supper had to be special. Just as in literature volume two must never be too similar to volume one, so he went not to a noodle place or a restaurant, but to a tavern. At lunch time Zhu and his friends savoured each dish and didn't take strong alcohol for fear that it might numb their palates, making them incapable of differentiating subtleties. At supper time they could drink to their hearts' content and then have a good sleep afterwards with no fear of insomnia. So they had to go to an inn or a tavern.

Suzhou taverns served alcohol but no food apart from snacks such as dried beancurd, peanuts, fried broad beans and peppery cabbage. That was all right enough for gentlemen but not for gourmets, who were richer than gentlemen. They must have food to go with the superior wine, and a wide variety too, so they turned to another field—appetizers.

One didn't get such things in just one part of Suzhou; they were scattered all over the place in little streets, at bridgeheads and crossroads. Some were sold in shops, some in stalls, some by small vendors. No one waiter could get them all; you had to send an errand boy out to buy them. Perhaps because of my long legs, Zhu one day asked my mother, "Your Gao Xiaoting is a clever lad; could he help me out? I'll treat him well."

My mother had no particular objection. She'd been feeling bad at living rent free with no housework to

do and wanted to do something for the sake of her conscience. But I didn't like the idea of being his errand
boy. How could a dignified secondary school student
be the attendant of a glutton!

My mother cried. We'd been poor since my father
died, reliant on my sailor brother to make ends meet.
"Go, Xiaoting, we're living here free of charge, we
don't even pay for electricity and water; that alone
could come to what we spend on food. A single word
from Manager Zhu and you could be out of school and
both of us out on the street. Your father left us too
soon; I beg you...."

So I had to put up with it. Every evening I would
wait at the tavern door with a bamboo basket. When
the neon signs went on, Zhu and his friends, clean and
fragrant, with ruddy cheeks and in good spirits, would
arrive in a line of gleaming rickshaws, bells ringing and
horns bleating, weaving their way through the
pedestrians like a festive dragon. Zhu was always at
the front, and A'er, spectacularly strong and vigorous,
would remove the blanket covering Zhu's knees so that
he could nimbly alight. Outside the tavern, they were
greeted not by the proprietor or the waiters but by two
rows of ragged, filthy beggars with their bony trembling hands outstretched. Zhu was prepared, and with
a wave of his hand a small bill would fly toward the
beggars' leader. "Off with you," he'd say.

The beggars dispersed with a cheer, and I, a beggar of a different kind, would walk up to Zhu with my
hungry stomach, basket in hand. This beggar was different because he knew a little about geography, about
history, about freedom and equality, and because he
disapproved of gluttony and believed in human dignity.
When the beggars had scattered, leaving me at the fore,
I was so ashamed and furious that I felt like throwing
my basket at Zhu. But I swallowed the humiliation,
took the money from his hand and, following his

instructions, would go off to get roast pork from Lu's shop, game from Ma's restaurant, fish from a delicatessen, goose from an old man's house, fried beancurd from Xuanmiao Temple, and other Suzhou delicacies from well-known stalls and stores.

That basket over my arm, I'd make my way through the small lanes and broad streets. Here were tall buildings bursting with music, and cobbled streets brightly coloured beneath neon lights. There were silent dimly lit lanes, where old women scavenged in the garbage. Here were lavish feasts; there, shadowy figures queuing outside the grain stores, numbers chalked on their backs, waiting for the following morning's rice ration. A family holding a wedding reception had taken up all the tables in the Pine and Crane Restaurant, filling Guanqian Street with carriages, pedicabs and rickshaws. The bride was wearing a long gown and a veil, while the guests were dressed in western-style suits with leather shoes. But in the corridors of the Xuanmiao Temple people who might not see tomorrow huddled together beneath ragged sacks.

Behind the scarlet gates meat and wine rot
On the road men lie frozen dead.

These famous lines kept coming back to me.

Zhu was generous with me, often shoving change into my pocket, with a murmured "Keep it," as if to a beggar.

I would stand motionless, humiliated to the core.

"Take it and buy some meat for your grandmother."

Insult was buried under hardship. I had been brought up by my grandmother, who was now in her late seventies, toothless, absent-minded and partially paralysed. But she had a good appetite and wanted to have meat every day, particularly roast pork cooked with fermented beancurd from Lu's shop, so well cooked that it melted in your mouth. She had no idea about prices or inflation. To her everything was still in copper coins and silver dollars. She suspected that my mother begrudged the money my brother sent home to get her pork. She accused her daughter of mistreating her and often nagged her bitterly, weeping as she cursed. My mother's explanations fell on deaf ears and she wept silently, her tears falling into the ration rice as she picked the sand and gravel out of it. Those tears broke my heart.

The meat I bought with Zhu's change moved my grandmother greatly. She would stroke my hair with a quivering hand and say, "You're a good boy, I didn't bring you up for nothing...."

When she talked like that I almost started sobbing, but I held back and squatted beside her bed. Why not let her derive some consolation from my insult money?

In heaven there is paradise, on earth Suzhou and Hangzhou. I don't know who invented the saying, nor why they put Suzhou before Hangzhou. It's said to be because Hangzhou became a capital only during the Southern Song dynasty, while Suzhou had been prosperous several hundred years earlier during the Tang. In the last hundred years, as Shanghai became infested with foreign adventurers and ambitious businessmen, those with foresight all bought property and owned homes in Suzhou. Since it wasn't a political or economic centre, Suzhou had much less official rivalry and was less of an investment risk. It wasn't a strategic military location either. For the last two thousand three hundred years, no war has ever started in Suzhou.

It has good weather, rich resources and beautiful scenery. Through the centuries, landlords and officials, wealthy merchants, butchers who'd put down their knives, scholars who'd failed to move up in the world, and ageing courtesans all retreated to Suzhou to pass their remaining years. This concentration of pleasure-

seekers made Suzhou a city with the best gardens in
the world and the most refined culinary arts. However,
scenery doesn't fill the stomach and loses its appeal
after a while, whereas three meals a day are indispen-
sable. The real reason for Suzhou being ranked above
Hangzhou was probably because of its superior food.

This source of Suzhou's pride seemed a kind of
crime to me, a sign of the terrible inequalities between
people. I didn't know if there was a "paradise" in hell,
but there was certainly a hell in "paradise" and most
people seemed to be hovering on its brink. To be
honest, I didn't start becoming a believer in communism by reading *Das Kapital* or the *Communist
Manifesto*. I was probably spurred on to it by Zhu and
his like, who made me realize that all extravagantly
elaborated "isms" were futile and only communism
could solve our problems. Zhu could hardly have
assumed such important airs if his property had been
confiscated.

I softly sang a song which was popular in Beijing:
On the other side of the mountain,
Rich and poor are all the same.
The rich must work to get their food,
No one slaves for them.
A simple song, easy enough to sing, but it helped me
understand the world and to know which road to take.
My future lay on the other side of that mountain.

In the winter of 1948, I decided to go to the
liberated areas. I'd read *Iron Stream* and *Débâcle* and
knew how hard revolution was, so I felt quite solemn
and heroic, prepared to die on the battlefield.

I was going to fight for Suzhou. That beautiful, suffering city was sending me into battle. Before my
departure, I went to the top of Huqiu Hill to bid
farewell to the town. That evening I took my insult
money and went to buy food for Zhu and some roast
pork for my grandmother for the last time. Three days

after she found out her beloved grandson had disappeared from home, she died of grief.

How profoundly one remembers what happens in one's youth! I erase from my memory the persecution, the humiliations, the insult of the Cultural Revolution as though it were all some fleeting, inconsequential game. But leaving my home and family over thirty years ago is carefully stored away. Perhaps I prefer to remember honour and forget injury, but why can't I erase the outrages of thirty to forty years ago from my mind? Every time I see films of wounded soldiers struggling to stand up, raising their rifles to charge the enemy, shouting slogans of revenge, my heart aches and tears come to my eyes. Although repeating the same scenes over and over again is boring, I forbid my children to say so and scold them when they do.

A Misunderstanding

I didn't realize I'd get to the liberated zone too late, that the gunsmoke would already have dispersed, the sound of gunfire already have died away. The soldiers and civilians were at the height of their triumph, preparing to fight their way across the Yangtse River. Students on their way to the liberated areas were stopped halfway and sent off with the army to work in the cities once they had been taken over. Since I came from Suzhou, knew the layout of the city and understood its beautiful but difficult dialect, I was naturally sent back there. At least I could take people around the place. No one cared about what they would do in Suzhou—if we'd brought up the question of our futures, our vocation, wages and accommodation the way young people do nowadays, we'd have been regarded as petty-bourgeois elements sent by the Kuomintang. Revolution was revolution and whatever you did was all right. But the officer in charge of assigning jobs wasn't careless about it and he wanted to make sure people were given work to suit their skills and interests. He convened a cheerful meeting of twenty or so students in a temple. We sat on either side of a table in the middle of the hall. On it were papers, pens and our files.

He was an educated man who had graduated from the Department of Mechanical Engineering at Jiaotong University and knew us students quite well. "Now, I'll assign you your jobs and will do my best to see that they fit in with your skills and wishes," he began. "I hope you'll think a little before answering my questions. Once I've assigned you your jobs, however, you must follow instructions."

But this solemn atmosphere was destroyed by a former classmate of mine nicknamed Bighead Ding. Actually his head wasn't really bigger than normal, but his extensive knowledge of astronomy, geography, history and philosophy made it seem so. He was the first to be called.

"What would you like to do?"

"Anything," he shot back.

The man rolled his eyes upwards. "What is 'anything'? Be a little more specific."

"More specifically ... anything."

Everyone burst out laughing. "He's a jack-of-all-trades, he can do anything."

The man laughed too and leafed through his file.

"Where shall I send a jack-of-all-trades? ...Can you tell me what you're most interested in?"

"Reading."

"Why didn't you say so before? Go to the Xinhua Bookstore."

That one sentence decided Ding's life. He later became the manager of a Xinhua Bookstore, and he was a manager who knew his job.

The second person called was a girl, a beautiful

Suzhou girl, attractive in her Lenin-style cotton suit and army cap.

After one look at her, the man asked, "Can you sing?"

"Yes."

"Will you sing something from *The White-haired Girl*?"

"*The north wind blows....*" In those days no one was shy since we sang every day.

"Good, you work in the cultural troupe."

She didn't do too badly either. Before the Cultural Revolution she was a famous folk singer. You don't hear of her these days; she's probably teaching singing somewhere.

When my turn came, I made a mess of things. I seemed to like everything except gluttony. I didn't have any particular skills and couldn't even sing properly.

The man asked impatiently, "You don't know anything at all?"

"Yes, I do, I know how to buy special food for people, and I know all the eating places in Suzhou."

"Right, go to the commercial department. Suzhou is known for its food."

"No, no, please, I hate eating."

"You hate eating? All right. I'll tell the cook to starve you for three days. Then we'll discuss it again. Next...."

Alas, my future was settled amidst general mirth. But I wasn't depressed, nor would I think of disobeying orders! The Yangtse River was surging angrily, the people on its south bank were suffering. We had to rescue them from the abyss of misery and overthrow the old society where people were cruelly exploited. The life-style of parasites like Zhu Ziye had to come to an end. Well, it's beyond your control now, Zhu. We won't let you starve, but you will have to cook your own meals. And A'er won't be pulling you around in a rickshaw. You've got legs, you can walk.

I returned to Suzhou and went back to live in the rooms in front of Zhu's house. Zhu treated me with respect: he addressed me as comrade, and I called him manager; he offered me expensive cigarettes, and I declined by producing my own cheaper ones. Don't pull that one on me, I thought. Just after Liberation Zhu was timid, afraid that the Party would put him in prison. Prison food would be hard to swallow.

After a while he was reassured, for during the movements to stamp out prostitution and opium, to struggle against local despots, suppress counter-revolutionaries and so on, he was never touched. He was no opium addict, nor did he have an eye for prostitutes. Apart from being a glutton he hadn't really done anything. So he would often give me the thumbs-up and say, "The Communist Party is good, getting rid of all those robbers, thieves, ruffians, vagabonds, gambling and opium dens. It's a lot better, much more stable."

So Zhu was not treated badly and kept right on eating, still riding A'er's rickshaw to restaurants and teahouses, and he still had someone to buy delicacies for him.

Those days I was up to my neck in work from morning till night, without even Sundays off. When special movements were in full swing I'd sleep in the office. But Zhu was even busier, leaving home before I got up and returning after I was asleep. Every time he got back he would step on the rickshaw bell, making a gong-like noise deep in the night. Sometimes he didn't come back and on summer nights, sated, would sleep in the pavilion in the cool, fragrant park. He gradually gained weight, growing a small paunch. My mother told him, "You're putting on weight, Manager Zhu; people in their forties tend to do that."

"It's because I have an easy life," he said. "Now I don't have to worry about thieves and villains. Despite all the money I had, life in the past was hard. I had to remember to give people gifts on their birthdays and on festivals too or they'd beat me up or throw dirt at the rickshaw. We didn't get any peace in the restaurants either. One time, a man walked in while we were eating and told us to move. I didn't know who he was and argued with him, but it turned out I had upset some gangster boss who had me beaten up and demanded four ounces of gold as an apology from me. You don't get that kind any more. They're either in prison, gone over to the Kuomintang, or hiding at home. The restaurants are less crowded and cheaper. I can snooze in the park after a good meal and don't have to worry about pickpockets." He patted his belly.

"So I'm getting fat."

I blinked in astonishment listening to him. I'd never expected that revolution meant liberation for him too.

Wakened by his rickshaw bell late at night, I was annoyed that Suzhou was still paradise for people like him. When the labouring masses won their liberation, these parasites benefited too. I couldn't budge Zhu, but now I had the right to preach communism publicly, so I decided to start with A'er, his rickshaw puller.

A'er lived at the lane entrance, just next to the public well. He was about my age, but taller, stonger and better looking. When we were little, we had often played together and he would always be the one to climb up on the roof if our ball got thrown up there. His father was a rickshaw puller too, who had come from north of the Yangtse River. When he could no longer work, his son took over. He took Zhu out three times a day and took other customers the rest of the time. He had a good rickshaw with a leather canopy, a horn, a foot bell and a blanket to cover customers' knees in spring and winter. A smart rickshaw and a handsome puller attracted a lot of business, especially from pretty artists who were story-tellers or ballad singers, attractively dressed girls with *pipas* under their arms. They felt they had to hire his rickshaw. As A'er wove through the noisy streets, horn bleating and bell ringing, all the pedestrians stared. When they got to the theatre, instead of slowing down he would brake in two steps with his feet firmly gripping the ground and his body leaning backwards, arms pressing the handles tightly, stopping smoothly like a Shanghai limousine. Holding the *pipa*, the actress would get off, wiggling her bottom, looking this way and that before disappearing behind a beaded curtain. What kind of impression would she make if she'd come in a broken-down rickshaw pulled by a hunchbacked old man?

Although A'er was a rickshaw puller, he had a reasonably good life. When I went over to talk to him, he and his family were having supper. The table was laid with a couple of dishes and good rice. His father was sipping wine and had a side dish of goose. I made a little small talk and then came right to the point.

"What do you think, A'er, now that we're liberated?"

An outspoken sort of person, A'er answered, "Things are good, we're no longer kicked around and beaten, and the customers always pay their fares."

I snorted. "Is that all? The working class are the masters of this country now; we do not slave for others."

"I haven't been slaving."

"Are you sure? What do you do?"

"Pull a rickshaw."

"Right. Down the centuries all vehicles have been drawn by animals except for trains and cars."

"What about a flat cart?"

"That ... that's for goods, not passengers. People

have legs, they're not ill or crippled. Why should somebody sit legs crossed on a rickshaw while you run in front of him like an animal? Do you call that equality? Do you call that being a master? And what about humanism?''

"Well, you've got a point there." A'er drew in his breath.

His father sighed, "We can't do otherwise; that's what they pay us for."

"Money...." A trace of scorn crept into my voice. "Do you know where people like Zhu got their money from? They exploited the labouring people and then gave you pennies to make you slave for them."

A'er frowned. "That man is quite fussy. He always wants me to go fast and doesn't like being jostled."

I seized this opportunity to tell him what the future would be like when the working people became the real masters of the country.

His interest was aroused. "That'd be something to work for. Dad, let's stop pulling rickshaws, you've been a slave all your life." A'er, I knew, wanted to be a car driver, the highest goal for all young rickshaw pullers at the time.

His father lifted his glass. "Finish your supper and get to bed. You've got to take Zhu for his noodles early tomorrow morning." I'd wasted my breath on him. Well, I'd forget about this conservative old man.

I invited A'er to my place to talk more. His consciousness raised, he decided to disobey his father and find another job. I spurred him on. "Good for you. You've taken an important step. The best thing would be for you to go to a factory and be an industrial worker."

A few days later, a despondent A'er came to see me. "I've applied to a lot of places but I can't even get into a restaurant, never mind a factory."

"Don't lose heart, you must hold out at all costs."

"I haven't lost heart, but I'm hungry."

I was worried too. "That's a big problem. We'd better get something sorted out for you."

I gave him some money and went off to the civil service bureau to look up a friend who'd come back to Suzhou the same time I did.

"That was a bit rash of you don't you think?" he said. "The factory owners are talking about withdrawing their capital and it's difficult to keep the factories open, so how can people expect to get jobs there?"

"Okay, I made a mistake, but we can't let him down; think of something."

He thought for a bit. "Well, at the moment I'm registering jobless people to do some work to earn their keep instead of just getting relief."

The work was dredging the small canals in Suzhou, strenuous but useful. The old society had left us with a lot of scum, so we had to clean the canal water and make this Venice of the East live up to its name. Making this paradise more beautiful was one aspect of revolution.

When A'er heard that this was also revolutionary work, he willingly went every day to dredge the canals and carry stones. It was much harder than pulling a rickshaw and he got only three catties of rice a day.

To make ends meet, A'er's father set up a little stall selling onions and ginger. He didn't do badly since they lived next to the public well. People often remembered they hadn't got any onions or ginger only when they were washing their vegetables. But the wine and goose disappeared from his table. Every time he saw me the old man turned away angrily. I felt rather apologetic and thought to myself, "Don't be mad at me, Uncle, some day you'll be able to drink vodka." His anger spurred me on. Every night, when I dragged my way past his door in the deserted lane, I'd think, "I haven't let you down, Uncle. I'm not afraid of hard work or fatigue; your A'er and I are fighting for tomorrow.''

My mother was very angry with me about A'er. "You ungrateful brat, what did Manager Zhu do to us? It's none of your business if he wants to spend money riding in a rickshaw. Now A'er can't support his family, and Manager Zhu has to hail a rickshaw when he wants to go out and sometimes gets caught in the rain.''

I decided not to argue with her. She'd suffered enough in the old society. Now that life was better I didn't want her to be upset. Besides, we just saw things differently. She still believed in the old feudal virtues, in loyalty to one's master like servants in classical operas. But it did keep me from approaching the man who ran errands for Zhu. He was so old he wouldn't even be able to carry stones like A'er if he lost his job with Zhu.

Zhu suspected I was behind all of this and no longer addressed me as Comrade Gao or offered me cigarettes. If we bumped into each other, he would lower his head and keep on walking. Without seeing his eyes I couldn't tell if he bore a grudge against me or just wanted to avoid me. He always carried a pair of galoshes and an umbrella, for he went out so early in the morning it was difficult to tell what kind of a day it was going to be. He didn't want to be drenched in case he couldn't find a rickshaw. I was secretly pleased. "You'll have to earn your own living sooner or later, Zhu. You might as well start practising now.''

The Attack Begins

Perhaps it was something the job-assignment fellow wrote on my file, for all my later jobs had to do with food. During the nationalization of private enterprise I was sent to a private restaurant to be manager since there weren't enough state representatives.

I knew this restaurant very well, though before

Liberation I'd never set foot in the place. I'd just watched well-dressed people go in and out, while the beggars crowded around the gate and looked at the delicious food in the display windows. After reading Andersen's *The Little Match Girl*, I always felt that the girl had probably died outside this very restaurant. It was winter when I started work there, and often snowing. I'd trudge through the snow to work, and suddenly my head would contract with fear that she'd be lying there dead, with her matches scattered all over the ground.

Inside the restaurant I couldn't be content either. I hated to see arrogant and wasteful behaviour. About one third of the food was usually left uneaten. If I let that continue, what kind of a revolution was I making?

I first of all got the restaurant employees to discuss the kind of people we had been serving. What proportion of them were workers or peasants, and what proportion were landlords or capitalists? This was meant to stir them up because they all knew that peasants never dared set foot in our restaurant; they were scared away by its appearance and cost. One meal cost as much as several bags of rice. They preferred eating at stalls in the Xuanmiao Temple where the food was good and cheap. Workers wouldn't come either except on very special occasions. But they all knew Zhu Ziye's likes and dislikes. Each waiter could recite a long list of regular customers, not one of whom came from the proletariat. During the time when private enterprise was being reformed, the capitalists were very unhappy. For some of them it was the end of this world and they'd often come to the restaurant to get drunk. They'd order a lot of famous Suzhou dishes and toss back one glass of alcohol after another, then tipsily declare, "Eat up, friends, we'll eat our way through their tractor screws." This was a way of attacking socialism, for in those days we looked upon tractors as a symbol of socialism. Socialist agriculture meant big state farms with lots of tractors like those in the Soviet Union.

I took this material, added to it my knowledge about the behaviour, past and present, of Zhu and his friends and wrote a long report, explaining my intention of making changes in the restaurant. It was animated and sincere and an obvious declaration against excessive consumption. My superiors were very pleased and gave permission for me to try out my ideas in my restaurant first and then see about introducing them in other ones.

I set to work. First I took down the neon lights at the door and the coloured lights in the windows. It seemed to me these sorts of lights represented dissipation and luxury that were the cause of wickedness. The old society of lavish display would never be resurrected, so why should we be left with its nauseating remnants?

The inside had to be changed too. We mustn't frighten off workers and peasants. The restaurant should be simply furnished and have plenty of room. Why should people eat in small private rooms? They could eat in public with money they'd earned from their labour. Only bloodsuckers wanted to eat in hiding. With the partitions knocked down we'd have a lot more room for ordinary labourers to dine in.

The service needed reforming too. The attendants weren't old-time waiters, they were working class. They didn't have to bow and smile, tagging after customers, wiping the tables and chairs with cloths they carried on their shoulders like people in Beijing operas. We were all comrades; why should they be a lower class, why should there be such hypocrisy? And people could fetch their own chopsticks, saucers and cups and whatever else they wanted, just as if they were at home. Who but the old masters didn't set their own tables at home?

These first three reforms the staff approved of and accepted as having a revolutionary flavour. But when I got to reforming the most important thing, the menu, things weren't so easy. Deep-fried fish, snowy chicken balls, crab meat and cabbage hearts...were all so aristocratic, who could afford them? An ordinary dish and an ordinary soup at 50 cents each were enough for one person. I had no objection to some people wanting something better, people had to have a little variety. In the revolutionary army we would often get special treats such as a bowl of stewed pork. Anyway, if what I suggested was too simple, we could have something like cabbage and shredded meat, garlic and liver, steamed fish or lion's head meat balls with green vegetables. That would be enough. No working class household ate like that every day.

Objections flowed forth, all of them from the older employees.

A waiter named Zhang took the lead. Grinning, he began, "Heavens, is our famous restaurant going to be turned into a little café? Why don't you do a more thorough job, Manager Gao? Give each of us two boards and let us set up stalls at the railway station."

I raised my eyebrows. "You can say what you think, comrade, but don't make fun. You're talking about revolutionary work, not joking with customers now," I cautioned him.

"All right, I've no objection. At least we won't have as much work to do," Zhang conceded.

The accountant chipped in, "I could be wrong, Manager Gao, but I'm a bit worried that we might not earn enough money." He spoke hesitantly since he'd been got at in past political movements for being a relative of the restaurant's former owner.

"I've thought about that too, but a socialist enterprise should serve the people instead of just earning money like the capitalists.''

"Yes, yes, you're right.'' He fell in line immediately.

But the celebrated chefs refused to be persuaded. These days they would be ranked among the top chefs and could have written books and gone abroad to demonstrate their skills. But back then no one had any particular respect for them, nor did they have any for laymen like me. Especially Yang Zhongbao, who acted as though I'd been flaying him alive.

"So that means we'll just be serving ordinary food, the kind people eat at home,'' he said.

"What's wrong with that?''

"Why bother going to a restaurant when you can get the same thing at home?''

"People don't cook when they come to Suzhou on business,'' I reasoned.

"Then they want to try the best food we can offer, and that isn't lion's head meat balls.''

"That depends on what kind of people they are.''

"All kinds, including cadres like you.''

"I get 50 cents a day expenses when I travel on business. If I spend that all on one meal I've still got two meals to pay for.'' I kept up the struggle.

"Not everyone is like you. People spend their own money too.''

"How much have they got? Some of them embezzle public money just because they want to eat good food when they go out,'' I said, trying another tactic.

"What if you get taken out to dinner?''

"Why should you accept? A lot of people have been corrupted by capitalists and it all starts with invitations like that. A lot of evil deals have probably been worked out right in our private rooms.''

"What about weddings?''

"Even less reason to be extravagant. Buy some sweets and have a party, that's what the government employees do.''

Yang flared up. "You're talking like a layman, Manager Gao. Government offices are different from restaurants. Why don't you transfer me to a government office to be a canteen cook? I'll gladly go.''

I glared at him, holding back what was on the tip of my tongue. I couldn't lose my temper with an old chef who'd worked longer than I'd lived, who had always been a member of the proletariat while I was an ex-student who belonged to the petty-bourgeoisie, something which couldn't be changed no matter how revolutionary I was now. At any rate, they had reason to object since their skills wouldn't be any use. Cabbage and shredded meat didn't require any high degree of skill; even I could do that…. It would be a pity if their talents went to waste. It would be better for him to go and cook for a foreign affairs department rather than in a mass canteen.

The room fell silent.

I turned to the younger ones, having discovered that the best way to save a situation was to stir them up a little. Even if they went too far it could still be put right later on.

"Haven't you young people got anything to say? You're in charge of this restaurant too; the future belongs to you.''

They only smiled, caught between the older chefs and me. One young waiter, Bao Kunnian, still only an apprentice, spoke very convincingly:

"Comrades, our restaurant must carry out thoroughgoing reforms. We will not serve the rich people any more; we must genuinely serve workers, peasants and soldiers. And our menu must show it. They can't afford crab meat and cabbage hearts. The cabbage hearts are put in that dish while they get the outer leaves. Stir-fried cubed chicken uses only chicken breast, and the claws and the heads are sold to rickshaw pullers. This is clearly a way of looking down on the labouring people. Once when a peasant came in and ordered beancurd soup he was sent away to the Xuanmiao Temple. This was a nasty trick because the Xuanmiao Temple only serves jellied beancurd. Yet when people like Zhu Ziye turn up, the waiters and chefs get cracking right away. He gets live fish, huge prawns and the tenderest cabbage hearts.''

Once Bao started, the others followed, criticizing the wastefulness in the restaurant and the way we took special care over big banquets but neglected small customers. A lot of these things I hadn't known and they infuriated me. I rapped the table, "Don't you see how badly in need of reform we are?"

Zhang hung his head in silence, possibly because it was he who had sent the peasant away. The chefs were silent too. Suzhou cuisine required a lot of superior ingredients and that made waste inevitable. And of course people like Zhu got taken good care of. Chefs relied on gourmets to spread their fame and appreciate the most subtle nuances of every dish.

Our policy was thus settled, thanks to Bao. He was later very active and carried out my instructions to the letter. I also gave him whatever help he needed to make progress.

He beat me half to death in the Cultural Revolution, but that's another story....

I threw myself into the reforms and never got home before eleven at night. I got the interior and facade altered, put up blazing red notices and sent a write-up to the local paper entitled "Famous Restaurant Serves Inexpensive Dishes to Ordinary People".

The first day a lot of people came—old men and women with their grandchildren, rickshaw pullers, vendors and people on business trips to Suzhou. Rickshaws, pedicabs and carriages lined the street outside. I'd seen this kind of commotion before Liberation when rich men and their wives came. While they were eating and enjoying themselves upstairs, their rickshaw pullers would be out shivering in the cold. Now these same shivering people were striding into the restaurant, heads held high. Human voices and the scraping of tables and chairs rose together in a hubbub. The atmosphere was electric. The waiters brought the food quickly since the dishes were cooked in large quantities and ladled out. Going in and out, people kept to the right as though they were in traffic. The restaurant was thronged with customers.

Surprisingly, Zhu and his friends came too. I wanted to see what they'd eat today. They read the notice outside, came in and looked around, bent down and scrutinized the dishes. Sniffing in contempt, they left, slapping each other on the back and sniggering. I was furious. "Disdain me if you like, that's exactly why I want to change this place."

But the reaction of the old men and women was quite different. "Before, we just heard about this place but never dared come in. Today we've really seen something."

One peasant choosing his meal observed, "Whenever I came here in the past I always had to go to the kitchens through the back door to deliver vegetables. I never dared poke my head into the restaurant."

Their praise made me forget my fatigue and touched me deeply. No matter how history might judge my work during this period, I firmly believed I was whole-heartedly and selflessly engaged in a great cause.

Our superiors paid a visit and were very satisfied. Although things were still a little chaotic, this was considered inevitable at the outset and we were asked to summarize and relay our experience to other restaurants.

A Happy Outcome

Zhu had been driven to the wall. Although the other famous restaurants didn't really follow suit and just made do with showing a few ordinary dishes in their windows, their specialities deteriorated in quality. The same dish at the same price was cooked with much less care. As soon as he tasted the difference, Zhu would frown, shake his head and complain. But he was misjudging the situation. No one paid any particular attention to him any more, no one called him Manager Zhu. A property owner, though still rich, no longer had any clout. Waiters weren't allowed to accept tips. It was up to you whether you came in or not; the volume of business didn't affect people's salaries. Anyone taking notice of Zhu's complaints would be labelled "a servant of the bourgeoisie".

Every meal was torture for Zhu and his stomach. He never ate his fill, and even looking at the food gave him indigestion. He wandered around like a lost soul, buying pastries which he'd find weren't as good as before and then leave them to go mouldy till my mother threw them away. His little paunch slowly dwindled.

One night a tipsy Zhu pushed open my door and announced, "I...oppose what you stand for, Manager Gao."

The bourgeoisie was counter-attacking. I had long been prepared for this: "Your opposition is welcome."

"You're making a mess of Suzhou cuisine; you're unfair to Suzhou."

"That's only your opinion. I haven't made a mess of anything. I don't make the landlords and capitalists very happy to be sure, but I think I've served the people of Suzhou well."

"You.... You're ungrateful to me."

"That's right; that's to be expected because you belong to the bourgeoisie."

"But I've been kind to you, Xiaoting."

Zhu was tactless enough to compliment himself for the very behaviour which had wounded my pride. I flared up. "I haven't made you or your friends happy, Manager Zhu. Three of them were landlords, two belonged to reactionary groups while you and two others still live on money the state gives you as compensation for your investments. Don't think you'll get that for ever."

Startled, Zhu sobered up and retreated a few steps. I declined the high-quality cigarette he quickly offered and took out my cheaper ones. He put the cigarette to his lips and inhaled.

"Ah, somebody bought me a chicken today somewhere outside Suzhou which was just as good as the ones I used to eat, so I ended up having a few too many. I don't even know how I got here; where's the door?" He turned to go.

"Wait."

He halted.

"Manager Zhu, I should have shown you my gratitude by warning you to change your way of living and learn to earn your own keep."

"Right, right I'll bear that in mind."

After that, I didn't see much of him and he never came to complain again. I often asked my mother about him. She didn't know much either except that he was seldom home and his room had a mouldy smell. He must be out doing something, I thought. Eating was his permanent necessity but it couldn't be his lifelong profession.

A while later, Bao gave me a report—he always used to report things to me.

"Chef Yang has opened an underground restaurant specially for capitalists and is earning a packet every night.''

"Are you sure?''

"Absolutely, I saw it with my own eyes. It's in No. 54, east of where you live. Every night a lot of these capitalists go there. Yang cooks while a seductive-looking woman collects the money.''

If there was any truth in what Bao said, how could I ignore it? I made investigations, sounded Yang out and unearthed Zhu's retreat.

No. 54 was the home of a woman named Kong Pixia, the former concubine of a politician-cum-professor, and her three tenants. She was not unusual among Suzhou residents. It was said she'd been as beautiful as a goddess when young, had been taught by a famous opera singer, and had even played a part in *The Goddess Scatters Flowers*. But even a goddess loses her attraction after forty, and on the eve of Liberation her husband abandoned her and her eight-year-old daughter and fled to Hongkong.

Probably because she'd once been on stage, Kong still liked doing herself up, and her every movement and glance were intended to look beautiful. When overdone, however, it was affected and coquettish—a little strange, in fact, since there was not much left to be coquettish about.

Zhu, who had never had any interest in women, got mixed up with Kong simply because of her marvellous cooking. Kong had prepared many banquets for her husband and his friends, men from political, industrial and cultural circles who were socially a cut above Zhu. To them Zhu was nothing more than a rich man and a glutton. No true gourmet dined in restaurants all the time. None of the banquets in *The Dream of the Red Chamber* were in restaurants. First-batch noodles were nothing to them. They were people who sipped tea in moonlit gardens and drank wine by balustrades overlooking streams. It was indecorous to eat roast pork that came wrapped in lotus leaves or fermented beancurd strung together with a rice stalk in noisy inns. People of taste and influence went to restaurants only when social occasions required them to and then only picked at the rich, greasy food. The pots and spatulas were not washed between cooking, so the food always had a mixed smoky taste. To them Zhu's delicacies were coarse fare indeed. What they ate belonged to another school of Suzhou cuisine, the crystallization of the highest forms of material and cultural accomplishment. Food as an art found its full expression in this kind of cooking.

Kong belonged to this school. When she'd been a celebrated concubine, she sang opera, cooked and painted. For over twenty years, distinguished people gathered at her home to play mahjong and to feast. She employed a good cook, but only as her assistant.

Just when Zhu felt totally despairing, somebody told him about Kong.

"You're kidding, my friend," he laughed. "I don't think home cooking can be so good. People don't have as many ingredients or as big a stove and pots as they do in restaurants."

"I don't know how I can prove it to you. In the past she wouldn't have given people like us a second look. I never managed to be invited to her place before Liberation.... But I hear she's come down in the world in the last few years and is hard up for money, so maybe she just might prepare a banquet for us. You two are neighbours, why don't you ask her and see?"

Zhu was desperate to find somewhere to eat, so he decided to make a visit and put forward the proposal.

Before Liberation Kong would have thrown him out. But now, unlike Zhu, she had neither income nor any property compensation and had to rent parts of her house out to three families. Even with this, she still had to sell pieces of furniture and jewelry from time to time. She was also keen to practise her cooking skills and win praise the way she had in the past. All the same, she didn't give her consent right away.

"Oh Mr Zhu, who's been telling stories about me? I only used to cook to amuse myself," she said in her lilting Suzhou dialect.

Zhu took the hint and unashamedly begged her, "Please do us this favour. Anything you do would be preferable to what we could get in restaurants."

"Restaurants!" Kong drawled contemptuously, "I don't understand how you men can bear to eat restaurant food. The smell alone is enough to put you off."

Zhu was stunned. What sort of smell did she mean? Some of them had wonderful aromas, ones which really picked up your appetite. But he said, "Yes, we're vulgar people who don't know anything about food at all. Please open our eyes for us."

"Very well, I'll try to do what I can. How many will there be?"

Zhu counted, "Nine altogether."

"No, no more than seven. You can't cook good food in large portions."

"How about eight? That'll be the right number to fill a table."

"You don't know the rules, Mr Zhu. One place must be for the cook."

"I beg your pardon," he said, wondering about cooks joining the meal. But to satisfy his palate, he had to go along with the rules. He produced a wad of notes and counted out fifty yuan. This he laid on the table, intending to give a ten yuan tip.

Kong looked a little hesitant. "Goodness, what can we get with so little money?"

The determined Zhu put the rest of his money down, eighty yuan all told.

Kong hesitated for a while as if calculating something. Glancing up at him, she finally said, "All right, if it's not enough, I'll put some money in too. You're a sorry lot."

Kong spent five days making preparations. People said she had to give up her plan to include eel in the menu because the eel had to be kept alive in a special manner for a week first, but Zhu just couldn't wait that long.

I didn't go to the banquet, so I can't really tell you what they ate.

Yang was there. He'd happened to run into Zhu while he was notifying his friends of the feast. One of them had fallen ill, and he had to find a replacement. "Come with me, it'll be an eye-opener for you," he told Yang, explaining his arrangement with Kong, and expressing again his disappointment with my restaurant.

A good cook himself, Yang never thought much of other people's cooking. Moreover, all the famous chefs were men, and he doubted a woman's ability. But he'd also heard from his master that ever since the end of the Qing dynasty, high-class brothels in Suzhou had served excellent food prepared by beautiful, intelligent women as exquisitely as if they were doing embroidery. He didn't have much else to do anyway, so why shouldn't he accept the invitation and learn something? If the food wasn't as good as Zhu had described, he could make fun of him and take him down a peg.

Yang was furious at the groundless accusation that he was running an underground restaurant and demanded to be transferred to a foreign affairs department. That was done quickly, so I never knew what skills Kong had displayed that evening.

Zhu's behaviour showed that it must have been a superb meal.

From then on, Zhu was seldom seen and stopped wandering about aimlessly. He never again went to the noodle place early in the morning and ate all his meals at Kong's. Soon the two of them, a rich man with a good appetite and an excellent cook and cunning shopper, linked up in marriage.

So Zhu finally married. A man who had already had countless houses got himself a home at age 45. A house is a wondrous thing; it can serve as a curb, can civilize a person. Zhu became decorous and decent, wearing smart suits with two fountain pens clipped to his breast pocket like a scholar. Kong spruced him up along the lines of her former husband.

Kong's housekeeping was as good as her cooking. After their marriage, she got Zhu to move in with her and moved her three tenants to Zhu's place. Her house had a little walled garden with trees, bamboos, rocks, a pool and bridge. They could live in seclusion and eat anything they liked. In those days, there were a lot of people who were opposed to good eating and fine clothes and who considered anyone who ate and dressed well as bourgeois. Therefore the rich had to eat behind closed doors. No one knew what they had in their stomachs. Of course people couldn't fail to notice the dressed-up Zhu and Kong when they went out shopping, arm in arm. They always drew a great deal of attention.

My mother never said anything bad about Kong, who she thought had done a good deed by reforming the errant Zhu. In fact, she often said to me, ''Zhu has changed for the better; they're in love and look after each other.''

I hesitated and thought to myself: Call this a change for the better? These people are evading reformation!

A Man and His Palate

Zhu evaded reform and I had no way of stopping it. He kept away from my restaurant and I couldn't freeze his bank deposits. It was no use criticizing him for having a bourgeois mentality either, since he was after all a member of the bourgeoisie. Let him eat, provided he abided by the law, stopped claiming that Suzhou cuisine had deteriorated and didn't storm into my room to voice his complaints. Revolution didn't happen overnight.

He never came again, and even when we met by chance he would ignore me and sweep past, displaying his re-emerging paunch like a victorious rooster.

What really got me was how so many other people had the same idea as Zhu and said that our restaurant had lost its reputation, that the service and the quality and variety of our menu had deteriorated. And more than ninety percent of these were not members of the bourgeoisie; they were cadres, workers, old men and women. Within a year, their support had turned to opposition. How quickly they had changed! I patiently explained to one old customer, "Now don't complain, granny, a year ago you wouldn't have been able to come in here."

"All right, now I'm in, and I want good food." She held out some money. "My son sent me this and told me to go out and have something really good when I felt like it. But what do you have here? I could do better than this myself."

"Then cook yourself. Home cooking's always best."

A slip of the tongue, I was thinking of Kong.

She was furious. "You sound like the manager of a den of thieves. If I cook myself, what do you do? Get paid for doing nothing?"

Bao butted in, "What do you mean by a den of thieves. Are you calling a socialist enterprise that? Why, you're attacking...."

I quickly stopped him. "Forget it, don't get angry, granny. If you haven't touched your food yet, you can have your money back."

When cadres criticized us I was less polite and would ask them, "Are you here on business, comrade?"

"Yes, I'm from Beijing," replied one. "I've come specially to your restaurant for a taste of the famous Suzhou cuisine, but is this all you've got to offer?"

"This is plenty good enough, comrade, what's your daily expense allowance?"

"I'm putting in some of my own money."

"We must keep to our tradition of frugality."

"Yes, yes thank you for your sermon. If I'd known, I would have brought a sack of corn buns with me and then your restaurant wouldn't need to exist." He left in a huff.

I sighed, thinking his bourgeois ideas were too entrenched. As soon as he'd got some money he'd got all high and mighty. Well, it seemed our restaurant had some problems. With the economic development and good harvests in the past couple of years, prices were low while workers and cadres earned good wages. People with money to spend shook their heads at the ordinary food we sold. I wanted to serve ordinary people but they criticized me. Some of them spoke their minds while most, not caring to waste their breath, simply avoided us and went to other restaurants which had only pretended to make reforms. Once the campaign passed, they dropped their pretensions and displayed exquisite dishes in their windows again. They were making people spend money and their business was flourishing. We'd had our day too, at the beginning of the reforms, but we soon went downhill and would be in big trouble if it went on.

Gourmets! When you were poor you would have had these classy restaurants torn down, but as soon as you get a little money you all pile in, worried you won't get a seat, and you want high-class meals too.

The spring of 1957 was a troubled time. The restaurant employees began to write big-character posters saying what they thought of me and hung them in the corridor. Their objections to the food and the drop in business didn't upset me, but one, signed "our employee", and accusing me of seeking personal glory at the expense of the restaurant and its employees, made me furious. The adjectives used in the poster and its tone meant it could only have been written by that scoundrel Bao! Of course I had to accept all the criticisms even if they had only the minutest grain of truth in them.

Just while I was so troubled and bewildered by all that was happening, my old schoolmate Bighead Ding, on his way to a conference in Beijing, stopped off in Suzhou to see me. It was eight years since we'd met and I was overjoyed. "You must come out to dinner, we can go to our restaurant," I said, a little surprised at myself wanting to take people out to dinner as soon as I saw them. It wasn't like me.

He shook his head. "Thanks, but I've been there and I've read the posters. Tell me what you have been doing all these years."

"What have I been doing? Well, just hold on a bit and I'll tell you all about it." I called my wife in and introduced Ding to her.

Ding bowed. "I'm Ding Zhen, Bighead was my nickname....But don't tell anybody else. I'm a manager just like you."

My wife smiled, scrutinizing his head as if trying to determine whether or not it was really bigger than average.

"Don't stand there gaping! Why don't you go and

buy some food?'' Ding had already been to my restaurant and I didn't want to become a laughing stock by taking him to another one. I'd better ask my wife to make something at home.

During the two years we'd been married my wife hadn't cooked very much. All she could do was give him tea and cigarettes and say, ''You two chat for a while. Mother has gone to a neighbourhood committee meeting. She'll get you something when she comes home.''

The neighbourhood meetings were always marathons. The food market would be closed by the time she finished. ''Why don't you cook something today? You can't depend on Mother all the time.''

''Have you forgotten?'' she retorted. ''You always say young people mustn't spend time on cooking if they want to get ahead. This ambitious young woman doesn't know where the oil is.''

Ding burst out laughing. ''I'll bet that's exactly what he said, so let him take the consequences.''

''All right, then go and tell Mother we have a guest and ask her to come back.''

After she went out I began to unburden myself, starting right at the beginning. ''You've read those posters. One of them was a personal attack by a young man. The rest were about my work. Where have I gone wrong in these reforms? You know what it was like in the old days. I have been working to eliminate that kind of wrong. Now those posters are attacking me for doing just that. But I haven't done anything bad.''

Ding fell silent, inhaling deeply on his cigarette. He was probably very troubled too.

''Well say something! You're well read, you've been working in a bookstore all these years. Pick up a book and give me a thump on the head. You'd better choose a hardcover one and give me a really good whack.''

Ding laughed. "That's no good, it'll spill your brains out. I would, however, like to draw your attention to a strange physiological phenomenon. It seems that the palate of the bourgeoisie is similar to that of the proletariat. The capitalists prefer shrimp to shredded meat and cabbage, and once they've tasted them, so do the proletariat. So when they've got the money they order shrimp, but you keep pushing shredded meat and cabbage at them. I'm surprised they haven't come after you with a hammer!"

I blew up. "You can't live on shrimp."

"Of course you can't; who can afford to do that?" he retorted.

"But we get so many people, you mustn't underestimate bad tendencies, comrade."

"It's you who've underestimated them. They've got money now. If one out of a hundred wants shrimp, that's enough to fill your restaurant to bursting. You keep rattling on about liberating the working people, but then you think they're not up to your expectations. People want to eat shrimp now and again and are quite happy to let you make a little profit, but this grates on you."

"It certainly does not! I don't have anything against them."

"I know you don't like that Zhu character, but what can you do about him when he shuts himself away?"

"He doesn't hide himself away entirely."

"Of course, a lot of people other than the working masses will be eating shrimp. I'll tell you: even when the landlords and capitalists have been eliminated, you'll still have hooligans and thieves among your customers, even escaped murderers."

I believed him. You needed an official letter and an ID card to get a room in a hotel, but only money to go to a restaurant. "You're right," I sighed. "But

I still think frugality is one of our national virtues. Why should we place so much emphasis on food?''

"I know, and from your personal point of view it's a fine thing. I hope you'll keep on being frugal. But you're a restaurant manager and you can't bring all your personal feelings into your work. Suzhou cuisine is famous; it's something created by labouring people over a long period of time. If you destroy it history will hold you responsible.''

I went cold. My schooling had taught me the importance of history. I would get nowhere if I resisted historical trends. Anyway I doubted that this cuisine was something created by labourers; it was obviously invented by people like Zhu and Kong.

On top of that, my mother shouldn't have given us such a lavish supper, five dishes and a delicious soup.

Ding was all smiles. "Look, this trend is sneaking into your home! You'd better watch out!''

Pumpkins and the Like

After Ding left, I did some careful thinking. Why did I want to get good food when an old friend turned up? Most simply, it was because I enjoyed doing it as well as showing my respect for a friend. Why didn't I do it before? When I said goodbye to him at Wuxi eight years ago, I'd given him a send-off with a bowl of dumplings that cost five *fen*. He was happy and I demonstrated my affection. Why couldn't I do that instead of spending five yuan on food? Because five *fen* was a tenth of all the money I had then. Now with my increased income, five yuan was the equivalent of five *fen* in those days. Even if Ding wouldn't have minded a bowl of dumplings, my mother and wife would have scolded me for being stingy. "You've missed Ding all these years, yet when he comes you won't spend more than five *fen*. What kind of person is that?''

Well, I had to be somebody who was consistent and didn't just follow bad tendencies. But had I noticed time passing, and life changing? To forget the past was a betrayal, yet refusal to change was also a betrayal, for it ran counter to the wishes of the people. Well, I'd forget about Zhu and let him have a good time in his cosy nest.

Just as I was about to accept these new ideas, the anti-Rightist movement started. It didn't hurt me; in fact I was almost a hero. People said I had a firm standpoint and had proved through my actions that the capitalists had been wrong in claiming that "the present was worse than the past". Still I wasn't really active enough since I had a change of heart after Ding's visit. I missed a chance of promotion.

That movement was followed by the Great Leap Forward and people were too busy to care about food that much. After that came the three years of natural disasters when people had nothing to eat. Ordinary food was a luxury; anything edible was welcome. No one particularly cared about the taste.

It was a bad time for Zhu. He'd spent his whole life satisfying his palate. Delicious tastes came from delicate foods like vegetable hearts, fish tails, egg whites, lean meat, mushrooms and ham. During the years when these were scarce even a good cook like Kong couldn't produce a tasty dish.

People are strange creatures. When there's food about their taste buds are highly sensitive—salty, delicate, savoury, sweet, hot, all can be differentiated. When there's nothing to eat, hunger takes over and three large bowls of plain rice give an indescribable contentment and satisfaction. Zhu wasn't exempt from this law either. Hunger drove him out of his nest to roam about, not for delicacies this time but to see where there were crowds of people about. Then he'd race over and squeeze in, try to buy sweet potatoes, turnips or peanuts at any price. More often than not, he would go home past my door empty-handed, exhausted and despondent. For the first time I saw him drop his airs; for the first time he realized that money wasn't omnipotent.

He complained that he was given less rice than Kong's daughter.

"You're seeing things," Kong snapped.

"Is it me or you? My bowl is practically empty."

Kong shoved her daughter's bowl at him. "Here, take this one too; she's not your daughter anyway."

The child sobbed while husband and wife had a terrible row. After that they ate separately, with Zhu cooking his own meals. No longer were they seen arm in arm, nor did people hear her coquettishly calling him.

I was hungry too. As a restaurant manager, there were ways I could get food. In times like this, power was more effective than money. But I never cheated and would rather have died of hunger than lose my integrity. Besides, I didn't starve. Both the women in my family took good care of their charge. My mother would always urge me, "You eat first, you've got to go to work and I'm staying home. I'll eat later." I knew what "later" meant, so I stealthily put some rice back in the pot. My wife made sure that our daughter had enough to eat. She was at primary school and growing and wanted to eat as soon as she got home from school. She'd eat as much as she was given, not like children today who have to be coaxed.

My wife had never been all that strong and she fell ill, her legs and face swelling up. This was a common illness in those days and could easily be cured with a chunk of pork and a chicken cooked with four ounces of rock sugar, but there was nowhere to get these.

With a heavy heart I was dragging my way past

A'er's door one day when he signalled to me.

When he was dredging the river he'd proved himself a very good member of the working class by working hard and not grumbling about being paid only three catties of rice a day. The leader had a high opinion of him and transferred him to a transportation unit where he'd become chairman of their trade union. He still trusted me and listened to every word I said. Hadn't history proved that the rickshaw had been consigned to museums and that pedicabs were hardly seen? Although he hadn't become a driver, he had become the drivers' boss.

I went into his place. His father was in the courtyard. After ignoring me for a couple of years, he'd started to ask me to have a drink with him after A'er began to earn a monthly wage, got married and got his two younger brothers working too. Where the stall selling ginger and onions had been, there was now a small table where he would sip a little wine every evening. But since things were taking a turn for the worse once again he'd taken his table inside. I still called him uncle, a greeting he acknowledged unsmilingly.

A'er took me aside. "How is your wife? She looked pretty bad when I saw her the other day."

"Yes, she's got dropsy."

"We sent two trucks to Zhejiang to get some bamboo but they came back with two loads of pumpkins instead. Bring a cart to the dock before dawn tomorrow and I'll give you some."

"You shouldn't do that! They're for the people in your organization; I can't take any."

"I'm not up to anything bad, I'm giving you my share. We often send trucks out to get food; I'm much better off than you."

"But..."

"No more buts, do as he says," the old man cut in. "And what's so special about pumpkin? I'm waiting for those big state farms and tractors and some of your vodka," he chided with a grin.

I laughed too. "Don't give me a hard time, Uncle. Remember how you used to ignore me when A'er was dredging the river? Then later you invited me for a drink every time you saw me. Don't be too impatient. These hard times are only temporary. The good times will come back."

He nodded and smiled. "I know, I know."

People like him who'd suffered in the old society and had a better life in the fifties never lost heart during those difficult years; they knew that there was no turning back and that hope lay ahead. So they patiently put up with hardships and waited for the good times to come back, though the waiting was long. I regretted that I hadn't given my customers more shrimps to increase their confidence in the future.

When I got back and told my mother the news, she was overjoyed and set off immediately to borrow a cart. The cart brought Zhu Ziye in its wake. He looked wary and pitiful. He wouldn't take a seat and just stood at the door looking foolish. I wondered if he had come to complain about something again.

My mother, as respectful to him as ever, made him sit down and gave him a cup of tea. "Say what you have to say, Mr Zhu. Did you have a row with your wife?"

"I haven't got that much energy! Look at me, I'm all skin and bones!" He sighed, patting his shrunken stomach, which had protruded twice before—a barometer of his existence.

That paunch gone and his ruddy face sunken, he looked haggard and old. "Have patience, Mr Zhu. Hard times temper you," I said.

"Right, you're right." He rose hesitantly and then sat down again. Mother had gone through hardships herself and knew that Zhu had a favour to ask. Before

Liberation, when she had to borrow money from Zhu, she'd gone in and out many times before she could bring herself to ask. Not wanting other people to suffer the way she did, she prompted him.

"Tell us what's on your mind; maybe we can help. Everybody has difficulties in their life."

"Pumpkins...I hear you're getting some pumpkins. Can I buy some from you?"

This was a surprise. As the pumpkins were supposed to build up my wife's health, my mother was at a loss, remembering old stories of loyal servants helping their masters in distress. She turned to me. "What do you say, Xiaoting?"

The Zhu Ziye who had perched arrogantly on A'er's rickshaw and who'd dined in all manner of eating places was pitifully begging for a few pumpkins. This was punishment enough for him.

I nodded. "You can have some."

"Thank you very much, I'll pay you." He shoved his hand into his pocket, never forgetting the power of money.

He'd managed to hit the wrong note. Disgusted, I said, "I don't want money, but I do have one condition."

"What is it?" He looked worried again.

"You must come along and help me cart the pumpkins. Those who don't work don't eat. You wouldn't want me to deliver them to your house, would you?"

"Of course not, I'll work. But...I don't know how to pull a cart. I might overturn it into the river."

He was right. "You can push while I pull," I said.

"Fine, I'll do my best."

"Good, come to the corner store at four tomorrow morning. Make sure to be there on time." A labourer must have discipline, I thought.

At 3:55 the following morning, I pulled the noisy

cart through a slumbering lane.

Zhu, wrapped tightly in a raincoat, had planted himself conspicuously beneath a streetlamp. I was pleased. Manual labour could reform people; at least he'd learned to be on time.

"Good morning, Mr Zhu, I'm sorry to have kept you waiting."

"I've smoked five cigarettes already." He took off his raincoat and bent down to push the cart.

I quickly urged him to put his coat on and told him that an empty cart didn't need pushing. And I showed him how to raise the handle a little. "See? When the front is higher, the centre of gravity is at the back and you can pull the cart without too much effort. When we've loaded it, all you need to do is give me a hand when we go up and down slopes and bridges. When we're on level ground, just put one arm on the cart, press your weight down and run along beside it."

Zhu heaved a sigh of relief. So pushing carts wasn't that hard! He walked along beside me, his raincoat over his arm, looking around animatedly as if seeing the city and the street cleaners for the first time.

"What time is it, Manager Gao? It feels like midnight to me."

"Three minutes past four. Haven't you got a watch?" I wondered if he had measured the time by the number of cigarettes he had smoked.

"I had a Longines watch in my first year at university but I only wore it for three days. I didn't like having it on my wrist."

I almost burst out laughing. That Longines watch must be in his stomach now. That was the best place for it.

"How did you get to class on time then?"

"I didn't go. It was a private university where you could buy diplomas. I regret that I didn't study hard now. There're still so many new words when I read a book.''

I looked at him in a new light. If he didn't push carts, at least he read. And reading was educational.

"What do you read?"

"Books about food, of course. Cookbooks. Now that food is scarce, I lie in bed at night remembering the goodies I had before and then all those exquisitely decorated dishes seem to appear right before my eyes. To tell you the truth, my memory is particularly good where food is concerned. I can remember what I had dozens of years ago from a certain chef in a particular restaurant, how it tasted and what the aftertaste was like. Don't you laugh. The aftertaste is important. Green olives are neither salty nor sweet nor crispy but they have a savoury aftertaste. Human beings are highly intelligent in creating so many good foods. They eat creatures that fly in the sky, that live on the land and in the seas and rivers. Otherwise they wouldn't exist today. Dinosaurs ate only grass. Where are they now? ... Don't sigh. It's a pity that I didn't keep a detailed diary of all the good food I've eaten. So I read cookbooks to satisfy my craving. Slow down a bit and listen to me. I sometimes get angry at cookbooks which are too general and don't include my favourite foods. What bothers me is that they don't give any space to Suzhou cuisine but to queer things that the emperors used to eat. The hundred dishes they had every day were only for show; how many of them were good? Why did Emperor Qianlong come to the south three times? For Suzhou food of course...."

I'd had enough. "Hurry up, let's go get the pumpkins." I stressed the word *pumpkins* to bring him back to reality.

"Right, we shouldn't overlook pumpkins; they can be made into something superb too. Your restaurant used to have a famous dish called 'watermelon bowl', or also 'watermelon chicken'. You cut the top off a medium-sized melon, take out the inside, leaving about one inch of flesh, and carve a design on the rind. Then you fill it with a well-steamed young chicken, replace the lid and steam it a minute. Serve the melon on a lotus leaf, which gives a cool green effect." After considering the recipe, Zhu shook his head. "Actually the chicken doesn't taste like melon and the sweet melon doesn't go with the salted chicken either, it's just to give it a pleasant cool greenness. We could invent a pumpkin bowl and fill it with steamed glutinous rice, nuts and preserved fruit. Sweet pumpkin would be just the thing for glutinous rice pudding; it would have a country flavour."

His long recital about food brought us almost to the dock. I didn't interrupt him, having no confidence in his transformation any more. People don't change their basic natures.

Landing in the Same Boat

It was beyond my wildest notions that an opponent of gluttony and a glutton would stand side by side one day. Yet in the Cultural Revolution I was labelled a capitalist roader while Zhu was called a bloodsucker. Every morning we stood in front of the neighbourhood committee with placards round our necks confessing our "crimes".

There was reason to call Zhu a "blood-sucking vampire". But I...maybe I was a capitalist roader. Once the years of natural disaster were over, I'd wanted to make amends for the reformation I'd carried out earlier and didn't force cabbage and shredded meat on the customers any more. Since times were changing, the higher-ups issued an order to open better restaurants selling costlier dishes in order to take a bit of currency out of circulation. It was incumbent upon famous restaurants like ours to take the lead. Those hard, hungry years had even made me, who'd never been greedy, crave good food. My mother went to the free market, where prices were unbelievable. She bought a chicken and made some chicken broth for my wife. "Eat, my child," she urged her, tears in her eyes. "You've had a hard time these few years." Actually my wife had recovered a long time ago, but my daughter was very pleased and told everybody, "We had a chicken today," as if it were something terrific.

Zhu and Kong came back to my restaurant, not arm in arm but carrying a basket filled with sweets and pastry, each holding one side and smiling at one another. Fresh from the hairdresser's, they were sleek and perfumed. Money had played its part in patching up their worn-out love.

Zhu ordered two fresh hams cooked with rock sugar and soya sauce at the exorbitant price of 20 yuan a piece and put them into two food boxes to take home. Ever since our pumpkin adventure, Zhu and I would exchange greetings and a few words on the weather whenever we met. The lean years were finally over and we could get provisions again. Exhilarated, I said to him, "I'm glad to see old customers."

He was all smiles and shook my hand, but his answer was not pleasant to the ears. "I don't have any alternative. We can't get rock sugar and fresh ham otherwise. Your prices are exorbitant."

"Eh.... Why don't you eat them now while they're hot?"

"Because they're underdone and tasteless. We'll cook them again, then put them on top of some green vegetables on a white plate to make them look nice, smell good and taste delicious. Your cooking still leaves much to be desired!"

This wet blanket made me regret ever having given him the pumpkins, but I decided not to show my displeasure. The food supplies were improved in 1963 and '64; I had to give my customers more shrimps so that they would remember the good times and I wouldn't feel remorseful again. But rehabilitation was a hundred times more difficult than carrying out reformation. It was always easier to go from refinement to coarseness, strictness to carelessness, diligence to laziness and from being humble to being unreasonable. To correct these tendencies was much more difficult.

Although Bao was still a waiter, he hadn't actually worked as one since I'd declared during the reform years that waiters shouldn't be humble and obsequious. He sat commandingly, like some president at a meeting, shouting to the customers, "Hey there, you're not to take any table you like. Fill the ones in front first. Hey, didn't you hear me? Why did you slip over to the window all by yourself?"

When customers asked him, "Could you come here, comrade?" he would demand, "You want to order? The menu's on the blackboard; read it."

"Comrade, I'd like to order a couple of your famous Suzhou dishes."

"Every famous dish has a name, and they're written on the blackboard." He wouldn't budge.

I would get complaints at almost every meal. "We've come to eat, not to be pushed around." I made apologies and called a staff meeting to look at our work, criticize one another and establish proper guidelines.

When the Cultural Revolution broke out, these became my "crimes". I was accused of restoring capitalism and forcing the revolutionary masses to wait on city lords.

Bao became a leader of the revolutionary masses and headed straight for me, thinking that if you overthrew a director or a manager you could take his place. Since the director had already been overthrown by others, he had to be content with me. And he did have the qualifications to attack me: he had a clean record, always supported the revolutionary line, and even more precious, he'd boycotted my restoration activities as early as 1963 and had been cruelly suppressed by me. That wasn't exactly a lie, for I had criticized him in 1963. His remark about every famous dish having a name had been quoted in the newspapers and although his name wasn't mentioned, he felt the pressure all the same. Therefore his condemnation of me had a particularly vehement tone: "It was a time when black clouds hung low over the city. I was alone and powerless and had to capitulate to his wishes. How I wanted to...." He often read novels during working hours and so had picked up a lot of colourful phrases which he lobbed like bombs. I'd taken him as my righthand man and had told him about my life, about things like running errands for Zhu and living in his house rent free and so on. I'd told him partly to show the injustice of the old society and partly to make conversation. Now he put it all together to denounce me.

"This unrepentant capitalist roader was bought by the capitalists when still a boy. Seeing the inevitable end of the Kuomintang, he sneaked to the liberated area with ulterior motives. After Liberation he pretended to be active in order to worm his way up to usurp power and restore capitalism when the opportunity arose."

His accusation, though groundless, was logical, for I had gone to the liberated area on the eve of Liberation, and had worked very hard before being promoted to manager. I had also intended to alter my way of management when the opportunity arose after the bad

years. You could look at a thing from lots of angles.
If you made up your mind to call any animal a horse
no matter what it was, then you could find horses
everywhere.

"Bao has a point. All property owners collect rent;
why didn't Zhu make him pay? It's been a long time.
What's their relationship?" People wondered. They
weren't malicious, just curious.

Bao went to our neighbourhood committee to
interrogate Zhu and try to dig up incriminating facts.

Besides being a glutton, Zhu's other weakness was
his fear of pain. As soon as Bao rolled up his sleeves
and pounded the table threateningly he started trembling and admitted to everything.

"Speak up, did you buy Gao Xiaoting?"

"Yes... I did."

"How did you do it?"

"I gave him money."

"Where did you give it to him?"

"At the wineshop."

"How much?"

"Hundreds of thousands of dollars."

"How could you get such a large sum out of the
bank?"

"I didn't need to go to the bank. It was all small
notes, devalued Kuomintang money."

"You call that money? What's the use of devalued
money? Tell me about your collaboration after Liberation."

"There wasn't any. He hasn't been very polite to
me."

"Rubbish! Take him away," Bao snapped.

"Have mercy on me, I remember now. During the
famine, he gave me a lot of pumpkins."

Alas, that was iron-clad proof of my "crimes". It
got even worse later when they finally got hold of
Kong, whose ex-husband in Hongkong had sent her

canned food during the bad years. A reader of detective stories, Bao could weave a convincing plot. An undercover agent, Kong received secret instructions in the tin cans her husband sent, while I supplied her with state secrets. Look, three-fifty in the morning, and Zhu, wearing an American raincoat and a cap (he hadn't worn a cap that night), smoked five cigarettes in a row. At four o'clock sharp, Gao Xiaoting had appeared with a cart, looked around and whispered, "Let's go...." This thriller had a good beginning and sold well. Bao was invited to speak at meetings everywhere. He spun his story out while I had to stand bending over and answering questions too.

"Do you admit your crimes?"

"Yes, I do." And I really did. It had been wrong of me to encourage and promote Bao instead of criticizing him when he came to me with the story about Chef Yang opening an underground restaurant with a coquettish woman collecting the money, when all Yang had done was have a meal at Kong's. If he could get promoted by lying, then what would stop him making up even more lies? The more he gained from telling lies, the greater his lies would be.

"Answer me. Are you guilty of a monstrous crime for which you deserve to die?"

I refused to answer. I didn't want to die. I wanted to live. I wanted to correct my mistakes. I wanted to live for the cause of communism, something for which I would gladly give my life.

Blows rained down on me. They weren't violent but they pierced my heart like daggers. I felt that I had practically placed the dagger in Bao's hand myself.

The neighbourhood committee couldn't just sit doing nothing, so since Bao had dealt with me, they made Zhu, Kong and me confess our mistakes in front of the committee every morning. Zhu and I were finally side by side.

Standing outside the neighbourhood committee with a placard round my neck was worse than standing on a platform being condemned. When I looked down at the large audience, I never knew how many of them actually knew me personally. At the neighbourhood committee everyone who went by was known to me. This old lady with a shopping basket had known me since I was a boy, that woman had invited me to her wedding, that boy always called me uncle. I lowered my head and looked at the ground. They would take a detour or quicken their steps, feeling bad at seeing someone who had neither stolen nor committed other crimes there like a man sentenced to death. I could identify them by their shoes and the way they walked, especially my mother, whose feet had been bound and later unbound. She'd hovered near me countless times over the years. Now her steps were heavy and hesitant.

A'er paid less attention. As he went by he would cough loudly and then whisper, "Hang on."

Kong couldn't take it. After half an hour, she collapsed and cut her face.

My disgust for Zhu increased tenfold. I stood as far away from him as I could to show that he and I didn't belong in the same category.

The following morning, A'er came with a big cart loaded with iron and wooden poles and ropes. Twenty burly porters wearing straw hats were following behind. Stopping right behind us, someone demanded, "Who told you people to stand here?"

Frightened again, Zhu blurted out, "The head of the neighbourhood committee."

A'er gestured to one of them. "Go and get him."

Five or six men dragged the man out.

"Did you tell them to stand here?" they asked him.

Sensing trouble, he replied, "May I ask which faction you belong to?"

"The rod faction. You mind that people are not allowed to stand here and block the traffic." The men began to take up their rods.

The committee head tried to calm things down. "We can talk it over, revolutionary comrades."

A'er spoke up: "If you feel you must punish them, then make them sweep the street round that corner."

A man who knew his way around, the head understood his intention at once, and avoided the beating he might get if he gave them a hard time. He quickly motioned us off. "Go home and get your brooms."

A'er threw me a cheerful glance. "Get going, don't dawdle. And do a thorough job."

I had to laugh. The street they were talking about was a dead end lane of only thirty metres or so; it wouldn't take us long to sweep it.

But I couldn't escape Zhu, who always tagged along behind me trying to find ways of expressing his gratitude.

"You have a loyal friend," he told me.

I could hardly stop myself bursting out, "Our friendship doesn't come only from eating and drinking together."

After a Long Absence

It was a full nine years before I saw Zhu again, during which time my family and I were sent to the countryside. He was probably still living in No. 54.

Nine years is a long time. What I saw and heard during those nine years made me think about the whole issue of food. I passed my fiftieth birthday deep in thought.

On my birthday, Mother killed a chicken and got a bottle of good liquor through a friend. I drank three glasses in a low mood, then was seized by fear. I'd turned fifty before I knew it! After Liberation, when I'd gone to meetings with men in their fifties, I'd taken it upon myself to help them up and down steps; to me they were old. In the country, a man of fifty with children of his line did not expect to carry heavy loads any more. "Greying temples without achievements make a hero tearful and sad." Though I was no hero, I shed a few tears of regret. Then tearful and tipsy, I let my thoughts run wild. "If I am given a post again, first I want to....Second, I want to...." It was like a dream. Dreams sometimes come true, but only with difficulty.

After those disastrous years, I went back to Suzhou, this time not with my belongings on my back but with my family, bits and pieces, furniture and farm tools enough to fill a truck. Suzhou felt both familiar and strange. The streets were still the same. But where had all the people come from? Suzhou people preferred window-shopping to going to parks when they had free time. Now, the streets were so crowded you had to pick your way carefully when crossing, and if you met a friend you could only shout loudly on the curb while a stream of people brushed past you. The city's population had swollen rather than decreased, although a lot of people and their families had been sent to the countryside. I'd been squeezed out of my home and had to stay at a relative's for the time being. This suited me fine, since I could keep my distance from Zhu, who was in another part of the city.

A man from the organization department came to talk to me. He was about my age. The man who'd wanted to starve me for three days and who'd later become the director of the organization department was no more. May he rest in peace.

"We've been considering sending you back to your old job. How do you feel about that?"

I was overcome by emotion. If that old director

had been there, I would have broken down right in front of him. You needn't starve me any more, director. I fully realized the significance of food now. And you can relax, Bighead Ding, I won't force cabbage and shredded meat on my customers anymore. I want to work hard and make up for lost time, work for you and for the old director.

"Don't be upset. What's done is done. We've still got a lot to get through."

I nodded. It goes without saying that food supplies are the first thing on the list to be affected whenever there is a disaster. And once the bad times are over, the first place people rush to is the food market; after that they buy clothing, electric fans and TV sets.

I wasn't wrong in my guess, although I'd overlooked two things. After the ten years of chaos, people began to look up old army mates, relatives, former classmates and bosses. Some of them had been held in custody for ten years, others had faded into obscurity ever since the 1957 anti-Rightist movement. People made inquiries: was so-and-so still alive, where were they, etc. Every household had their surprises, "My goodness...where have you been all these years?" Opponent of gluttony though I was, I couldn't resist dinners in such situations. I was human; I had feelings too. If Ding could come and see me now, I would have feasted him for three days running.

One other thing I hadn't foreseen was the rise of tourism. The word "tourism" was seldom used before, and such activities were called "enjoying the mountains and rivers", which was considered somewhat vulgar. Now "tourism" took on a new meaning— seeing and appreciating our native land. Anyway, whatever the meaning might be, I had no objection to people sightseeing. We particularly welcomed foreign tourists to see our city and spend their foreign currency. The rockery and pools of the Suzhou gardens might be artificial, but all earth's culture was made by man. Real mountains and rivers might be wonderful, but they aren't culture. Besides, without boasting I can say, the artificial gardens of Suzhou are more characteristic, more concentrated, perfect and unique than natural ones.

And what about Suzhou cuisine? Well, manager, in this ancient paradise food was always on a par with scenery. If I wasn't opposed to dinner and tourism and foreign visitors, my restaurant had to catch up.

We had a hard time in the beginning. My customers just weren't satisfied. Not enough seats, too little variety, bad service, so on and so forth. They carped and complained. Some had a go at me about it. Once Bao even came to blows with a group of young men.

After the fight, he came to me with an embarrassed look on his face. "I...I treated you badly in the past, Manager Gao."

I brushed it off. "Forget it, it wasn't entirely your fault. If you've come to apologize, you can stop right now. If you've come about something else, then just say what's on your mind."

Bao hesitated a little. "I've...got a bad temper. I don't think I'm much of a waiter; my attitude annoys people. In the past I had wild ideas about being somebody. I know now that you can only get on in the world if you've got qualifications. So I want to learn some kind of skill."

"You want to quit?"

"No, that wouldn't be very practical. I want to learn to cook. I think I can learn to do it better than others."

"Well." I thought about it. Bao's attitude couldn't change overnight. He might come to blows again. Then again the kitchen was short of hands; we needed more chefs. I gave my consent.

Bao was pleased. "You can relax," he told everyone. "That capitalist roader isn't the sort of person to bear a grudge. Although I beat him up before, he hasn't paid me back. Since all you've done is write a few posters about him, you don't have anything to fear."

Don't belittle Bao's declaration. It had a reassuring effect. After those chaotic years, people wanted a more peaceful life. If they grumbled a bit, it was because they were impatient for improvement. This was no bad thing. Impatience gave some kind of impetus; it was better than indifference.

We studied the customers' comments book. Apart from our bad service, other things were brought up too, such as the quantity and quality of the food, quick service for those eager to go sightseeing, patience with those who wanted to be left in peace when old friends got together. Some of them placed more importance on famous specialities and others on reasonable prices. Some of them lost their tempers at having to wait too long, others complained about the cost. My conclusion was that I should neither force cabbage and shredded meat on people nor do away with it entirely, but should improve its flavour.

I introduced foreign ideas into my restaurant by serving fast food—one dish, a soup and a bowl of rice. Tourists could eat quickly. Actually the fast food wasn't much different from ordinary mass-produced food; it just sounded more efficient. I had the ground floor seats changed into booths, so it seemed like being on a train.

Young people liked the idea and the lower prices.

When I was young all I knew about was tractors, while youths abroad could enjoy revolving restaurants. How they revolved I had no idea, but my booths had a feeling of motion too. And the fast food wasn't bad:

there were also dishes of fish, spare ribs, shrimps and chicken. One young man even snapped his fingers at me and said, "Hey, bring me a bottle of whiskey." This I couldn't agree with—I was afraid whiskey and vodka were more or less the same.

Upstairs we served hot food and the space was repartitioned and furnished with square tables and imitation redwood chairs. Big round table tops could be put on the ordinary tables for large groups. Green plants decorated the corners. Old people nodded in approval, "It's just like it used to be." Actually it wasn't exactly the same, otherwise they would have said, "What's the matter with these people? It's all run down after twenty years."

While I was up to my neck in renovation work, I heard the odd comment drifting by: "In the past this old fellow tore down the partitions. Now he's putting them back again; why couldn't he have been smarter before?" My heart sank; I'd become an old fellow. Well, I might be old, but why did they call me "old fellow"? Anyway, my repartitioning was certainly an improvement; only it had taken twenty years to do. That I felt bad about.

Renovating the place and introducing a few foreign methods were easy enough, but traditional cuisine posed a much more difficult problem since our skillful chefs were few. Yang and his peers had all retired. The young chefs were ignorant about a lot of traditional dishes, but they wanted to learn. They'd heard about Yang's skill and were eager to learn from him. They must have heard how I'd treated him too. History is recorded by word of mouth as well as by books.

I decided to look Yang up and ask him to give lectures to the staff, hoping that he wouldn't bear old grudges. We would pay him well and treat him like a professor.

It was raining hard that day, but I decided to go anyway. Yang was quite moved that I'd come in the rain. "You still haven't forgotten me," he said. He'd aged a lot, was hobbling and a bit deaf. When I told him why I'd come and asked his forgiveness about the past he grasped my hand and said, "Save your breath, I've already forgotten. I still think of the restaurant as my home; that's where I learned, that's where I grew up. Whether you'd invited me or not, I'd still have come to visit my old colleagues before I kick the bucket. I've heard you're doing pretty well."

I was moved by his magnanimity. He was still enthusiastic about our work, and his enthusiasm was even greater than mine.

He came, accompanied by his grandson. He looked around the place, nodding with approval all the while, saying it was incomparably better than before. Spacious kitchens, refrigerators, ventilators, white stoves and modern cooking utensils—it was better equipped than the kitchen of the foreign affairs office where he'd worked. He studied our menu very carefully.

The whole staff came to his lecture. I asked him to speak openly and concentrate on our shortcomings. He spoke well, with a due sense of propriety.

"I'm impressed with your work. Your menu includes almost all of Suzhou's specialities and the cooking is good. Of course you're hampered by the lack of ingredients and the large quantities you have to prepare. But that can't be helped; you've got a lot of people to serve and they don't mind what they spend. I've been told that you've never heard of some of our most famous specialities, which is because one dish can have a lot of different names. For instance, what's rather grandly called the 'supreme dish' is only baked rice soup...."

The audience burst out laughing.

"Yes, baked rice soup, you've got it on your menu,

but there are a lot of famous dishes that you can't put on the menu. Take fish lung soup for example. The fish lungs are only the size of broad beans. Where can you buy those in quantity? Actually the lung itself doesn't have much taste; what makes it delicious are the other ingredients and the monosodium glutamate. It became famous only because Yu Youren, a big Kuomintang official, wrote a poem about it after he had it in the Shijia Restaurant. Then both the restaurant and the soup became well-known. Some dishes have become known half from word of mouth and half for their quaintness.''

I sat back and heaved a long sigh of relief.

"But there are a lot of improvements you can still make. Why kill the fish the day before and keep it in the fridge? Why leave your fresh vegetables in the sun? Everything except your alcohol should be fresh. In the past we took only three minutes from killing a chicken to cooking stir-fried chicken breast.''

Bao raised his hand. "Can you tell us the secret of that kind of speed, Master Yang?''

"Actually there isn't one. You just have to have everything ready and work fast. You kill the chicken, plunge it in hot water, pluck the breast only and take the meat. Then dice and stir-fry it. Of course this was a demonstration dish and could make a chef famous.''

Yank talked for about two hours and then went to the kitchen to give a demonstration. He was in good spirits and refused to take a break, but he tired himself out and had to rest for a fortnight afterwards.

I'd thought of sending in a report asking permission to have Yang supervise our chefs and be given extra pay. But now I thought I'd better not bother him and just let him enjoy his retired life in peace. However, the young people were very enthusiastic and wanted to keep on. I regretted that I hadn't valued their talents and paid more attention to training them. I racked my brains trying to think of a way of making up for it. I asked my staff to recommend good cooks if they knew any. They would be paid well and we would arrange cars for those who needed them.

But alas, this was to bring back Zhu Ziye.

A Diner Gives Lessons

I don't know who first brought Zhu's name up, but everybody supported the idea. I was thoroughly surprised that a glutton could be so famous.

I suppose there was every good reason for Zhu to give lectures. He'd been making the rounds of Suzhou restaurants from 1938 to 1958, and before that had frequented Shanghai restaurants too. Though he had nothing to eat in the three lean years, he'd never stopped reading about food. I heard that he wrote a cookbook during that time. Although during the Cultural Revolution he'd confessed to anything put to him, he'd kept his mouth shut about his manuscript, wrapped it in plastic and buried it in a rockery. This action alone put him on a par with scientists, theoreticians and men of letters. Bao put it well: "He could have taught us a thing or two just by telling us what he's eaten all his life." I agreed to do it. I shouldn't put my own likes and dislikes above my work. At any rate, I hadn't seen him for the last ten years. In ten years a man could become a scholar. But I didn't go and get him myself. Bao went in a taxi. At 68, Zhu was qualified to be picked up in a taxi. Bao said he wanted to take the opportunity to apologize to Zhu and Kong for his past bahaviour. I thought it was better for him to make his own apology. People should do their own apologizing. I couldn't take on everything.

I presided over Zhu's first talk. Remembering his fantasies about pumpkins, I wondered what other ideas had occurred to him during the last ten years.

Zhu wasn't a good speaker, particularly in front of an audience. He stuttered and trembled. But when it came to food, he was a different man. He was eloquent, interesting. As soon as he got on stage he asked an interesting question.

"Comrades, who can tell me what is the most difficult thing about cooking?"

The audience's interest was aroused, and they began to make guesses.

"Choosing the ingredients."

"Chopping."

"The actual cooking."

Zhu shook his head. "No, you're all wrong. It's the simplest yet the most difficult thing to do—the adding of salt."

They were riveted. Nobody thought he'd mention something every little girl could do. When old ladies went to the well to wash rice they would call out to their granddaughters, "Put some salt in the pot for me, would you, dear?" Some of the old chefs nodded in agreement: this simple thing required great skill.

Zhu elaborated, "Sour in the east, hot in the west, sweet in the south and salty in the north. People all believe that Suzhou dishes are sweet, but actually apart from dessert, Suzhou cuisine is very careful about salt, which enhances all tastes. A fish lung without salt is tasteless. Salt makes the fish lung tasty, ham more savoury, the water chestnut more slippery and the bamboo shoots crisp. It brings out all these tastes and yet itself vanishes. The right amount of salt is not salty; if there is too much you taste nothing but the saltiness. Then all the skill in the chopping and careful cooking is wasted."

I was astonished that he could be so convincing.

He went on, "The quantity of salt varies with the people and the time. The first few dishes of a banquet should have more salt because the diner's body needs it and his palate is still not ready. The dishes that follow should have less and less salt. The soup that comes at the end of a forty-course meal should have no salt and people will appreciate it all the same, because after so much wine and food, the body is already saturated with salt and people need water. And water with a little MSG is delicious.''

Zhu interspersed his talk with interesting anecdotes too. ''Not putting salt in soup was an accidental discovery by a famous chef. The dinner had been going on from 6 p.m. to midnight and he was so tired he had forgotten to add salt. When he realized and hurried into the dining hall with it, people had already finished the soup and commented that it was the best course of the evening.''

He went on nonstop for two whole hours impressing the audience with his extensive knowledge. He ended to applause and returned to his seat with his chest all puffed up. His ruddy face and silvery hair gave him an air of solemnity. Bao picked his way through the audience and walked up to grasp his hand. ''That was excellent, Mr Zhu. I tried to take notes but I missed a lot. Could you repeat what you said if I bring a tape recorder to your home?''

''Well...yes, but please come after three in the afternoon. I take a nap at noon.''

''Certainly. I won't trouble you to repeat your talks in future; I'll just record them right away. Then I'll transcribe them from the recording.''

''That's not necessary. I just talk off the cuff.''

''It's very valuable information. It would be a pity if it wasn't taken down.''

''Well, let me read the manuscript when you've done it.''

''Of course, I'd like you to have a look at it.''

Since he had after all been to a private university, Zhu did have something of a professional air. Bao always liked to collect material, so I asked Zhu to continue his talks over the next few weeks.

Zhu gave three talks. Bao borrowed a four-speaker tape recorder and recorded everything he said. In his second talk, people began to get a little impatient. He went on and on about the importance of adding salt, but never told people how to do it. The chefs weren't amateurs like me, they knew the importance of salt. They wanted Zhu's consummate skill of using salt. But unlike Yang, Zhu didn't go to the kitchen to demonstrate. The third time, he began to talk about when and with whom he had had a feast on a boat in a lake; how refined the feast of crabs was that he'd had one Double Ninth Festival when they'd used sixty-four solid silver pieces of cutlery to eat them with. And he kept harping on about the dishes today being a far cry from those in the past. I remember how he'd belittled the emperors' palate, but now he was praising the imperial food of the Qing dynasty to the skies. I took it in stride. Food wasn't like works of art, the older the better. A primitive mural found in a cave was precious, but was the ox roasted in a cave in ancient times also the best? The chefs began to yawn and some of them left for home, saying they were fed up with his bragging. In his fourth talk he even started in about singsong girls, flower girls and actors who performed at banquets.

I decided to put a stop to it. Bao protested, saying that history would hold me responsible if I didn't preserve such precious material.

The mention of history left me cold. If Zhu disclosed something valuable in his future talks or if he had already done so and we'd missed it, then I'd take the responsibility. Yet I refused to be cornered now, having learned the trick of not committing myself. I would wait and see and only speak when things were clear. Then I could always be in the right.

"How about this? Zhu needn't give his talks any more because no one wants to listen. You can go on with collecting material since you've already started. I'll provide you with the things you need."

Bao was delighted. "Let's buy a four-speaker recorder."

"No. I'd have to get permission for that. But you can buy some cassettes on our propaganda fee. Don't get all foreign ones only, get some of our Chinese-made ones too."

He was very pleased. "Thank you for your trust in me, Manager Gao. I'll do my best to do a good job."

So the lectures were settled that way. We paid Zhu his fee and the taxi expenses. But the matter was not quite finished. Bao kept on buying cassettes; every two weeks he bought a couple more. When I signed his receipt one day, I inquired, "When will this mission end?"

"My dear manager, it's become a big thing now. I've made contacts for Zhu to give talks at a lot of places, so it's not going to end. Nor do we want it to. We've decided to set up a Culinary Society, so that we can have a proper name when we make contacts. Zhu will be president, I'm vice-president. You're one of the sponsors too. Since you're so busy we thought of asking you to be an honorary councillor."

"What?" My head was spinning. Bao seemed to be organizing another attack force the way he had in the Cultural Revolution.

"I can't," I protested. "I don't know anything about cuisine."

"You don't have to, just give us your support."

"No, we don't have money to throw around."

Bao laughed. "Manager, you're such a....You don't need money, we can make money by selling mimeographed notes of his lectures. The street stalls sell sewing books at a hundred percent profit.

Cookbooks will sell well too. Besides, we can sell them at Zhu's talks for people to buy with their office propaganda funds.''

I had to hand it to Bao; he was a much better businessman than I was. I'd never thought of tapping the propaganda fund, which of course was much easier than taking private money. I had no right to forbid them and could only give them a warning.

"You mustn't have things like singsong girls in your notes.''

"We won't. I'll do the actual writing, all purely academic. Nothing about love.''

I smiled and signed his bill. "Remember, next time buy domestically made ones.''

"Don't worry, there won't be a next time.'' He waved the bill. "We're going to buy a four-speaker recorder and a calculator.''

I didn't take Bao seriously. They were dreaming. Bao's cooking skills and Zhu's theories about salt didn't warrant research. Bao liked to follow the fashion, he'd turn back after a while.

But I was a simpleton; I underestimated Bao's ability. A good cook he wasn't, but he was an old hand at manoeuvring and gauging situations. Well-known restaurants were gathering places for all sorts of people, particularly well-known ones. You could set up relations by being friendly, giving good service, helping people make orders and reserving seats for them. You could get to know the younger generation if not the older one, and the young could influence their parents. Bao had helped them organize receptions for their sons' and daughters' weddings or get-togethers with old friends. They didn't mind spending money but they just couldn't cook well. Although Bao was no expert, he could get skillful cooks for them. Good cooking, Zhu's boasting and Bao's arrangements would doubtless make the banquets a success. They would explain the aim of their Culinary Society at these parties and get support. A culinary society which laid sumptuous dinners right before your eyes was more likely to get support than a nutritional society, which was difficult to grasp though it might keep one fit and healthy. The word "society" had its appeal. Anti-academicism had been crushed and now everyone knew a little learning was better than no learning, so you wouldn't be in the wrong by supporting a society. Even if it was a mistake, it was still an academic problem to be thrashed out. And the more you discuss and debate something, the more famous that something becomes.

Zhu's fame grew. He was said to be an expert who had written a book during the Cultural Revolution which had brought manager so-and-so to his knees. This manager had sent a taxi to get him to give lectures and offered him 200 yuan a month to be an adviser, but Zhu had declined.

News of Bao's activities and Zhu's growing reputation reached my ears. "Watch first and make comments only when the time is ripe." Now the time was ripe, yet I had nothing to say. I couldn't say Zhu was just boasting and that people shouldn't pay attention to him. What was the harm in listening to theories of adding salt? Nor could I claim Zhu had been a glutton all his life and would never change....That would sound more like a compliment, since people who want to achieve something should devote their entire life to its pursuit. There was nothing I could say about Bao either. I couldn't say he was opening an underground restaurant, nor was he asking me to sign his bills any more. I would only be picking up a rock to drop on my own feet. Some people drop that rock as soon as they pick it up, but others drop it dozens of years later.

A Sumptuous Meal

Not long after that, my old friend A'er came to see me. Even though we were no longer neighbours, we often called on each other. The day I moved into my new place, his whole family came, even his father. "Well, congratulations," he said to my mother. "Now you'll never have to worry about being thrown out by a landlord any more." My mother, who was getting on now, didn't reply and just wiped away tears. A'er often dropped in for a chat, a cigarette or a cup of tea. This was the first time he'd looked me up at the restaurant.

He waved to catch my attention. "I wouldn't have bothered you today, only I wanted to ask you a favour."

"What is it?"

"My eldest son is getting married this Sunday. I tried to book two tables for the reception but was told I'd have to wait three weeks. Can you help me?"

That put me on the spot. "So you do this too. Other people give banquets in restaurants to show off, save themselves trouble at home and collect gifts. Is that what you're up to? How much should I give?"

"Come on, I'm not inviting many people. The bride's and bridegroom's families and yours, less than twenty altogether."

"You could have a party at home by putting a couple of tables in your courtyard. Look at this place; it's so noisy you couldn't even hear people's congratulations. Once it gets near closing time, the staff are so eager to knock off they stand next to you holding brooms. How could you possibly enjoy your meal?"

"Listen to you! Running down your own restaurant."

"It's not that; our food's not bad. We get a pile of complimentary letters every month. But I just always feel a party at home is nicer. Besides, we have a regulation that no employee may sit down at a friend's table. Should I just stand beside you and watch you eat?''

"Of course not; this time I want to do something special for you. If you hadn't persuaded me to dig ditches, my life would have been quite different.''

"Good. Then have a party at home. I'll get you a good chef, first-rate.''

"There's no need,'' A'er laughed. "We've got a big family and everyone can do something. Times have changed; everyone's got a couple of specialities.''

"Splendid, everybody can cook one dish. I'll do the soup.''

A'er washed his hands. "Thanks, but don't bother. I know how to do it. You just come over early; I'll be expecting you.''

I was really looking forward to the wedding reception. I'd brought trouble to this household once. A'er's father had had to sell ginger and onions because of me. Now, the same courtyard where A'er had promised to give me those pumpkins would hold two tables of food. I felt thoroughly happy.

Just then Bao raced in, looking really pleased. When everyone was happy, the world became a better place.

"Here, Manager,'' Bao cried and thrust a red invitation inscribed with gold characters into my hand. It read: "In celebration of the establishment of the Culinary Society, prominent figures from all walks of life are invited to luncheon on Sunday the twenty-eighth at No. 54, X X Lane.'' Another dinner party. I quickly said without thinking, "Sorry, I've got an appointment on Sunday. I'm going to a wedding.''

Bao scratched his head. "What time?''

"Six o'clock.'' Another thoughtless answer.

"Excellent. Our luncheon is at noon; there's no conflict.''

I looked at the card again. Yes, it said twelve noon.

I had to make myself clear. "I can't come. I'm not a member of your society and I'm no prominent figure. It would be inappropriate for me to come."

"My dear manager, your refusal to be our councillor has helped a lot. The councillor's seat is still vacant. Otherwise we would have split up quarrelling long ago."

So my not joining them was an even greater support! How subtle these things were.

"Please come. Everyone's coming; it wouldn't be right if you didn't. Besides, it's not a meeting where you'd have to make a speech. It's just to eat. It would be a shame not to eat such good food."

"I don't care for good food."

"You don't have to eat much. It would be an eye-opener and a kind of vocational study for you too. To tell you the truth, it's going to be something very, very special. Zhu will give the directions and Kong will be cooking. We've spent four days making preparations. Kong insisted on no more than eight people. We had to do a lot of persuading before she'd agree to use a round table which could seat ten people, including you."

I wavered. Yang had praised Kong's cooking to the skies after eating there. I still didn't know what he'd had that day. I'd regret it all my life if I lost this chance. Besides, I had already given them my support whether I was present or not. If I left a seat vacant once again, what would happen?

"All right, I'll go,"

"Fine, then it's decided. I won't come to pick you up. You know No. 54 well."

"I certainly do. I could find it with my eyes closed."

When I'd been in secondary school I went by No. 54 every day and saw the shining rickshaw parked outside the door. Occasionally a Ford would drive up and squeeze the pedestrians against the sides of the lane. The black lacquer door, invariably closed, had a slit and a burglar eye. The slit was a letter box, and the eye enabled those inside to see out, but not vice versa. In those days there were beggars, and families had such devices to keep them away. I never saw inside the tall courtyard wall overgrown with creepers, but the scent of osmanthus wafted out in autumn. Now the osmanthus were in bloom again and I had come to No. 54 not as a boy, but as a prominent member of society.

Inside the opened lacquer door stood a beautiful girl in high heels, sleek trousers and a silvery blouse with white ruffles at the throat and a drawstring waist. She walked up to me smiling. I held out my invitation card, but she bowed with a smile and invited me in.

"Manager Gao is here, Mother," she cried.

So this was Kong's daughter by the politician and professor. Yes, she would have grown up by now; my own daughter was already a mother. I turned to look at her. She was the very image of Kong, who must have been just as beautiful when she was young.

Kong walked along the gravel path lined with flowers. I could hardly recognize her; she seemed to have given her own face to her daughter while turning into a mature lady herself. She had put on weight and looked much younger than when she had stood in front of the neighbourhood committee. She wore her hair piled up high in a pompadour which gave her more height and disguised her plumpness. Her dress was tasteful; time had taught her the art of dressing. A young girl was beautiful no matter what she wore or how she made up, but the dress of an older woman should bring out elegance and character. Her simple clothing suited her age and figure, and her blue jacket was well tailored and of good quality.

Kong was extremely friendly towards me. People as meticulous as she always remember the small things.

"I was afraid you might not come, Manager Gao. You've got on in years too; are you a grandfather now?"

"Yes, my daughter had a baby."

"That's nice. Do come in, please, we're waiting for you."

I followed her through a quiet little garden. A stone bridge spanned a square pond on three sides of which were trees, flowers, bamboos and rocks. The bridge led to a big pavilion overlooking the water, which must have been the study of the politician-professor. It was spacious and had a long row of French windows opening onto the pool. Looking in, I could see a large round table set in the eastern end, while the "prominent figures" were seated in the west.

Bao came across the bridge to meet me and introduce me to the important people. Among them were two of Zhu's old banquet companions for whom I'd bought food in years gone by. One was a former superior of mine, whose speeches I had listened to when I was a young man. The other three I didn't recognize. One was very quiet; the other two were talkative and seemed to be businessmen of some kind. Dressed in an old western suit complete with an old tie tucked inside his vest, Zhu didn't look too bad. I didn't know which trunk he'd dragged the suit out of, but it had a strong smell of mothballs. This kind of clothing was familiar to me, but from where? Oh, yes, in my secondary school days my teachers had divided off into two groups. Half dressed in dark blue long gowns and the other half in western suits and leather shoes. My Chinese language teachers were always seen in long gowns and my physics teachers were always in suits. Cuisine was a kind of science. A long gown would be too old-fashioned, an ordinary uniform had no particular impact, and there was no particular reason to wear a brand-new western suit. An old suit was just right. He seemed like an old scientist who had been overlooked for years, now suddenly discovered by the world. This must have been Kong's handiwork, since Zhu had always been a careless dresser.

Zhu hadn't worn a western suit for ages and seemed uncomfortable. He bumped into several chairs and then stuffed a mimeographed manuscript on cooking into my hands. Ill at ease, I sat in front of my former superior. Having worked with him for a time just after Liberation, I was under the impression that he was a sombre and strict person and did not approve of intellectuals. We "petty-bourgeois" elements were always very careful and disciplined in front of him. Meeting him in this setting, I was flustered and at a loss for words, so I slowly leafed through the mimeographed sheets.

"Young Gao."

"Yes?"

Then he discovered I was no longer young. "Er, Old Gao, you should read this material carefully and learn from the author."

"Yes, I shall certainly do that."

"Non-professionals cannot direct professionals any more; they really must know what they are doing."

"Definitely. I've made mistakes in the past."

"As long as people recognize their mistakes, there's time to correct them."

I nodded, continuing to finger the manuscript. Narrated by Zhu and written by Bao, it had nothing new in it and was only copied from a lot of other cookbooks. There were many mistakes, or maybe they were just printing mistakes. I looked up at Zhu, meaning to ask him a few questions, but he avoided my eyes and showed us all to the other end of the room.

We each politely asked one another to go first and finally persuaded my former boss to take the lead.

The table dazzled us. The white drawnwork

tablecloth had been set with an exquisite dinner service: very thin porcelain with a semi-transparent design and a latticework blue rim which looked as if it would leak. There were no flowers on the table but the twelve cold dishes were just as colourful. The shrimp, ham, green pepper, beans and chicken were pretty in themselves. The beef and fish were decorated with all kinds of vegetables, red crabapples and green plums. Salted fish cooked with shrimp roe was usually not good enough for banquets, but since it was a Suzhou speciality and had been unobtainable for many years, it was a rare treat. It was surrounded with white lotus strips partly as decoration and partly to take away the saltiness of the fish.

At the centre of the twelve colourful dishes was a large rose, crocheted perhaps by Kong's daughter, to be used as a mat for hot dishes later on. The entire table was like a large blooming lotus or water lily.

This astonishing sight was greeted by many "oohs" and "aahs".

Another criticism came before we even sat down. "Look at this, Gao, this is real skill. That restaurant of yours is nothing more than a noisy market."

I remained silent and just glanced around. Outside, trees were swaying in the breeze and the reflections of the verandas shimmered in the water as the scent of blossoming osmanthus wafted in. Birds chirped in the garden, just as they had when the politician-professor had sat in his studio....

Zhu again urged us to take our seats. He loosened his tie a little and made an impromptu speech.

"Gentlemen, please follow my instructions. There's a lot to knowing how to drink and eat. You mustn't wolf the food, especially at the beginning. Try a little of everything first. The best comes later, so you have to leave some room for it."

Everybody was in high spirits and laughed.

"Although everyone can eat, some people never really enjoy their food. It takes years of experience to learn to do that. I'll explain every dish to you in the hope that you'll give your comments freely. Now let's start; bring the wine glasses."

Bao opened a cupboard and took out a set of wine glasses and two bottles of port. Even without Zhu's explanation I knew one mustn't start with alcohol since it numbed the palate. But I liked alcohol. I'd learned to drink it during the lean years and could drink nothing weaker than 128 proof.

Bao poured the wine into the glasses, making them look instantly like beautiful red rubies.

As vice-president of the society Bao spoke briefly, not so long to outshine Zhu of course. He raised his chopsticks and urged us, "Let's start, comrades, help yourselves...."

Ignoring Bao, Zhu stopped us, "No, no. You don't tuck into the cold dishes at a sumptuous dinner. They are just to fill the gap between courses so that you can keep on eating and drinking." Then he called out, "Serve the first course."

All eyes turned to the opposite side of the pool. Since ancient times, a gentleman always kept his distance from the kitchen.

I seemed to be watching a film: Kong's beautiful daughter made her way through the trees and bamboos to the bridge. Walking lightly with a tray in one hand, she and her reflection in the water floated toward us like a modern goddess from the Moon Palace. This beautiful scene, directed by that damn Zhu, would make any food on her tray, even if it were only coarse corn buns, seem like one of the Empress Dowager's feasts.

Of course the dish wasn't corn buns, but we were all astonished to see ten scarlet tomatoes when the plate lid was lifted. In Suzhou cuisine, the first course had always been a hot dish like stir-fried diced chicken, fish or shrimps. I'd never seen a meal start with tomatoes. Was this a dish or a fruit?

Zhu served them calmly, putting one on each plate. Then, like a magician, he took the top off his tomato, which was stuffed with stir-fried shrimps.

In high spirits, we all did the same.

Zhu explained, "Stir-fried shrimps are nothing special; you've all had them many times. Apart from improving the ingredients and way of cooking there haven't been any changes for many, many years. In recent years, people have started stir-frying shrimps with ketchup, but that tastes too western. Shrimps in a tomato are both delicious and attractive, but please don't eat the bowl."

I had to admire Zhu. I'd been wanting to give my customers shrimps for a long time, but it had never occurred to me to stuff them in tomatoes. Autumn tomatoes were expensive, it would be a shame to throw them away. I would have liked to eat the tomato too.

The shrimps did taste better with a hint of sourness from the fresh tomato. Bighead Ding was right in saying that people's palates were more or less the same, unlike Zhu who claimed that some people ate without tasting anything. The difference was that some people could describe it better than others. All some people could say was "Good, superb," while Zhu's talent was in description and exaggeration. He had the ability to exaggerate in a way which could stimulate nerves that had been desensitized by excess.

The goddess floated back and forth across the bridge. I lost count of the number of dishes she brought except that a sweet followed each three. We'd had three desserts already: lotus seed broth, glutinous rice balls cooked with osmanthus and Gorgon fruit with lotus root starch.

I lost interest in Zhu's explanations. The beginning was too superb to be sustained. The later dishes, like hibiscus chicken slices, snowy chicken balls and chrysanthemum fish, could be found on the menu of my restaurant too.

The praises and exclamations were unceasing.

"How did you learn all this, Mr Zhu?" someone asked.

"It's difficult to say; from experience perhaps. You can't learn it from any teacher or book."

"You've had a happy and comfortable life, Mr Zhu. We're much too far beneath you."

"Not at all, we were all in the same boat during the bad years and the Cultural Revolution."

"That's all in the past now; come on, let's eat."

"All right, when we reach communism we'll eat like this every day."

Hearing that made me feel sick. If we ate like this every day then who would be working, robots? Maybe. But we mustn't start eating right now: the 58th generation of robots has still to be invented.

"Old Gao."

"Yes?"

"Why are you so quiet? Did you never discover Zhu's talents?"

"Oh yes, I knew about them a long time ago."

"Then why didn't you ask him to help you improve your restaurant?"

"I...did, I asked him to give talks."

"That was only temporary. He didn't have a proper title."

Everyone suddenly fell silent. All eyes turned to me. I was on the alert. Some kind of deal had been planned for this dinner, it seemed.

"What kind of title?" I asked.

"Well, he's a sort of expert."

"What's he expert at?" I waited for an answer.

A scientist, writer, actor? He was none of those.

"Eating...." They couldn't go on; that was hardly complimentary.

"Someone who knows...." That was no good. Who didn't know how to eat?

Bao raised his chopstick. "Foreigners have a term called 'Gourmet'."

"Excellent."

"That's absolutely right."

"A gourmet, a gourmet," they all exclaimed.

"Let's all drink to our gourmet."

Zhu was extremely satisfied, and couldn't resist unbuttoning his old suit and walking round the table to toast me, giving my delicate glass such a powerful clink it almost broke. This was the high point of his eating life. No one had ever paid him any attention for this lifetime of diligent eating; all he'd had was opposition. His real value was something recognized only by foreigners.

I hated myself for my ignorance, which had enabled Bao to defeat me. All I knew about was introducing fast food. I hadn't been on guard for the introduction of gourmets.

People were enthusiastically starting on the tenth course when Kong entered to solicit comments. We thanked her and asked her to have a drink.

"Mrs Zhu, thank you for your superb cooking; thank your daughter too for bringing the food," I said. I wasn't that well disposed towards Kong, but I still had to admit that she was an excellent chef. Actually, she ought to be the president or vice-president of their Culinary Society. That's the way things were: those who worked weren't up to those who bragged. Those who cooked weren't up to those who ate.

Kong was delighted. "Why, thank you for your compliments, Manager." She raised her glass and made a circular gesture to indicate all the guests. "I must offer my apologies to all of you, I'm not satisfied with the cooking I've done. I had to use tinned bamboo shoots since I couldn't get any fresh ones."

"You're being too modest."

"Let's drink to Madame Gourmet."

After everybody had drained their wine, Bao removed the glasses. But this was far from the end of the banquet; he was only changing them.

Zhu produced a set of Yixing pottery wine cups in the shape of peaches with twig and leaf handles. A jar of mild yellow rice wine was brought in. It seemed that the vintage of wine rose with the guests' spirit as the feast advanced. I stole a glance at the two bottles of *wuliangye* in the cabinet. They would probably be opened just before the soup. I wondered who was paying for the meal. Was it Zhu, or somebody's propaganda fund?

Kong withdrew to raise the curtain on the second half of the banquet. Hot dishes and desserts came in a stream until a "three-in-one" brought the meal to its climax.

The "three-in-one" was a pigeon, a chicken and a duck stuffed one inside the other. It looked like a huge duck sprawling on an oval plate, surrounded by quail eggs.

Everyone exclaimed in admiration.

"Old Gao."

"Yes?"

"Now, isn't this the height of perfection?"

"Yes."

"Doesn't this alone make Zhu a qualified adviser for your restaurant with, say, a monthly allowance of something in the region of one hundred?"

I realized that this was the crucial topic of the day. I quickly found an excuse.

"That's very flattering, but my restaurant is much too small to warrant the help of someone so distinguished.''

"It's not the size that counts, it's how the manager feels."

Luckily, the three-in-one came to my aid at this point. Once it was divided up, people were too busy to talk.

I stole a glance at my watch; three hours had passed since the dinner started. There was still my favourite *wuliangye* and a delicious soup to bring it to an end and then there would be fruit. But I dared not stay to the very end; people would chat over their tea and try and put the rope around my neck.

"I'm very sorry, but I have to leave for another appointment. Please allow me to express my thanks to Mr Zhu and to everyone....'' I stood up as I spoke, retreating all the time. After I'd gone five steps I hurried across the stone bridge. When I looked back I saw the stunned expression on the faces of everyone in the room.

I had fled in a totally ungracious and impolite manner. Kong would be very hurt if I didn't say goodbye to her.

Kong and her daughter were still busy cooking. When she heard I was leaving, she was disappointed.

"Perhaps you don't like my cooking."

"Your cooking is excellent. One of these days I'm going to ask you to talk about it at my restaurant.''

She laughed. "It's nothing special, you could do just as well. The only problem is that you don't have as much time to do things meticulously. It takes almost two weeks to prepare things really well. Why don't you stay a while longer? I'm just making the soup....''

I suddenly remembered something. "Mrs Zhu, why aren't you having a pumpkin bowl for dessert? When your husband came with me to collect those pumpkins he claimed he would invent a pumpkin bowl with a pastoral atmosphere.''

"Don't listen to him," she laughed. "All he does is brag."

Chocolates

To the west of No. 54 was A'er's home, where another dinner was waiting for me.

I was already full. The "three-in-one" sat heavily on my stomach and their proposal weighed on my mind. I just wanted to drink a little 128 proof with A'er and his father to warm me up so I could have a long sigh over the joy, sorrow and hardship of life.

Autumn is the golden season in every city and Suzhou is no exception. This year the temperature was mild, the sky blue and the humidity low. The fragrance of osmanthus drifted out from the courtyards. The sky above the little lanes was seldom so blue with so many clusters of white clouds. It was Sunday and the lane was quiet. People were doing their housework, the most important part of which was cooking. Steam floated out of windows which opened on to the street, and the sizzling sound of things frying could be heard.

On the way to A'er's I had to go by my old home. It hadn't changed a bit. The black lacquer door, the white walls, the five rooms set back from the street with Zhu's old house behind them. For just a moment, I seemed to see A'er waiting with his rickshaw at the gate and Zhu coming out in a long gown to sit on the seat, step on the bell and head off to Zhu Hongxing's for noodles. For forty years he had been the incarnation of food, had haunted me like a ghost, had unintentionally decided my career. I hated and despised him, tried to keep away from him. Yet instead of getting rid of him, I had been asked to give him a monthly allowance to be my adviser. I would happily give more money to Yang if he could come. But what was Zhu, this man who could only teach people how to squander and waste; what bearing could he have on our work?

Just try and squeeze your way in, Mr Gourmet! As long as I'm here you're just daydreaming.

I felt better as soon as I got to A'er's. It was a happy world, with no social rituals, no hypocrisy, no extravagance. The courtyard was full of people cracking melon seeds and eating wedding sweets. My family was already there. My one-year-old grandson was a happy chubby baby who could smile, grimace and wave his plump little hands. Now that each couple could only have one child, each baby had six grownups to look after and admire him. He was the centre of attention. All the guests gave him sweets, talked baby talk to him and passed him round.

Somebody gave him a fruit drop which he pushed out with his tongue.

"Doesn't he like sweets?"

"He does, but he likes good ones."

"Then let's give him a chocolate."

And sure enough the little boy stuffed half the chocolate into his mouth and sucked greedily.

Everyone laughed. "What a clever baby! He likes chocolate."

My head was spinning. When he grew up he would be another gourmet. I had spent my whole life unsuccessfully trying to change Zhu; surely I could change this little creature. I grabbed the chocolate and forced a fruit drop into his mouth.

He started to wail.

Everybody present was stunned, thinking to themselves that the old fellow had finally gone off his rocker.

1982

Graduation

1

ALONG THE LANE they used to call her Comrade Lee. At that time she had a job, went to the office every day and didn't have time to fetch the vegetables, milk and breakfast cake or to mind the little girl. Since she'd stopped working two years ago, they started calling her Mistress Lee, because her husband Wu Li hadn't yet retired from his university post. Professors are teachers and for thousands of years their wives have been called mistress. By tradition of course, women should take the husband's name, and she should have been called Mistress Wu. Mistress Lee, reflecting her own name, was technically inaccurate, but marked a certain progress in society and respect for women's rights. But the other baby-sitters—standing as she did in the afternoons with her granddaughter in her arms at the end of the lane, making "honk-honk" noises at the traffic in the main road—could never work out if she was Lee or Wu, comrade or mistress. So they followed the child's example and called her Granny.

One day everyone in the lane learned the old lady's real name. The postman came with a large brown envelope, knocking on doors and shouting, "Lee Manli! Where does Lee Manli live? The number on this envelope is wrong."

Two old men drinking tea in a doorway tried to help. They had an air of authority, as if they knew all the households in the lane. They put their heads together over the envelope and tried to puzzle it out.

"Lee Manli is a girl's name. But the teenagers around here are known by their pet names—we don't know their real names."

"I seem to remember someone called Lee Manhua."

"You old fool! You're thinking of the filmstar Zhou Manhua. Remember when he came over to the Reds 40 years ago?"

"I went over then too. I was working in a foreign company in Shanghai..."

"Number 28 is Lee Manweng, the painter."

"No, it can't be him. He's eighty if he's a day."

"Sorry, comrade postman. She probably lives in the new apartments there. I see fashionable girls coming and going there every day."

The postman looked up at the ugly six-storey block. A row of old houses had been knocked down two years earlier to build it. The residents came from all over and no one knew anyone else. It would take at least half an hour to go up, knocking from door to door, and he couldn't spare the time. So he yelled at the top of his voice, "Lee Manli, anyone here called Lee Manli?" Lee Manli was standing making traffic noises with her little angel at the end of the lane when she heard her name called out. At first she thought he was calling for someone else, but on looking around she saw that the postman was facing the very place where she lived.

The onlookers were all gaping up at the building in hopes that a fashionable woman might appear. The fourth floor windows opened and a man's head poked out—"Who do you want? Not here!"

From a second floor window, a child cried, "Don't shout. My dad is Lee Baili."

Lee Manli carried her granddaughter over to the postman and saw straightaway that the envelope was official. "Oh, this letter is for me."

Everyone looked amazed. "You?"

"Yes, I'm Lee Manli. It's on my residence card as clear as day."

The postman was not appeased. "Really Mistress Lee, in future you should ask people to write Professor Wu's name. With his name, I'd know to put it through your letter box even if it didn't have a number."

"What do you mean? I'm not supposed to have a name of my own?"

"Sure, here's your letter, Lee Manli." The postman turned to the little child: "Hello darling, what's your name? I'll be a grandfather before you start getting letters!" With a wave, he mounted his bike and sped off.

People crowded round Lee Manli. "Mistress Lee!" The name Lee Manli still felt unnatural, this fine name hardly fitted the sallow, stooping figure in her outmoded clothes. So they couldn't bring themselves to say it. "Mistress Lee, we've lived in the same lane for all these years, we used to see you coming and going before the old houses were knocked down, but we never knew your name was Lee Manli. The newcomers even thought you were a hired baby-sitter."

"Mistress Lee, what's in your envelope? It's an impressive size!"

Lee Manli knew what was in the envelope, and she would let them see. Whoever thought of her as the Professor's wife, the baby-sitter or Granny should know she was Lee Manli! The envelope was stapled closed, but slowly and carefully she worked each staple open, then pulled out the sheet of stiff paper, and smoothed it over. A graduation certificate, resplendent, dazzling, the name filled out in fine handwriting—Lee Manli. This was a proper document from a university recognized by the Ministry of Education—not churned out by some evening school! If Lee Manli could have shed 20 years this would have brought promotion, a big job, a better salary. Sadly, the graduation date on the certificate was 1949, a bit late to talk of promotion.

Most of the lane's inhabitants had never seen a university graduation certificate, but they knew that such things were worth more than a gold medal. Everyone craned to catch a glimpse of the paper as it was passed carefully from hand to hand, amid warnings and advice on how to keep the precious object from getting soiled. When the examination was over, the neighbours, full of respect, tutted as they looked at Lee Manli. Who'd have thought that this insignificant-looking old lady was a college graduate!

Some were puzzled: "Granny, tell us why you've only got the certificate now? You graduated before Liberation. The red tape must be something!"

The old man scolded: "Don't be stupid. Documents like this were either destroyed in the Cultural Revolution or burned by their owners. Plenty of people got classed as counter-revolutionaries on account of papers like this. With the new Pragmatic Policy, they're reissuing them."

Lee Manli shook her head. "No. Before Liberation I did three years at university, then I did revolutionary work. There's a new rule that people in my position should be sent certificates to recognize that they are graduates and offer them some consolation. In fact I never graduated, I only spent a few years in college."

"Oh no, that's all wrong," said the old man. "In those days, universities were high quality. Three years then is worth five years now."

Lee Manli didn't reply. Instead she took the certificate back, replaced it in the envelope and pressed it into her granddaughter's little hands, saying, "Maomao, this is for you, what good is it to Granny...?" Then she bundled up the child and hurried off into the building.

The bystanders were disappointed. "She's right, what good's a certificate when you are retired? It doesn't change anything, you don't get paid for looking after children, in fact it probably costs you money.''

"They should give it to our Dashan. He hasn't got a decent job, he can't even get his foot on the ladder.''

But the old man who had worked for the foreign company wagged his finger and said, "There is something about her, you know. She was a student then. When she was young I bet she was very modern, you can tell from her name—Lee Manli, really lovely name. You know what Manli is? It's Mali, Mary; all the names had a foreign ring to them back then—you can just tell she was really modern. People nowadays think they're following foreign ways, but they only want jeans. They haven't even thought of changing their names to Lucy, George, John... they don't know a thing!''

2

When Lee Manli got back to her apartment, she put her granddaughter into her little chair, took the certificate out of her grasp and put it on the cupboard. She gave the little girl a rattle and then wiped away her own tears, which had surprised her a few moments earlier in the lane. You don't cry much when you get older, not many tears come.

"Graduation...I've graduated...'' Lee Manli sighed softly and breathed out. What a long slow course— altogether it had lasted 35 years! Thirty-five years in the university of life leading to retirement, another graduation, in fact. Who'd have thought she'd get her retirement certificate and her graduation certificate at more or less the same time? Retirement first, then graduation. The two certificates bore witness to a lifetime, but Lee Manli felt that neither documented the real achievements of her life. The old man had only understood half the story—in the past, not all universities were good; it depended how you studied, and in what subject.

At university she had studied useless stuff. Then for all those years she'd been an ordinary office worker soldiering on and doing her bit, but her retirement papers said nothing worth remembering. On reflection it had all been routine, trivial—if you didn't think hard, all that remained was a blurred memory.

By contrast, this place and everything in it was absolutely vivid and concrete. In the teeth of all hardship, she had set up house, somewhere to come home to, a nest full of bits and pieces where every object recalled her efforts, recorded her history. An important history, unrecognized by certificates. It would not be mentioned in her funeral oration.

Lee Manli felt a little uneasy because the kind of certificate she'd have preferred would have honoured these things. Just now she felt that her history was under attack from the future. The future in itself was nothing terrible, but it had a way of creeping in through small openings. For instance Wu Li and the children were unhappy about the untidy mess of useless objects in their house. They were forever suggesting modernizing schemes, all of which required consigning her history to the waste recycling centre, secondhand shop or rubbish dump.

Lee Manli considered it foolish to talk of spending money on modern decorations and furniture, compared to looking after her granddaughter properly and later preparing her to study at university. The second generation had been neglected, but it must not happen to the third. Lee Manli pulled over a little wooden chair, knocked together its loose joints, sat at Maomao's side and kissed her on the face. This was really the best kind of chair, she thought. It might be ordinary, even shabby, but those imitation leather sofas couldn't be moved around to where you needed them.

Lee Manli's daughter and son-in-law came back from work. One went to make supper, the other to collect the laundry from the balcony, avoiding Lee Manli's room in case Maomao grabbed them and stopped them getting on with their chores. Later Wu Li could be heard returning. Although he was nearly bald, he still had a spring in his step as he climbed the stairs. But then with a resounding crash, the Professor tripped on a metal bucket, giving his knee an excruciating knock. This roused Lee Manli from her reverie, but when she heard his 70-kilo frame fall she rushed out of her room into the sitting room to help Wu Li up.

"Where have you hurt yourself? Get up, get up, let me see."

As soon as Wu Li had dragged himself up, he pulled away. "Let go. I won't die this time, but if I did you'd use the space to pile up more junk."

Lee Manli realized that he hadn't fallen badly—if he had, he wouldn't be capable of anger. The bald old man was simply taking the opportunity to play variations on his favourite theme. Nursing his knee, Wu Li looked around, but there was nowhere in the so-called sitting room for him to sit. The large square table with four hard stools crammed underneath, the enormous glass-fronted cupboard plus a few other cluttered furnishings left only one-and-a-half square metres of floor space empty. On this valuable space were the offending bucket and the small wooden chair, used by Lee Manli for peeling potatoes. Every seating place was piled up with clothes, knitting, even a pair of shoes their daughter Qinqin had bought the day before.

Wu Li's eyes widened: "Look at it! This place is like a pigsty."

Lee Manli hastily gathered up some things and turned on her daughter. "Qinqin, do you actually want these blasted shoes? They're all over the place."

Qinqin dashed in from the other room and took

the shoes, keeping well out the way while her parents argued—making sure she didn't get caught in the crossfire.

Wu Li sat down, rolled up his trouser leg and saw the full horror—he had grazed his knee and it was bleeding. "Look! All your fault!"

Lee Manli felt bad. "Oh dear, I didn't mean to hurt you. Here, come on, I'll get you some iodine solution."

Lee Manli began looking everywhere for the iodine—her home was like a department store, with something for every contingency, but for the moment she couldn't think where she'd put the iodine. She opened cupboards and drawers. "Qinqin, have you seen the iodine?"

"Don't know," came the reply. Qinqin didn't show her face.

Their son-in-law dashed out from his room, saying, "I think I noticed a black bottle down in the corner there." He crouched down, stretched into the space between the cupboard and the wall and pulled a bottle out, blowing the dust off. It was indeed an iodine bottle, but it had lost its lid and the solution had dried, so he made to throw it into the bucket.

Lee Manli stopped him. "No! Even if it's dry it's okay, we just need a little water."

Wu Li began his refrain as soon as the iodine was applied.

"Rooms are meant for people, but this one is full of things. Things and people are fighting for survival space. Things have pushed people into a corner!"

He went onto develop this theme. "I once saw a play called *The Chairs* in which nothing happened. It was just two people on the stage endlessly moving chairs, making chair-mountains, being pressed down by chairs like insects, sticking their heads through chairbacks, talking all sorts of nonsense. At the time I didn't understand, but now I do. People have made a material universe, and they themselves been squashed into the bottom of it, so they can hardly move..."

Professor Wu moved smoothly from theory to example: "Our house is as absurd as that play—four adults living in 64 square metres, so you could say the State is doing well by us, but look—things everywhere, even on the chairs, and they're all broken anyway. If you add everything up, there are probably only 10 square metres left for us, everywhere else is piled up with stuff. We've got to change, it's disgraceful if we don't. And if foreign students came to visit us, they'd think it was a mess. We're damaging the nation's honour!..." The Professor's voice became more and more heated.

His family stood listening to the lecture. his daughter with interest but little hope, holding young Maomao. Qinqin knew that her father's passions were easily roused, but he had no staying power. Young Maomao listened attentively, but naturally without understanding. She was interested in her grandfather's voice and gestures—it was better than any cartoon.

Their son-in-law was hoping that Father could keep up the attack, so he could follow through and break down the defences. He had made plans for the place, and had his strategy prepared. He wanted to put another layer of cream-coloured concrete on the floors, with lines and grooves to make it look like a wooden floor. There would be wallpaper or distemper (shade green 106) on the walls, wall-mounted lights, hanging lamps, ceiling lights, and double curtains on all the windows (nets to allow light in by day and heavy curtains for blocking out the light when watching TV). The furniture must be brought up to date—there was too much at the moment, and none of it any good. Everything should be discarded in favour of a sofa, some folding chairs, and a rectangular table where guests could be seated on both sides. In the bedroom there would be a collapsible bed with a teak-finish headboard, and built-in shelving which could be extended upwards if necessary. The Professor's study too, should be sorted out. The two rows of bookshelves should go from floor to ceiling, to stop him piling books under the bed. The effect there should be scholarly, with no sofa but a bamboo chair. Right now the place, far from looking like a professor's residence, was worse than a street vendor's hovel. Putting this ambitious plan into practice would be perfectly possible. He worked in a sawmill and knew lots of private companies doing carpentry, people who could turn their hand to anything, at a good price. The problem was not money, but his mother-in-law.

Lee Manli was standing in front of the young man. She had not absorbed any of Wu Li's speech, it was as if she hadn't even heard it. But since Wu Li had skinned his knee she was a little more considerate than usual. Suddenly Lee Manli cupped her hand to her ear and said, "Shh, quiet, I think I hear someone knocking." Two more knocks. She said: "Professor Wu, class is over, someone's come to see you."

Lee Manli moved towards the door. When it opened, there was a jumble of girlish voices. "Mary..." "Hello, Sasha, Feifei." Judging by their voices, the two visitors were no more than 18 years old, but the two old ladies who came in were of an age with Lee Manli. The three of them were slapping and hugging each other, just like young girls.

"Have you got your graduation certificate?"

"Yes it's just come."

"So, we've graduated!"

"Hey Professor Wu, now you can't lord it over us, we're graduates too, with certificates to prove it!"

Wu Li knew his wife's old college friends and had heard about the decision to make good the lost certificates. But when he saw the three old ladies rejuvenated, he was infected by their high spirits.

"Have you really had your certificates? Manli, you too?"

Lee Manli pointed at the glass cupboard. "Over there." Wu Li unrolled the envelope, flattened it and turned it 180 degrees, his heavy frame seeming to lighten a little. "Aha, you ladies have graduated! Shasha, you should all have a graduation party, I'll organize it for you."

Lee Manli gave him a look. "What a lot of fuss!"

Shasha said, "You're right, that's why we came. Wu Li, do you remember Fatty Wang? He's still a good sort, he organized the certificates being sent out and suggested we should find all the graduates still living in town, so we're having a party this weekend at my house. He's looking after the refreshments, I'll give the party, so it will be fine, you can rely on it. Fatty Wang is a good organizer."

In the old days the universities all had a character known as Fatty Wang, little fatso or some such — usually a goodnatured fellow who would help the female students and be sent out to buy sweets and peanuts.

Lee Manli smiled, "That Fatty Wang is an idiot. He put down my old address from thirty-odd years ago."

"Well you can't blame him, even I only knew you'd just recently moved house but I didn't have your exact address. It was the old man in the lane who directed us. Manli, I hear you've got a pretty big place, may we look around?"

Lee Manli protested. "Aya, no, it's in a terrible mess. I'm so busy I haven't had time to tidy up."

"Have a look, go on, tell us what you think," Wu Li insisted, for his lecture was not yet over. The two curious friends pushed past their hostess, even sticking their heads around the toilet door.

"Manli," Shasha had some comments to make. Years ago she had been a girlfriend of Wu Li's. As time went on she found him a little too outspoken, while Wu Li found her too flighty. The two of them had stopped seeing each other. The leopard doesn't change its spots, and Shasha was still as unrestrained as ever.

"By the look of it, studying domestic science didn't do much for you, even now you have the certificate you can't call yourself a graduate. You've made this place look like a junk shop!"

Feifei added, "Didn't you study interior design in the domestic science department? Why don't you make use of what you learned?"

"I've forgotten it. Besides, I changed over to social education." Lee took back the certificate. "Look, from the social education department, isn't it? Social education only looks at society, it doesn't deal with putting homes in order."

The daughter and son-in-law couldn't understand what the old ladies were talking about. They'd heard of studying physics and chemistry, Chinese and law, but what on earth was domestic science?

"Father, what's domestic science about?"

Wu Li puffed up with pleasure. "Ah, a great subject! It disappeared from China years ago, it was brought in by the missionary colleges. Taught women how to keep house, interior design, childrearing, shopping, clothes and so on. You see, all the students were destined to become happy housewives. Unluckily for your mother, her destiny was to end up with a hopeless fellow like me."

Lee Manli disputed all this, "You're talking nonsense, we used to study social reform, the structure of the family, English and French."

"Eh!" The son-in-law was surprised. He'd never imagined that his mother-in-law knew two foreign languages. If she hadn't forgotten everything she should stop teaching Maomao to say "honk-honk" and start in on ABC, begin her foreign language training at an early age.

"What do you mean 'eh'?" Shasha assumed the authority of age. "We were much more with it than you are now. These wretched-looking suits like the one you're wearing used to be sold from stalls on the street." The son-in-law pulled at his lapels. "Huh? We got them from the factory."

"...Your mother was even more fashinonable, you know, she used to wear a fur coat in winter, fox it was, and a muff that doubled as a purse. Long silk trousers, high-heeled shoes, a little Misvando lipstick—right?" (Shasha spoke English to Lee Manli again.) "Misvando was the best French brand!"

Lee Manli shook her head. "Shasha, stop going on about how westernized I was!"

"It's just to tell the youngsters that we're not old fogies, we've seen it all!" Shasha tugged at her woollen overcoat. She stood on tiptoe, as if she were about to make a stage announcement. At university she had enjoyed being in the limelight, dashing around at parties and so on.

She certainly looked eyecatching, and fashionably dressed for an old lady. Her honey-coloured coat was belted at the waist, her trousers were cut long and slightly bell-bottomed so they fell over her high-heeled shoes. Her hair was permed and she wore a little make-up so her skin didn't look sallow like most old ladies'. Lee Manli felt a little envious. "Shasha, you're the same as ever, just as full of life."

"Yes, no need to show our age. There's a long way from leaving work to leaving this world; we should keep our end up. Manli, you should get a perm and have yourself a couple of decent outfits made, sort out your house and live a bit more comfortably."

Shasha pulled Manli towards her to straighten her

collar, as if she were stroking a lost sheep. "Dear Mary, what a sight you are! Wu Li, you've brought so much suffering to Manli with your free-speaking. No, don't laugh, I'm serious! If you don't turn over a new leaf, I'll get our classmates to come and 'struggle' you!"

Wu Li spread out his hands. "Heaven knows none of this has anything to do with me."

Feifei was not a great talker, but she felt that Shasha had gone too far, so she urged, "Let's go, Shasha. We've got other people to tell."

"Ok, let's go now. Manli, you must come on Sunday, otherwise I'll send Fatty Wang looking for you!"

After the guests had gone, Wu Li was about to resume now that he had even more arguments, including the opinions of outsiders. But Lee Manli clapped her hands. "All right, don't go on, I'm not such a diehard after all. We'll change, you'll see. You can count on me ."

The daughter and son-in-law were jumping for joy. "Hooray for Ma!" Even Maomao was cheering, although she had no idea what was going on. Lee Manli seemed to sparkle with life. "If we're going to reform, everyone must help, and the first thing is to clear out all the rubbish."

Wu Li clapped. "Right!" He bounded forward and gave the bucket a resounding kick. "Let's begin with this thing, we're always tripping over it!" Wu Li carried the bucket outside the door and threw it into the rubbish chute. Down it crashed helter-skelter from the third floor to the rubbish heap on the ground.

3

The next morning as Wu Li was washing he looked around and saw the bucket large as life in the sitting room. He called out, "Who brought that broken bucket back?" Lee Manli leaned out of the kitchen and whispered, "Quiet, Maomao's sleeping."

Wu Li pointed at the thing. "You?"

Lee Manli smiled. "On the way back from market, I saw it on the rubbish heap and it looked so sad! When you think about it, we've had that bucket for so many years, through thick and thin, it seems inhuman to throw it away just because it's old. And I bought three pounds of potatoes, so I've brought it back for the meantime."

Wu Li shook his head. "My dear, you can't even bear to part with a broken bucket, so how are you going to sort out this mess? Last night was just talk, wasn't it?"

"Don't get worked up, reform is a gradual process, let's take it step by step. You want it to be like when we went off to the countryside, emptying the whole house in three days? Ah... that winter in 1969 was so cold, we used the bucket to melt ice. Isn't it strange, it's got warmer and warmer lately. There hasn't been another winter like that one."

Lee Manli sat down on the wooden chair to peel potatoes. They thudded into the bucket as she talked.

"Ah, Wu Li, you were snoring last night and I didn't sleep a wink. So what are we going to do with this house?"

"Complete reform!"

"Sounds right. But whatever way I look at it the three beds are hard to get rid of. Take Qinqin's bed, the big one. It's old and awkward. The mattress has been mended four times, but it was my mother's. Do you remember, when we got married we were issued with two rolls and quilts, and two straw mats that we laid together. My mother cried when she saw them — what a way to begin an important thing like marriage! She was so poor, yet she gave us her own bed, said I was born on that bed, it was my birthplace. That bed has been good to us, we had no chests, no cupboards, all our clothes went under the mattress or under the bed. The girls used to play there—how they loved tumbling around in the bed! We used to sit on the edge and laugh. And all four of us slept there without knocking into each other. It's so big you can't buy mats to go with it any more... Wu Li, we forgot to go to Mother's grave at the grave-sweeping festival this year. Who knows if her memorial tablet is still there...?'' Thud, another potato fell into the bucket.

"As the children grew up they needed their own bed so we bought another one, that little metal-frame bed I sleep on now. When we bought it in the second-hand shop, I didn't want to, we had beds like that at university. They're not really beds at all, just metal frames, they need a mattress, but you were determined to have it—you've always been mad for foreign things. You said it didn't need a mattress because it had a wire mesh base, but of course the girls rolled into the middle pushing against each other and fighting all the time.

"I had a real battle about that bed, remember? When they had the 'Smelt Iron' campaign, it seems unreal now, all those backyard furnaces burning night and day, hardly turning out any molten iron! God knows who decided to mobilize the whole city ... they took away doors, windowframes, shelving, pots and pans and threw the lot into the furnaces. Then they'd say they'd met their targets—that way they were safe from criticism. That government boss was so tough, I couldn't get rid of him. He brought people around to take our bed away and melt it down. They said anyone refusing was against the whole movement. If you were a Party member they could take away your Party card, if you weren't it was some other punishment. I wasn't having any of it—Chairman Mao told us to make iron and steel, not to melt down what we already had!

"I refused to hand over the bed. You were already

branded a Rightist then and couldn't speak up. So you just said, 'Don't argue, give it to them.' If I'd done that, where would the children sleep? I almost went mad. Whatever he said, I countered. He said I had problems with my ideology; I said he was distorting the sacred directive and going off on the wrong road. The children helped, they just lay on the bed, crying and fighting—no one could have moved it. So in the end they left it, but I was left with an 'iron hat'—from then on they said I was 'opposed to the Three Red Flags'.... That official fellow probably has grand-children of his own now. I really ought to keep that bed. It's a key piece of evidence. After all, who was right, him or me?" Thud, another potato went into the bucket.

Wu Li only sighed, "Try to forget. Forgetting is a kind of progress."

"Forget? It's not that easy. Remember when we accepted the big bed from Mother, they said we were 'not drawing a demarcation line between ourselves and the bourgeoisie'? When we kept the iron bed we were 'opposing the Three Red Flags.' From then on even with my education I had to do clerical work. I did it for thirty-five years, girl and woman..." Thud, another potato fell sharply into the bucket.

"Come now, that's all past, don't get worked up...."

"Past? Perhaps as far as you're concerned, Professor. Now you can study your classical texts, your *Dream of the Red Chamber*, you've woken up from your nightmare. But mine isn't over yet. At night I dream I'm still at university, wanting to do my bit for society—you're laughing, you think I have no idealism, that I wanted to be a rich lady! If I'd wanted that, I wouldn't have married you. And why did you drop Shasha for me if it wasn't because I've got more brains than she has? So I'm a 'stinking intellectual' like you!

Just look, Shasha got through that time unscathed, she wasn't roasted alive like us. Of course she's more fashionable than I am. Look at me, empty-handed— even those beds that I traded for my political reputation are on the way out.''

Wu Li knew now that things had gone wrong. The beds would not be moved. "Let's keep them then. We'll get rid of my small wooden bed, take it to the dump."

Lee Manli's hands stopped and she looked up. "Is that an ordinary wooden bed? You created it with sweat and tears. If it doesn't mean anything to you, it does to me. Have you forgotten 1969, that terrible winter when we were sent down by the sea? That wind from the north west howling like a wolf and tearing the grass matting from the roofs of our huts. The day you went off to the purchasing station to buy wood, I looked out from the doorway, hoping the sun wouldn't set. As soon as it did, the place would be freezing. We were all cold and hungry enough to freeze to death.

"I saw you coming from a distance—one nice thing about the seaside, always so deserted. I could tell it was you, you were thin as a rake then, carrying that big plank on your back. I couldn't see your face, and in the distance you looked like a letter T in English swaying and tottering along. As you came closer I could see your face was ashen, and the beads of sweat on your forehead were as big as beans. You were trembling. I came out to try to help, but you pushed me away and let the plank crash to the ground. Then you fell, grazing your forehead. Funny, you never used to complain or lose your temper in those days. As I dressed the wound you were quiet, then you began to weep and said, 'I've let the children down and you too.' I just cried, for what good did that kind of talk do? Rightists weren't the only ones, so many people were sent down to the countryside—but you always felt that you were cursed, dragging the girls and me down with you.

"How you wanted to give our eldest a bed, to let the two girls sleep apart and more comfortably. It wasn't the *Dream of the Red Chamber* you were studying then, but carpentry, and trying to make a living from it! Well, there's another dream. You really were healthy in those days—low blood pressure, no heart trouble—you carried loads, fetched water and kept busy all day long. That time we were snowed in, you worked feverishly on the wood at home, getting up before dawn, working so hard you didn't need warm clothes, we couldn't get you to rest. A bed made with so much care, it should last for a hundred years. When you finished it, all four of us sat on the edge and jumped together. The bed didn't move, and I could see you were pleased. But when one of the girls asked, 'Daddy, are we going to sleep here for the rest of our lives?', you put your hands over your face and said, 'Dear child, I've let you down.' You were shaking with sobs…"

Wu Li's eyes were streaming. "Hush now, don't go on. We'll keep that bed too."

So none of the three beds could be parted with, and half the modernization scheme had come to nothing overnight. Whether in a home or a hotel, beds take up a lot of space, and the appearance of a room has much to do with beds. A rusty iron bed, even with a smart teak-finish cabinet beside it, still looks ill-matched. If you then put up wallpaper and install lights, it's rather like those portraits of the Empress Dowager—brocades and precious stones on a pockmarked old lady.

When their son-in-law heard that none of the beds could be moved, he shook his head. The room he and Qinqin lived in was 14 square metres, with the huge bed inherited from his mother-in-law's mother occupying two-fifths of the space. Then there was a three-shelf wardrobe and a bedside cupboard. In his grand plan, besides twin beds, they would install a pair of lounge chairs, an occasional table, a Lark brand round table and four French-style chairs. But where could he put them? Even if you went ahead and jammed them all in, how could modern lounge chairs coexist with a late-Empire wooden bed? Those beds were designed for old-fashioned rooms, measured in traditional room-widths or numbers of doors, not square metres. One of those old rooms could be as large as a whole modern apartment. Multi-storey blocks were the norm now. They were the model which dictated a change in the design of furniture, whether one liked it or not. Of course, the family could muddle along for a few more years, but in the end they absolutely must change. He had looked into interior decor quite thoroughly, had read articles, seen TV programmes. His conclusion was that modern life demanded spareness and refinement. Interiors ought to be imaginative, practical, multipurpose, and adaptable, with room for upward expansion. Old-fashioned plane-based design had to make way for the three-dimensional. People had to make an imaginative leap—but with bed, wardrobe and cupboard all in a fourteen-square-metre room, where was there to leap?

The son-in-law explained his viewpoint to the old couple. Wu Li nodded and said, "You're a young man of the eighties with forward-looking ideas. You see things with a fresh eye and what you say makes sense. We're the ones who must change—the new ways are here, but we can't bring ourselves to cast aside the old ways. Granny, what are we to do?" Wu Li, usually so loquacious, fell silent. Qinqin smiled. Her father was behaving true to form.

Lee Manli saw no reason to be particularly polite

with her husband or daughter, but she was more sensitive to her son-in-law. She didn't want him to be too despondent. Anyway, he was no fool, and he wasn't talking nonsense. She began to look for a compromise.

"Listen, we'll take the double bed back. We're old, we don't need your new-fangled stuff. I came into the world on that bed and I can leave for the other world from there too. The metal and the wooden beds—wrap them in plastic sheeting and store them on the balcony as a memento of the past so we can show them to Maomao when she's bigger, to remind her that happiness can't be taken for granted."

The son-in-law disagreed. His reforms were an integral plan, he had no thought of looking after his own narrow interests. If you put the double bed into the old couple's room, how could you sort that room out? The odds and ends would pile up sky high and the overflow would spill into his room, for nature abhors a vacuum. Mother was up to her tricks again. Reform inevitably required loss and gain, birth and death. You couldn't just redistribute. How could they put more things onto the balcony? It was already crowded with jars, bowls, buckets, ropes and old wood so that you could hardly dry the laundry there. It should be completely emptied and they'd put out tubs and pots of plants. In summer they'd have two deckchairs for the old couple to sit out and enjoy the breeze, since for the time being there was no air conditioning inside.

Wu Li turned the matter around in his head and came to the conclusion that the crucial difference between his wife and son-in-law was the double bed. Suddenly he had an idea.

"How about this? We'll sell the double bed and use the money to buy a new one. The connection with the past won't be broken, the bed won't be destroyed. Sleeping on the new bed will feel like sleeping on the old one, because the new bed will come out of the old.'' The day before the Professor had taken the theatre of the absurd as his subject, today it was metamorphosis.

Lee Manli blinked, thinking that this just might be possible. She asked her son-in-law, ''How much do you think we'd get for it?''

He had already looked deeply into the matter. ''Three years ago that bed could have fetched 200 yuan. The peasants liked them then. They'd put on a lick of paint, touch them up here and there and they'd be fine for a wedding bed. But not now. You know how rich the peasants are in the suburbs, they either have things made new or buy mahogony. If our bed were mahogony, it would be worth at least 1000 yuan. Maybe your family weren't such great capitalists after all, since they thought a mulberry bed was so precious! Mulberry is strong, but it warps.''

''So how much is it worth?

''Hard to say, but you might find someone who'd give you 50 yuan.''

''What!'' Lee Manli jumped to her feet.''Only 50 yuan for a bed that size! I spent over 20 yuan having the supports repaired! All that rubbish about the essence remaining unchanged. At two stokes you'd destroy the best part of it. My mother would damn us for ungrateful wretches from beyond the grave!''

4

For three days there was no movement on the issue. No overall plan could be fixed. Life went on as usual, through habit. Lee Manli went out in the morning to buy vegetables, milk and breakfast cake. In the afternoons she took Maomao out to the end of the lane to go ''honk-honk'' at the cars and then brought her back. The only difference was an extra person to pass the time of day with. The old man who'd worked for the foreign company was now an acquaintance, and he had decided that Lee Manli was an expert on all things foreign. He was a strange old man: he wanted to grasp not the essence of China, but the essence of the West. He was certainly not anti-foreign, but he felt that westernization today was not up to scratch. It had no style, wasn't authentic. Lee Manli found him amusing. Although she'd forgotten her English almost completely, her accent was correct and she could make out a pidgin flavour in the old man's foreign phrases, probably acquired as a messenger for that company years ago.

By the fourth day, Lee Manli had to decide if she was going to the graduation party or not. There was no great attraction, but Shasha would be crazy with excitement, and if she didn't go Fatty Wang would come for her anyway.

Wu Li was strongly in favour. "Retired people should get involved in social activities, not stay at home and brood. Too many men are healthy at the time of retirement, then sit around without moving, never going out. Gradually they fall into a daze, sitting and dozing all day—really dangerous. Events like this which help people to recall their youth are especially good. Even if the improvement is temporary it's better than nothing."

Qinqin also encouraged her. "Go, Ma! It's so boring for you at home all day cooking and looking after Maomao. Go out and have a good time."

Lee Manli thought that Wu Li was certainly off beam. He was talking about men, but where could you find a retired woman sitting with her feet up? Even if she wanted to doze off, she wouldn't have time! Qinqin was right. She'd go for the change, to see her old friends and hear what had become of them.

Lee Manli, the student of domestic science, was

fairly conscious of social niceties. She went to have her hair set (she didn't have a perm) in a style which lifted her hair back off her face, but was full at the temples. It made her pudgy face look a little slimmer. She even had them put on a pomade, to disguise the white hairs which peppered her head.

It wasn't true that she had no decent clothes. She'd had a suit made before she retired, from fine material. It was well-made; the only problem was the cut, which was unfashionably wide. Never mind, she knew about such things. The important thing about western clothes was material and workmanship. Good quality material and meticulous workmanship meant she would at least look distinguished. Styles change every year. Lengths and widths alter constantly, and only people who change style all the time can be considered fashionable. But such people are rather lacking in good breeding. Of course, it wouldn't do to be completely out of fashion—this was a sign that a lady or gentleman, once comfortably off, has recently fallen on hard times. Lee Manli was dissatisfied with the suit she'd had made. She'd worn it to her retirement party to show that she was not completely past these things, but it didn't have the effect she'd hoped for. She remembered how all the ladies had been very well turned-out and how the old men had sat at the back of the room, boasting about how they'd still be able to do a night march of 80 miles if there was another war.

Now Lee Manli put her suit on again. She stood in front of the mirror, patting her hair. Then she straightened her collar. She turned to Wu Li. "Well, what do you think?"

"Ah, you look 18 again!"

Qinqin was thrilled by her mother's appearance. "Wear my shoes, the high-heeled ones. They're new."

Lee Manli nodded. Of course, you couldn't wear Chinese cloth shoes with western clothes. She put on her daughter's shoes and took a few steps. Good God—she looked taller, her back and shoulders were straighter. High-heeled shoes pushed your centre of gravity forwards, so to keep your balance you had to push your chest out and hold your head high. In this way Lee Manli's stoop was corrected.

Qinqin clapped and said, "Ma, you look really nice in western clothes. They look better on you than on Shasha. Her clothes were nice but she looks a bit vulgar."

"Rubbish! Now get your new handbag out and let me borrow it." Lee Manli was in her element. She used to carry a handbag in the days when she had a fur coat.

With her leather handbag and high-heeled shoes, her graceful posture and chest held out, Lee Manli went downstairs and walked along the lane at a leisurely pace. When she saw the old man, she raised her hand and waved. It wouldn't have taken much for her to call out, "Hello" in English!

The old man jumped up from his tea, as if he had seen his old boss's wife, Mrs, Johnston. He lowered his voice repectfully as he said to his companion, "Look. She wears western clothes like the rest, but what a difference. She looks like a real *gen-ter-man!*"

5

The graduation party lasted a good four hours, only ending when all the refreshments were gone. They couldn't get official money to hold the party, so everyone put in three yuan. Lee Manli was flushed when she got back, and still in a party mood. Her voice was very lively. "Qinqin, hurry and get my plastic sandals. I haven't worn heels for ages, I think I'm paying the price now, my feet are aching." She bumped down onto the wooden chair, but sitting down felt no better. At Shasha's she'd been sitting on lounge chairs or high-backed chairs, and the wooden one felt too low.

Lee Manli took off the high-heeled shoes. "You know, it's a pity you didn't come, it was packed. Lots of people brought husbands and wives. It was crazy, they all started behaving like children, and there was dancing. At first I didn't want to because I thought I'd forgotten how. But it's like swimming, if you go into the water, you'll float. The problem is that I've become clumsy. You used to say that dancing with me was like holding a willow branch, I'd bend wherever you wanted. Fatty Wang danced with me and we were crashing around like elephants—God, I'm tired!" Lee Manli moved from the little chair to the bench, finding it more comfortable to be a little higher, but a sofa to stretch out on would have been better still.

Suddenly, she found her own home uncomfortable, like someone who's been abroad coming back to China and seeing everything in a different light. She looked all around, feeling that her own home was really in a terrible state. Overall Shasha's house was no bigger than hers but it wasn't strewn about with useless junk. There were several chairs lined up against the wall, so that over a dozen guests could find a seat. In the middle was a folding table and folding chairs, which could be put away to make room for dancing and set up for the food—in fact just as her son-in-law had suggested.

"Son, today I've seen your ideas on home improvement in action, and they do make sense. Especially those long folding sofas, they're really handy. Put them against a wall and they take no space at all. Do you know how much they cost?"

"Not much at all, and you can have them made even cheaper." The son-in-law's eyes lit up.

"But the folding chairs were really ugly, all those metal plate frames and plastic seats, they're really vulgar. Wood is best, with fabric seats. And you wouldn't want to have nothing but folding chairs, lined up in rows like a meeting, they look a bit impersonal. You should have a pouf, round or square. Cushioned on top and hollow inside so you can store things. It's hard to find them nowadays but they're really practical and very light. When guests sit on the sofa you can move the pouf over beside them. It's good for conversation and it looks very welcoming. Oh, and you've thought about wallpaper and wall-lamps, but how about hanging pictures? Houses today are low-ceilinged, so western paintings look best, long and narrow if possible. A house without a few paintings looks uncultured. Professor, don't you agree?''

Wu Li wagged his finger at her. "Aha, all your domestic science is coming out now!"

The son-in-law was pleased too. Perhaps there was something to this domestic science after all. Qinqin smiled, "Ma, all this dancing has gone to your head. You're talking nonsense to make him happy."

"No, no. I've always wanted to change, it's just that I don't want to rush into anything. Do you know what is holding us up? Beds? No, one bed more or less doesn't really matter. The greater problem is content, not form. Old wardrobes, shelves, mirror, boxes, baskets, suitcases—they may look terrible, but how can we move them when they're full of things? If they were all empty, what would I need them for? We should get to the root of the problem, and begin at the beginning."

Lee Manli was really roused now. "From tomorrow, you'll have to take pot luck for your meals, and let's take Maomao to her auntie's for a few days, so I can get down to a big clear-out. To be honest, I don't want to pass on a broken crock from one generation to the next."

Wu Li was excited. "Aha! You really have graduated now, the party was not held in vain! Qinqin, Son, let's get down to it together and help Mother to clear out.''

Lee Manli immediately called a halt. ''Don't get involved. How would you know what's useful and what's not?''

The next day, Lee Manli's house was in chaos—but a chaos which was necessary. She threw open cupboards, pulled out drawers, prised open boxes and rummaged through chests. She would look everything over one by one, deciding what should go to the rubbish heap and which rarely or never used things could be sent to the waste centre and secondhand shop.

Their belongings could be divided into clothes, utensils and toys. There weren't many toys, and clothes and bedding made up the biggest group, so Lee Manli decided to begin there. When she'd done, the chests and boxes would be empty. She also knew that the clothes and bedding were in a dreadful mess, so she gritted her teeth and focused her attention on things which hadn't been worn for three years or more, dividing them up and sorting them into bundles ready for the secondhand shop. But the floodgates of memory were thrown open again. Each piece of cloth told a story and for Lee Manli such things were not trivial. Writers get their inspiration from the dramas of important people, but ordinary people have to rely on themselves, sing their own praises, comfort themselves.

Nobody cared what that cotton swatch was for, but Lee Manli recognized it for one of life's little victories. When Wu Li had a cadre-suit made, she'd worked out that there must be four inches of cloth left over. The tailor hadn't wanted to hand it back. She'd stuck to her guns and argued until she got it, meaning to use it for patches and a new collar. Later when Wu Li was doing labour reform at the State farm, the collar of his jacket was ruined. Lee Manli cut off two inches of cloth and faded it in salt water before replacing the collar, so it looked completely natural. When Wu Li was young, he was rather sloppy in his dress, but after his marriage to Lee Manli his clothes were tidy, his shirts were clean, and he never had a button missing. "From the husband's clothes you can judge the wife," goes the saying. Wu Li's colleagues used to sing her praises: "That wife or yours is a good woman!" Lee Manli still felt pleased when she thought about it. "They're right; without me, who knows what would have become of him?" Lee Manli pulled out the well-washed cadre-suit from a pile of old clothes and put the two inches of cloth into the pocket. She thought to herself: "If a canny peasant woman buys this jacket, she'll know what those two inches of cloth are for!"

When Lee Manli pulled the jacket out, it brought with it two white rabbit hats. She felt such a wave of happiness, she couldn't help turning them over in her hands. They really were like little animals with red-lined ears, pink eyes and red noses. Wu Li had brought these back for the girls from Beijing before they made him a Rightist. There was only a year between the two children, they looked like twins. When they set off hand in hand for nursery school wearing their little hats, people used to stop in the street, look at the two of them and call out to passing cyclists, "Watch out, let those little rabbits cross the road!" How proud she felt. The children were delighted too, they often gave little performances at the nursery, playing rabbits without even dressing up. Afterwards they'd come home and tumble around on the big bed, full of high spirits. At that time they only had two rooms, but the house was happy and full of hope. Wu Li often used to sing, "Onwards and upwards every day, the future shines brighter in every way." Lee Manli too thought that the sky was the limit. Before long her dreams from those days studying domestic science would come true.

A husband widely respected, two beautiful daughters, a fine large house. There would be built-in open shelving by the front door, plenty of hooks in the top for hats and coats, a rack at the bottom for umbrellas. The rooms would have more shelves, red carpets, and there would be an open fire in the parlour, naturally with sofas and so on. Separate bedrooms for husband and wife. In the lady's bedroom would be a huge vanity unit where she could make up before she met her husband in the morning, so that he might never see her looking tired or weary and would always think of his wife as youthful and lively... This was the dream of her youth, undimmed by time.

In a way, these dreams were returning. But what was she to do with the rabbit hats—throw them out or not? Hang on, wasn't there a photo somewhere of the sisters in their hats? If she still had the photo, the hats could go. Any other way, the clear-out would be pointless. Lee Manli piled the rabbit hats and the old jacket together. Until she could say if the old photo was still around, she wouldn't be able to relax, because if it was lost, the happy time would have vanished without trace. She rummaged in a drawer, pulled out an old photograph album and turned over to the second page. There it was, two children in the top right-hand corner, wearing rabbit hats and patterned jackets, one looking merely vacant, the other excited. Children really were at their nicest when they were little, she thought. They became such a pain when they grew up, always wanting something. Lee Manli, forgetting about clearing out, went on turning pages in the album. After a while she came across a picture of the sisters in pigtails and dresses. That was when she remembered that, yes, those dresses were still in a cardboard box.

Lee Manli put down the album and started tearing the boxes open. From the heap of old clothes she pulled out the two dresses. She could scarcely believe that they looked so garish, in her memory they had been lovely. Spotted red and green material with a white bodice, square collar and no sleeves, with a border of lotus flowers around the shoulder. Lee Manli went into a daze as she fingered the dresses, as if she could hear the children calling and see them rushing about. She flushed and broke into a sweat. She could see a Children's Day festival one June 1st. Usually it was a joyful time, but that year dark clouds were all around, and a terrible load weighed on her mind. Wu Li had been sent to labour reform camp after he was classed as a Rightist. He was with criminals and although he wasn't treated as one, he was not allowed to come home. Lee Manli had to work and look after the children, and travel to see Wu Li when she had time. She was worn off her feet. There were meetings, too, until 10 p.m. every night. She had to give the children a house key on a chain round their necks, leave their lunch ready before she went out in the morning and let them make their own supper and put themselves to bed. Just as well there was nothing much to eat in those hard years, that made cooking easy. But although the children grew up quickly, one of them would forget the oil, the other the salt, so the food they made was inedible. The two of them were usually asleep when Lee Manli got back, and the elder girl would leave a note passing on some news to her mother: "I got 100% at school today" or "Xiaohu from next door beat Qinqin up again."

That evening Lee Manli got back shortly before ten, but the girls were not asleep. They were waiting up for her. Lee Manli was surprised. "Why aren't you asleep?"

"We were waiting for you!"

"What's wrong?"

"Ma, do you know what happens tomorrow?"

"Oh no, I completely forgot about your festival. No presents, Daddy's not here and I can't take you out..." Lee Manli couldn't go on. Had Wu Li remembered Children's Day on the State farm?

The elder daughter was a bright girl. She lowered her eyes when her father was mentioned. Without Daddy, the house was joyless, but when he was here you couldn't hold your head up. She wasn't allowed to be a prefect at school, and the teacher wanted her to "draw a demarcation line" between herself and her father.

Qinqin, the younger one, didn't care. She was determined to have her say. "Ma, there's a big parade tomorrow. Teacher says the boys have to wear shirts and the girls have to wear dresses. The ones in dresses can stand at the front and carry the red flags, and the ones without dresses have to stand at the back. Ma, we want to wear dresses."

Lee Manli was annoyed. "Why didn't you say before? Where can I get dresses at this hour of night?"

"Teacher told us this morning. You weren't back so we couldn't tell you..."

"Oh, it's my fault, nothing you could do..."

The elder girl could see her mother was embarassed so she tugged her sister's arm and said, "Forget it, we'll stand at the back."

"No way! I want to be at the front and carry the flag. We can't always stand at the back, with people laughing at us." The little girl started to cry—the fog of politics even clouding over small children's eyes.

As one designated "politically backward and ideologically stubborn", Lee Manli wasn't going to be defeated by a little thing like this. She wiped away her daughter's tears. "Don't cry. Go to sleep now. If you don't peek, I'll work some magic and tomorrow you'll both have dresses!"

The girls fell asleep halfway between tears and

laughter, while Lee Manli took out some patterned material she'd bought with the intention of making curtains. She also found some white cotton, bought to make a shirt for Wu Li. But he was working with cement and couldn't wear white because it was impossible to keep clean.

Lee Manli started sewing, without a machine. It all had to be done by hand. Each stitch carried her along a thread of memories and longings. Children's Day in past years had been so happy, it was the children's festival but it was also a day for adults. Wu Li and she would buy presents and put them by the children's beds, so June 1st always began with sounds of laughter and joy. In the afternoon they took the children out, bought them ice cream and lemonade and then took them to the shops where they'd squeeze in front of the toy counter. They could have stayed for ever. They'd buy a doll or toy dog. The children would get wildly excited and exhausted, and on the way home they'd beg their father to carry them one on each arm, since he was so tall, all the way to the lane. A happy couple, lovely children, a joyful festival. Everyone who saw them was open-mouthed. The world was full of smiles, but then everything had changed.

A cold wind, dark clouds. Was rain coming? Lee Manli hoped so. Rain meant a rest at the State farm, Wu Li might have a breather. He'd got thinner, weaker; there was nothing to eat.... But no, don't let it rain. Then the parade would be cancelled and all her efforts would be wasted. Lee Manli sewed on and by 3 a.m. had finished the first dress. After that she felt even sleepier. Like someone who has been deprived of water, she felt hollow, and her eyelids kept edging down. The needle blurred over as she worked and she kept pricking her fingers. Blood spotted the patterned cloth in several places. When Mother sews, the stitches are supposed to be fine and close, but Lee Manli just couldn't do it. The stitches grew longer and longer.

It won't rain, she thought, the dawn star is bright and clear. The girls wakened early, but when they saw their mother huddled by the window and the dresses not yet finished, they shut their eyes again and pretended they were asleep. When Mother called out, "Time to get up!" the dresses were there. The girls jumped up together and hugged their mother. The older girl said, "Ma, you haven't slept all night!" Lee Manli didn't cry, instead she tried to pick them up together as Wu Li used to do. She had not an ounce of strength left.

Lee Manli's office looked over the main road and the procession passed under her window. She stood in a daze leaning against the window, looking out, trying to see where her daughters had been placed.

Here they were, the brightly coloured ranks marched past and the girls were indeed at the front, carrying the flag, delighted with themselves, the edging on their shoulders fluttering like butterflies. Lee Manli couldn't help calling out but the girls didn't hear, they kept on holding the flag high and shouting slogans, and Lee Manli likewise wanted to yell to the skies, "Wu Li, I've seen the children all right, and I've done right by you, I didn't let them stand at the back!" Tears streamed down her face.

…There were tears in plenty back then. Once started, you couldn't stop them. Lee Manli cried now, but only a trickle ran down the sides of her nose. She gathered up the two old dresses and dried her nose with them. She went to get a sip of water, then sat down for a few moments on the little wooden chair. She was tired, she couldn't do any more. Wu Li's old fur jacket lay beside her but she couldn't lift it up.

Lee Manli sat on the little wooden chair and her anger welled up. She thought, "All the Rightists have had their names formally cleared, but what has anyone said to their wives?"

6

Lee Manli had only got through 50% of the clothes and bedding. Things needed time for reflection. Take the eight-pound quilt padding, so hard and thick. It would never be used again. But Wu Li's mother had given it to them. When the old lady in her village heard that townspeople only had three or four-pound quilt paddings distributed to them, she was incensed. Wu Li had always suffered from the cold, it made him shiver and turned the corners of his mouth blue. The old lady grew a dozen or more cotton bushes at the back of her house and got around the local restrictions by insisting they were grown for the flowers. She gathered cotton for five years until she had enough to make this padding—the bales were twisted by her own hand. Lee Manli was keeping the bed her mother had given them, so how could she get rid of the quilt padding from her mother-in-law? They were both dead, but she was still trying to hold the bowl of water level between the two of them.

Wu Li, Qinqin and the son-in-law came home from work, and brought Maomao back. Now they felt elated and amazed by the mess. Elated because Mother had really made up her mind to have a clear-out, and amazed there was so much old rubbish in the house. They could see that the job was not going to be easy.

Wu Li showed his concern: "My dear, you must be tired."

"Yes, Wu Li," she sighed, "I feel as if I've been winding up my own affairs."

"Hey, you can't talk like that. You should say you are taking leave of the past with a smile on your face."

"I can't raise a smile."

"Then wipe away your tears and take leave of the past anyhow. It's less dramatic, but that's how things are."

"Yes, I've wiped away the tears, but how long will this leave-taking last? Look, I've been at it all day and I haven't even scratched the surface."

Wu Li declaimed lines by Li Houzhu, the tenth-century poet.

Still drawn by severed ties,
Still tangled up in threads now ordered,
This is the sorrow of separation....

"Of course," he went on to explain, "the poet's imprisonment, the destruction of his family and the national crisis at that time are in no way comparable to ours. We and the country are flourishing. But the sentiment is appropriate, don't you think, Manli?"

Lee Manli rolled her eyes. She was irritated by his lecturing, his Rightist's fear of what other people might think.

Her son-in-law had a plan. "Mother, how about this. You have a rest and sit down, let us do the work. We'll take things out for you to decide on. We'll put the ones you want to keep on the left and the ones you want to throw out on the right. In two hours I guarantee we'll have the whole lot sorted out. When it comes to choosing what has to go to the recycling centre and what to sell you needn't concern yourself, I can deal with the outside world."

Lee Manli thought this was a good plan—otherwise when would she ever get done? "All right, let's make something to eat and then we'll set to work. Come on, let me hold Maomao." Qinqin passed the child to her grandmother who gave her a big hug. Maomao put her little hands round Lee Manli's neck and pursed her lips to kiss her on the cheek. Ah, that was better. Lee Manli relaxed and thought how much nicer it was to hold her granddaughter than to clear out all those damned things.

After supper they began working. The son-in-law placed two stools in the middle of the room for his

parents-in-law to sit on, while he and Qinqin squatted on the floor.

Wu Li lit a cigarette, full of high spirits as he sat
by Lee Manli's side. They were like judges at a joint
hearing—although this was a court with a difference.
Lee Manli gave Wu Li a shove and said, "Get away,
you're just in the way here. You'll drop ash over
everything and ruin it all." Just as well, Wu Li had no
desire to listen to his wife's ramblings. Even less did
he want to hear about her sufferings.

The son-in-law was a bright character. He had a
few tricks up his sleeve, like putting the most useless
things out first, so Lee Manli could give an immediate
verdict of "Out, out, out!" Old people are creatures
of habit, and he hoped the laws of inertia would then
work in his favour.

He took out a pair of plastic shoes, now gone hard.
"Out," said Lee Manli. Next came a pair of shorts.
"Out," again.

But almost immediately, Qinqin began stirring up
trouble. She'd grown up hearing tales of all the
marvellous things the family had owned. Take that fox
fur jacket which Auntie Shasha had mentioned just the
other day. Or a pair of white leather shoes, worth three
sacks of rice many years ago. "Ma, you know that fox
fur jacket, I've never seen it, only heard about it."

"Ah, it's just like all of us, it looks terrible now,
Son, take it out, it's right behind you."

Her son-in-law turned round but could not see a
fur jacket.

"There, by your hand, with the silk top." Lee
Manli pointed at something halfway between an overcoat and a padded jacket. Son-in-law picked it up and
passed it to her, noticing it felt a bit heavy.

Qinqin was terribly disappointed. "You mean that
one! But I've seen you airing that jacket!"

"Don't look at the outside, look at the inside."

Lee Manli put the jacket on her knees, opened it up and turned it inside out. The inside was lined, and she turned the lining over to disclose a hint of red fox fur. ''Well? Real fox—you can't buy it now, and even if you could you wouldn't be able to afford it. The best fur is mink, but it's reared on farms whereas fox is hard to farm, foxes are so slippery. All the smart set in the 1920s used to wear fox — starlets, socialites and rich ladies. And they used to drape fox stoles around their necks. Sun Yatsen's wife Song Qingling had one, I've seen the photo.

''I was just 18 when I had this fox fur. Second Uncle gave it to me for my birthday. He was rich. It was a really lovely style, better than what you see today. Last year on TV they had a fur coat fashion show, but the coats were all man-made from chemical fibres.''

Her son-in-law glared at Qinqin, thinking all these digressions were her fault. If she hadn't started in on this, they could have thrown out five things by now. Qinqin wasn't interested in all the history either. She'd heard it at least three times before, all about what a lovely coat it was. But here before her was a horrible fur-lined jacket like shepherds wear.

Lee Manli understood her daughter's feelings from the look in her eyes. She spoke more quietly of things she'd not mentioned before... ''It is a shame such a fine coat hasn't survived in its original shape. After Liberation I couldn't wear it any more. We'd had a revolution, and we all wore great coats of rough cloth and caps. If I didn't wear those things people would have started raking over the past, calling me an aristocratic young lady. They'd have said I wasn't ideologically reformed. I was so frightened I put the coat away in a chest and didn't even dare take it out for airing. It must have been, yes, 19...59, when your father was sent to the State farm for reform through labour. The farm was at a lakeside, absolutely terrible in winter, just like the place they sent us to afterwards by the sea.''

Qinqin shook her head. She knew that tone of voice.

"At first he was heaving rocks around, but then he got a better job assignment, as a night watchman guarding the granary, the haystacks and the winter vegetable stores. The peasants were starving to death then, so they used to come to steal from the State farm. The farm guards were afraid to arrest them because they all had carrying-poles, and in any case if you caught them and locked them up you had to feed them. So they got people like your father to keep watch at night. They were conscientious, responsible, and wouldn't take risks. When they saw people stealing things they didn't run to catch them, they spoke nicely, 'Take pity on us, we're all here for reform through labour. If you steal this, we'll have nothing to live on!' Peasants are good people, so they might turn around and go home. Your father's job never changed after that—all night out in the cold, walking around in the ice and snow, afraid to stand still in case he froze to death. I used to go down to see him twice a month, and it cut me to the quick to see him like that, but what could I do? It looked as if he was going to freeze to death by that lake.

"When I got back home, I took out my scissors and forced myself to cut the coat up to make him a fur-lined jacket. I used old cloth for the covering, new would have been too showy, and the lining was covered, so you couldn't see the fur. Labour reform campers couldn't wear fur jackets—that's what landlords used to wear. Your father wore this jacket all that time by the lake, then later all that terrible time we spent by the sea. Even last year he remembered it. Said it had saved his life.''

The son-in-law had changed his mind. "Look, we'll keep the jacket, okay?"

Lee Manli stared blankly for a while, then flared up as if Wu Li might be the family's unlucky spirit. "No, throw it out! He won't wear it in any case. He's so determined to change with the times, he even complains about wearing his woollen coat—wants to buy a parka. I say he's forgetting himself!" She flung the jacket at Qinqin. Of course, she knew none of the other professors would be seen wearing something like this either—they all wanted to wear those quilted ski jackets with what looked like inflated packs on their backs.

"You know, if things had been different, Qinqin, that coat would have been perfect for you."

Qinqin smiled wryly. Her husband quickly pulled out a nylon shirt. He wanted to move on.

Lee Manli clapped hands. "Put that down. First get out the white leather shoes. Look, they're under that basket." Lee Manli wanted to cheer the girl up by giving her something nice. Qinqin smiled. Naturally, after the fur coat came the white leather shoes. If they'd been worth three sacks of rice in those days they must be pretty special. The price of leather had gone up lately, but you couldn't imagine shoes costing as much as three sacks of rice.

The son-in-law was surprised by the shoes he pulled out. The white leather had yellowed a little, but the style was very nice, with good quality workmanship and materials. They were summer sandals, open-toed with sling backs, but the fronts were not so open that you couldn't wear them in spring and autumn too—and they were high-heeled.

Lee Manli took the shoes from her son-in-law and held them back to back. She knocked them together a couple of times. "Well, listen to that! Leather high-heels have a sound of their own—quite jaunty. It shouldn't sound like a hammer hitting stone, more like the clicking of mahjong pieces. These shoes make a good noise—hollow, not solid. Try them and see, they feel like gloves when you hold them.''

Lee Manli handed the shoes to Qinqin and pointed out the elasticated linings.

''Unlike other shoes which rub about where they're too big and pinch where they're too small, shoes like these are never too tight or too loose, they fit the whole foot. Try them on and see. Since your sister isn't here, I'll give them to you.''

Qinqin lost no time in pulling off her shoes and putting on the sandals. They were the right size, light springy and comfortable. She couldn't help herself, she just had to jump. Pop! The shoes burst open. The leather had perished. Qinqin stared. Her husband laughed.

''Wearing them is one thing,'' said Lee Manli, hurt. ''But what did you have to jump for? There was nothing wrong with those shoes, but when you put them on look what you did!''

Qinqin was unconvinced. ''Stop moaning, if I hadn't jumped I'd certainly have made a fool of myself in town and had to walk home barefoot. All this old stuff of yours is only good for looking at, you can't use it.''

Her husband couldn't suppress his smiles. ''Mother, you can't blame her! Leather isn't as strong as iron, how can it withstand forty years of storage? Even iron would be a pile of rust by now, you know!''

Lee Manli flared up. ''All right, my stuff is all worthless, not fit for the likes of you! Throw it out! Out! Out!''

7

At last the things were divided up into ''keeps'' and

"discards". In the end, most of it had to go. There were four baskets for the waste centre and three large bundles of clothes for secondhand shop. For the time being they would hold on to the quilt lining, since their son-in-law said it could be used for a sofa base, so that the old lady could make her contribution to the world of the future. The chain would go on and nothing would perish.

"All right then," said Lee Manli, "what's the point of keeping things that the children don't even want? Let's sell the fur-lined jacket and buy a heater for Wu Li. The object changes its form but keeps people warm just the same. Let's sell the two rabbit hats and buy an electronic game for Maomao, or one of those remote-control boats that turn around automatically when they bump into something. They're quite expensive, aren't they? Never mind, put the two dresses in too. It's all for the child."

They fixed on a Sunday afternoon and Lee Manli set out with her daughter and son-in-law to sell the bundles. Wu Li advised her to let the children go by themselves. "You've been worn out lately, stay here and take it easy."

Lee Manli disagreed. "What? How could I do that? They only know about buying new stuff, they don't know anything about selling to a secondhand shop. And also...these things are going away and I'd like to see them off." Lee Manli was a little depressed. Wu Li soon changed his tune. "All right, smile as you take leave of the past!"

The son-in-law and Qinqin were in high spirits. They pushed the bicycle along with two bundles tied on either side of the back wheel. Another parcel went on top of the luggage rack.

Lee Manli led the way. Like an old horse on a familiar route, she knew all about where the second-hand shops were. At first, Lee Manli hadn't really

known these things. As a stylish young woman, she
wouldn't have wasted a glance on secondhand goods.
But then in the 50s, when she was setting up home
and starting work, she was always on the lookout for
a good buy. Wu Li had an artistic bent. He found new
things vulgar and boring, less refined than the old, so
he was always dragging Lee Manli off to putter around
the secondhand shops. Wu Li was not terribly
disciplined about what he bought. The salesmen were
good talkers and he was frequently taken for a ride.
There was the metal bed, then the glass-fronted cupboard in the sitting room, so big it would be a real
headache to get rid of.

There used to be lots of secondhand shops. In the
50s they sold old wooden furniture, bowls and curios.
In the 60s, it was watches and cameras. The 70s was
the decade of confiscated property, and then there
were heated arguments in the shops. Into the 80s, and
for a while these shops disappeared completely. Just
recently they had reappeared in a new guise, selling
jeans, nylon shirts, odd makes of cassette recorders,
good electric fans, and washing machines. They had
changed from Chinese goods to foreign and had abandoned the old in favour of the new. Lee Manli led the
young couple for quite a way, without passing a single
shop which bought used goods. After much trouble,
they found one, but the salesman shook his head when
he saw their bundles. He told them he didn't take old
clothes, but if they had any old four-speaker cassette
recorders, he would think about it. Lee Manli was wide-
eyed with astonishment. "My cassette recorder only
has two speakers and we bought it new last year."

Lee Manli went to and fro passing plenty of shops.
They were all the same, selling foreign goods. But the
foreign goods weren't much, not one pair of shoes like
her white sandals, not one fur coat. All they did was
deceive the fashion conscious. Every doorway was

called some company or other, but the names were
patently false. A company looked like that? And they
had loudspeakers on the counters blasting out music
that made your ears ring! Lee Manli began to get cross.
If they wanted to make money, they shouldn't try to
make people deaf. So this was modernization, things
laid out on mats! In the old days stall-holders had
attracted customers by playing on the trumpet. Qinqin and her husband trailed along behind, craning to
look at the foreign goods.

Lee Manli snapped, "Hurry up. Let's go, I
remember there was a shop behind here, but I don't
know if it's still here...Qinqin, I'm telling you these
things are no good, if you want a western dress, have
one made, don't get them from those 'companies.'
They're all factory-made and people will laugh at you.
For shoes you should go for custom-made too. I know
the shoe factory boss, his brother was at school with
me."

Qinqin didn't know what to say. She thought,
"What about the shoes of mine you wore to go dancing? They were bought from this company!"

The shop in the back street was still there. It had
been a pawnshop with an entrance three room-widths
wide and box-shaped shelving. It was still imposing.
The shelving was piled high with old clothes and there
were clothes hanging everywhere in the rest of the
shop too. But there were no customers, only one old
and one young salesman sitting chatting behind the
counter. The old man looked like a court official and
the youngster sported a little beard.

Lee Manli directed Qinqin and her son-in-law to
put the bundles on the counter. The two assistants
didn't move; they saw all right, but they looked as if
this had nothing to do with them.

Lee Manli took the initiative. "Comrade, we want
to sell some things."

The beard sat motionless, calling in their direction, "What have you got?"

"Old clothes."

"More old clothes! Madam, I'd better tell you straight, there's no demand for old clothes just now, we can't sell them."

"Take a look, some old clothes are worth a bit and some aren't, they're not all the same."

The beard realised that this was an educated lady; she certainly looked out of the ordinary. So he decided he might as well take a look. He walked over to the counter, arms folded, and pointed at the bundles. "Open them up."

The bundles were opened and the things were spread out on the counter, one by one, in a long row. Lee Manli took a last look, finding it terribly painful. A lifetime's experience spread out in front of this cold, arrogant bearded young man, ready for him to judge its price.

The beard cast a professional eye on the things, walked back and forth and opened in an aggrieved voice, "Madam, I don't want to offend you, but most of this is rubbish. If we were in America it would not only be unsellable, you'd have to pay to have it taken away".

He sounded as smug as if he'd been to America himself. Throwing in a little reference to life overseas was designed to take the wind out of the old lady's sails. "Of course, we're not at that point yet, some of this stuff here will make a little, but what are you bringing this in for? It's only good for rags and dusters, you should take it to the waste centre." The beard picked up the cadre jacket and shook it, looking at Qinqin as if he wanted her to join in the joke.

Lee Manli couldn't see what was so funny. Jackets like this had been in vogue for 30 years. Everybody used to wear them. You got married in a new one and worked in it when it was old. Why should it be made into dusters? "Sell it to a peasant, there's even a piece of cloth for the collar in the pocket."

The beard started to laugh. "Peasants! You think peasants still wear rags? Times have changed, they want fine materials...you know who the western fashions are sold to now? Most of them are bought by peasants. Don't think about selling that jacket, they wouldn't have it if you gave it to them. They'd think you were looking down on them, so please take it back, we don't accept things like that."

"What about fur?" Lee Manli played her trump card. So he thought he could patronize her!

"Fur? What fur?" The beard was not impressed.

"You haven't looked properly!" Lee Manli pulled out the family heirloom and handed it to him.

He stroked his beard, blew his nose and leaned backward as if he'd smelled something disgusting. "This...What is this? Did you find it on a rubbish heap?"

"What?" Lee Manli was really insulted. "Rubbish heap did you say? Where do you mean, in America or in China? In America they protect wildlife, you won't find fur on rubbish heaps. My boy, if you want to do business in China you shouldn't talk about rubbish heaps."

The beard was at a loss. All he could do was point at the fur jacket and say, "Look at it! What can I say?"

"Of course the outside is old, but selling fur isn't about the outside. The outside and the lining are worth nothing." Lee Manli turned the jacket over to show the lining and spread her hands over the fox fur. She felt its warmth and thought about the bitter wind still blowing by the lake and the sea. "Look. Lovely fur."

The beard knew all about fur, his master had taught him. First he stroked it against the grain to see if it was autumn or winter fox. Winter fox has coarse hairs while autumn fox is fine-haired. And no one shoots fox in summer since that's when they shed their coats. Then he checked the pelt to see if it had perished or hardened, by holding it between two fingers and rubbing. Next, he held the fur up against the light to examine the tips. If they were worn down, it was a sign of heavy wear or rubbing against a sweater.

The beard was busy for a few moments. He thought the jacket was all right, and easy to sell because the peasants had faith in fur. They thought it protected you from the wind, kept you warm and was quality stuff, since all the landlords used to wear silk in summer and fur in winter. The beard wanted to do a deal, but one look at Lee Manli told him that she wanted to put the price up, so he had to take her down a peg or two.

"Huh, this is nothing special, it's old and beginning to perish. No one wants these fur jackets nowadays, everyone wants quilted or synthetic-cotton mix, they're so light and cheap. Old fur jackets like this... we could take it and sell it as winter shoe linings."

He really was letting his tongue run away with him. Lee Manli's expression changed. Shoe linings! A good fur jacket to be used for shoe linings, so that people could trample on it! It had been trampled on all that time and now it would be trampled on some more....

The beard picked up the two rabbit hats and put the two dresses to one side. He played with the hats, pretending they were puppets. Qinqin was beginning to get angry. This man was really awful. "Hey, we've come to sell, not to bring toys for you! If you want to play with them then buy them, and the dresses too, it's all stuff my sister and I wore when we were little."

He snapped back, "So what if you two wore them, there's nothing but one-child families now. They get hats from one auntie, dresses from another, and they can't wear everything they've got. No one wants secondhand children's clothes. People think they've got germs and they'll spread infection.'' The beard pushed the hats and dresses back at Qinqin. "Here, take them back please.''

Lee Manli screamed at him. "Right. We'll take it all back. Qinqin, Son, pack it all up, we're not selling, never! I'll take them to hell with me first!''

The old shopkeeper saw that the bargaining was becoming heated and came across smooth things over. "Now now, don't get angry. We can't let our feelings affect business. Let's talk, Madam, we'll give you a price.''

"No price. I don't care how much you offer, I'm not selling. Let's go.'' Lee Manli was white with rage, her voice trembling. Youth, hardship, wifely affection, mother's tears—the bloodstains on the dresses...a bitter past reduced to a pile of rubbish, with germs to boot!

Lee Manli walked out without a backward glance. The old man turned to the youngster, "Well, you blew that one. You went too far.''

The beard felt uneasy. "I did what you taught me, didn't I? When you see an old lady coming in to sell, first tell her all the stuff is rubbish that no one wants, otherwise she'll think her junk is like the crown jewels and hold out for a very high price.''

The old man tutted. "Huh, you're not as smart as you think. Old ladies come in different shapes and sizes. This one knew about wildlife protection in America, you can see she's not just run of the mill. She's not selling for the money. Perhaps her house is full of stuff and she's having a clear-out. You have to take a different line with people like her. Madam, your things are really interesting, I can see your family has had a good life. You're doing so well now, your needs have changed. No one appreciates old things these days. This fur jacket is not bad at all, but no one wants to wear them now, we can't sell them. If we pay out to buy it from you we have no guarantee when it will be sold. It's all I can do to pay off the interest at the bank. Look how sweet these rabbit hats are. Little girls look cute in them, but children today are so spoiled, no one buys secondhand for them. If we buy them for 20 cents, of course it's not a proper price, but it's a joke to talk of a price for things like that, it's not even enough for half a pack of cigarettes—we could put them in the display case and perhaps a nursery school would buy them, for when they put on shows....Then you play about with the rabbit hats and bow to the old lady, doing the one about waiting for mother to come home... I guarantee you'd have her eating out of your hand. Better still, tell her which nursery would buy them, and she'd hand them over for nothing!''

The beard rolled his eyes. It was a good line, but what a lot of bother. ''Master, I think you should let me leave. I'd do better with a stall for imported goods on the main street. Before you know it I'd be making three times what I'm getting here. The stalls make 5 or 6 yuan a day, that's 150 yuan a month...'' He was having a sulking fit.

8

Lee Manli led her daughter and son-in-law home, bearing the three bundles. They walked fast and they didn't utter a sound. Qinqin and her husband followed closely, not daring to talk, nor to look at the foreign goods in the shops. Mother was furious. If you scratched her she'd probably explode. Fortunately they bumped into the old man who had worked for the foreign company, so Lee Manli had an outlet for her fury. Otherwise, Wu Li would have had to take the full force. The old man stood up when he saw Lee Manli. "Manli, why are you carrying these three bundles back and forth?" He was getting familiar, calling her "Mary".

Lee Manli sighed. "Don't talk about it. They're all ganging up on me, wanting to modernize the house. We don't have room for all this stuff, so we thought we'd sell it, but we didn't sell anything, just had a blazing row."

Qinqin pulled her husband's arm as if so say "Let's get back home, if we stay here she'll start in on us." At the same time they would tell Father and get him prepared.

The old man laughed nervously. "Did they say it's not worth anything?"

"Yes, they went on and on about how it was all worthless, they're really insulting. It's America this and America that—what do they know about America?"

"Oh, I see, always talking about how things are abroad, but of course the comparison stops before it reaches themselves—they didn't say anything about what we have in common with foreigners! Manli, don't be angry, they're pathetic, these people. They think they've got foreign style but they don't know the first thing about it. Eventually they turn into real idiots with no style and no standards."

"You're right. When I see these teddy boys on the street, not one of them looks right." Lee Manli didn't linger to talk with the old man. She was afraid he might start speaking pidgin English again and make her break out in a sweat.

She climbed slowly upstairs to the third floor. Only now did she feel tired, and her legs felt wobbly. She pushed the door open and went in to find Wu Li and the others sitting nervously. Even Maomao was sitting up straight in her little chair.

Lee Manli was puzzled. "What's the matter with

you? What are you planning now?''

Wu Li said. ''Nothing. We're waiting for you to throw a fit.''

Lee Manli sat down on the high stool and her son-in-law instantly brought her a cup of tea. Lee Manli smiled. ''No need to butter me up and pretend that you have come round. You know I don't throw fits just like that. I think I understand now. All your plans were about fashion and following the tide, but none of it was properly thought out. Putting up vinyl wallpaper, laying linoleum, all these chemical products, all poisonous! Those sofas with artificial leather get sticky, with foam plastic over a wooden frame. They say it's French style but the French wouldn't have it! If we're going to do something, let's do it properly, not like someone wearing a baggy, ill-fitting suit. Yes, we'll put up shelving and lay carpets but not artificial fabric carpets because they give off static electricity. Have you seen a real leather sofa, a big one...?'' Lee Manli waved her hand, describing a sofa as big as a third of the sitting room. Then she talked about the interior design she had learned years ago from her domestic science classes and seen in the homes of her American headmistress, French professor and the British missionaries. Her son-in-law was dumbstruck. ''When could we ever have that kind of stuff?'' Lee Manli said: ''Don't worry, we'll do it gradually. You can wait. I can't, but never mind, I'll not be disappointed. Qin-qin, Son, let's get moving and put all this stuff back where it came from. Wu Li, you can help too. There are newspapers all over the place in your study, tidy them up!''

Clearing out is really hard, but putting things back is easy. You know where everything goes. The son-in-law was a good worker, he put things back more neatly than they had been before. Lee Manli had a good sweep-out, cleaning away the dust and gathering up old papers and bottles.

In under two hours the house was back to its original state. Everyone thought it looked less chaotic and run-down than before, and it was all neat and tidy. This feeling arose from the chaos of the past few days when things had been spread all over the place and there was nowhere to stand, nowhere to sit and it was even difficult to find somewhere to sleep. Now everything was packed away and it looked neat enough.

Lee Manli was quite satisfied. "Wu Li, look, this is a fine way to live, isn't it? Why give ourselves all that trouble? If we made our home look like Shasha's I would feel depressed, as if I was living in someone else's home, far from the things I'm used to. Things are people—the traces people leave. People who walk along a beach will always leave footprints, don't you agree?"

"Even though after the tide turns they vanish without trace, before the tide comes in you must be able to see something. Otherwise you feel as if you've never walked along the beach, it's been empty all along."

"Ah, Wu Li, you are a good sort, you do understand me." Lee Manli patted Wu Li's hand.

He in turn patted hers. "Yes, yes."

Their son-in-law smiled. The old couple were really affectionate. Lee Manli turned round. "What are you smiling at? Why aren't you off to the waste recycling centre with the things we don't need?"

He was surprised—was there anything they didn't need? Lee Manli pointed to a corner. "Look, over there!"

The old bucket's moment had come. All it was good for was tripping over. It was now full of old bottles and glass, including the empty iodine bottle with no lid.

He took the bucket to the waste centre and got seven cents for it.

1985

World of Dreams, a Valediction

I HAVE BEEN to many places but the world of my dreams will always be the narrow lanes of Suzhou. The myriad times I have walked here, it is as if my youth had flowed away through these lanes, carving a deep gully in my mind, full of enduring impressions.

Thirty-eight years ago, clad in a long, blue cotton gown and riding in a wooden sailboat, I touched at a lane leading into Suzhou. It was paved with long flagstones underneath which water gurgled. It was known as a thoroughfare but it was impossible for two rickshaws to pass each other; on either side there were low one-storied houses, and bamboo poles used for drying washing stretched from the eaves on one side to those on the other. Above the eaves were square brick blocks with holes in them which looked just like archers' slits in an ancient wall.

At the corner my view changed. On each side there were now higher buildings with black tiles, crimson railings and white walls. Along the lane ran a long wooden gallery, in the eaves of which were set painted boards, each carved differently, some with squirrels and grapes and some with the legendary Eight Immortals who crossed the ocean. Both the crimson railings and the painted carving had turned black or yellowed with age. Bamboo drying-poles were slotted into the carved boards and bamboo blinds hung down, concealing windows. It seemed to me that I had known something similar to this in an old painting or novel.

Now shops appeared with their living quarters above. The majority were tobacconists, groceries and the kind of teahouse that also sold boiled water. The teahouses were the busiest and noisiest of all, for there were always men there, left hands on the table-tops, right feet sticking up on the long benches, holding up those shiny dark brown earthenware teacups and pouring dark brown water down their gullets. People in Suzhou call this phenomenon *flesh covering water*, whereas the evening bath is known as *water covering flesh*. The tea-drinkers all naturally wished to engage in elevated discussions, but in the overall buzz it was impossible to distinguish what was being said. Only the sound of vendors' cries stood out clearly. These were girls with baskets peddling melon seeds, sweets and cigarettes. And then there were the blind men in dark glasses playing the *erhu,* huskily singing. I say ''singing'', but it came closer to weeping than anything. The narrow lane unrolled before me like a scroll-painting.

I stepped through the painting and climbed up into a small building. In fact it had two parts, a building at the front and one behind, with wings on either side connecting them to form a square. The courtyard was small and deep as a well, with only two jars below for collecting rain water. If you leaned out and looked down from the front building you could see people going back and forth, a bustling market-place; leaning out of the window in the back building you could see the big river flowing.

On the river sculls creaked, the sky was bright, waves rippled and the wind and sun seemed quite unhurried. On either bank were people's homes, each house having a long window by the river and a stone jetty. The jetties were built in a marvellous way, simple yet ingenious, using rows of many long stone slabs.

One end of each slab stood out in space while the other end was embedded into the long stone wall along the river's edge. The slabs advanced in ranks toward the riverbed, like stone ladders hanging from the back door of each household. Women washing vegetables or rice would ascend or descend the ladder, appearing and disappearing in the shimmering light and the cloud shadows.

Small single-oared boats would move slowly out into the current, letting it take them where it would, their holds filled with fish, shrimp, vegetables or melons. At a gesture from a window that someone wished to buy something, a little boat would shoot over like an arrow. When the transaction was completed, a basket with money in it would be lowered, filled with the goods bought and hauled back up again. Then the window would be shut with a creak and the little boat slowly followed the waves once more.

Opposite the back building was a fork in the river spanned by a very high arched bridge, the balustrade of which was a stone wall which curved like a melon seed. When people crossed the bridge only their heads would appear above it. The bridge itself was exceptionally broad, having within its arch on one side an old Buddhist temple where one could still make out the word "Namah..." on the yellow wall. On moonlit nights there was poetry in the swift flowing current within the arch, that sheet of shimmering silver carrying the moon's reflection, while the temple bells spilled out after the waves of light. On the stone jetties suspended between moonlight and waves, women were washing and chanting—"On a moonlit night in Chang'an/Comes the sound of pounding linen."

From the front building I could see the brightly-lit land with rickshaws rattling past, *wonton* sellers banging bamboo clappers and sellers of spiced tea-flavoured eggs with their small stoves in baskets. At night the teahouses became resorts of storytellers, and then the strumming of *pipas* was accompanied by the soft lilt of the Suzhou dialect. Suzhou-style storytelling and ballad-singing were high-pitched and beautiful, while the vending cry of those selling spiced tea-flavoured eggs was filled with sadness. I had not realized that a small winding lane could change so infinitely, be so different within and without, with its rows of houses dividing land and water, silence and movement. On one side was the world with all its joys, sorrows and hubbub. On the other side were waves and moonlight, and also that low, reverberating sound of an evening Buddhist bell, making it seem as if the world could be forgotten.

I once lived in another kind of lane with high surrounding walls on either side, so high that one had to crane to see the top; no pink apricot could reach over these walls, and only the spring vines were able to climb up and hang down in tassels from the top. The heavy main gates were always tightly shut so that not a morsel of intimacy could squeeze out. Two mounting blocks like strange beasts lay on either side of the gates, glowering at the screen wall opposite, sombre and fierce. The screen wall had a carved stone border and a plain centre. There were few passers-by in lanes such as these, but occasionally a flower-seller would utter the long drawn-out cry: "Who will buy my white orchids?" For the rest, there were only the sparrows cheeping and chattering on the gatehouse and magpies hopping on and off the eaved walls.

You could imagine a princeling or high official still riding through the lane on his fine steed. The black lacquer gate with brass knockers would creak open while four servants waiting within lept up to help the Great One step onto the block and slide off his horse, which would then be led off and tied by the side of the screen wall. Or you could almost hear the horns and firecrackers, see lanterns and decorations hung by the gate, and a bridal sedan-chair being carried through the lane. And after a few years a memorial to a widow's fidelity or chastity would be raised where that bridal chair had passed. In the yellowing pages of local records it would perhaps be possible to find the name of that upright woman, but her memorial would have fallen, leaving only two large square stone pillars standing there.

I would brush past those stone pillars as I entered the lane and stopped before one of the doors. A bamboo plaque was nailed to it, and the door was never closed. In the entry way an old tailor-cum-watchman would do his business, watching the entrance in return for a reduced rent. Or there would be an old woman in glasses, half-blind and bent over an embroidery frame full of dragons, phoenixes and bright butterflies. She would be one of those seamstresses who spent their whole lives making bridal clothes for others. Even though her eyesight was going, when wearing glasses she could still split the coloured silken threads into eight strands. Down entryways of this kind there were often six-leaved doors, some cream-coloured, some with gold-leaf on a dark-blue ground, but here the gold had turned black in uneven blotches. Only the first panel of the door would be open so that it was impossible to see at one glance what went on within. I might slide inside but still could not see very much on entering, coming instead into a dark, dim world, a seemingly endless corridor. There were many arched entrances and small doorways on either side of this corridor, but each was shut tight, with only a faint light filtering out from windows dispersed far between. Peering on tiptoe through the windows I could see a row of halls down the left side, all dark and gloomy, while on the right side there was a series of courtyards with rockeries, tall bamboos and small buildings with crimson balustrades—a green and shady place. This had once been the home of a wealthy family in which each wife, concubine, son or daughter had private quarters with a garden attached.

I once spent half a year living in a garden like this, almost one-third of an acre in size. It could be described as either a courtyard or a flower garden, yet this confined space had all the characteristics of a park, with an artificial hill made from rocks brought there from a nearby lake. On top of the hill was a cobblestone path which twisted and turned, dipping and rising abruptly, one moment passing through a cavern, the next crossing a small bridge over a gully—the gully was just a chink and the bridge was like a toy model. If you were to follow the curves of the path the distance would be surprising, but going straight to the top of the hill was only a matter of four to five paces. The hilltop was masked by towering old trees through which the sunlight shone down in rays of gold while around them dappled spots of light and shade flickered. There was a lotus pond at the foot of the hill with a crooked stone bridge across it. The crooked bridge was connected to the gallery, which in turn was connected to the waterside pavilions then curved back to join up with the small building which served as my living quarters. On a rainy day you could stroll along the gallery and watch the raindrops close-up on each layer of branches and leaves or watch the fine shrouding rain submerge all the buildings and pavilions in mist. If you sat in a pavilion for a brief rest you would see the pond slowly flooding until the little crooked bridge was buried beneath the water.

The garden was wild and unkempt; white guano spotted the ground and the caves were the haunts of foxes. Apart from birdsong, the most animated thing there was the lotus pond: there the plants grew luxuriantly, crowding the water-lilies up against the low embankment, and in early summer charming little tadpoles floated in the clear water within the rock crevices. The pointed tip of the lotus leaf seemed incomparably sharp, capable of poking up between other thickly growing aquatic plants and boring out onto the water's surface in the space of one night. Yet there were some which did not make it, for carp are very fond of soft, young lotus leaves. At night, the pond was very active, the croaking of frogs like drumbeats, now loud, now silent, and in the time of silence you could hear fish spouting. With a great whoosh a large fish would leap out of the water, startling the sleeping birds awake so that they twittered restlessly. Peace came again only when the croaking of the frogs rose once more. It was lonely, living in that high-walled, deeply receding courtyard with only books for company. I often sat on the artificial hill and read, becoming so completely immersed that ants would climb onto me. One mustn't crush that sort of ant, for they had a strange smell like powerful turpentine, making me think they had grown up feeding on the resin of the pine trees.

Among lanes I prefer a different sort, combining high walls, concealed courtyards and stone pillars with tobacconists, flatbread-makers and shops selling boiled water. Here a canal might run alongside, but the lane looks very different from those on the outskirts of the city. Here the houses press desperately close together on either bank, squeezing the canal so that it is no more than a narrow channel, a sight already familiar to the Tang dynasty poet:

> Little spare space there is in old palaces
> And many small bridges span the
> water channels.

Enter a lane such as this early on a summer morning. The mist would be lifting and at the bottom of the lane women would be drawing water from the public well, languidly pulling on the rope attached to the bucket as if they were still asleep, still clad in their voluminous striped pyjamas. Of course the place would really have awakened long before. The elderly retired men would already have gone off to the tea-gardens in the parks or to teahouses to practise shadow-boxing, drink tea and chat. Those too old to leave home would be puttering about the courtyards, tending their miniature landscape gardens or sitting blankly in rattan chairs, pouring cup after cup of strong tea down their throats. The housewives would already have whisked through their chores and left for the small, noisy food market with baskets on their arms. They would bustle into the narrow lane, discussing whether or not there were certain kinds of food available, if they were good or bad, cheap or expensive. It was only after the bell of the rubbish cart sounded that people returned from the market one by one, the morning struggle to buy food now over.

Not long after the food-buying brigade dispersed, activity would reach another peak. All those going off to work came crowding out almost at the same time, some leaving the lane to head eastwards, others entering it and going towards the west. Some with satchels were bouncing and full of energy, others carrying children stopped for the kids to wave goodbye to their grandmothers. The flash of bicycles and the ringing of their bells filled the air. The lane became an exhibition riding track through which insufficiently skilled females had no choice but to push their bikes. Like the peak of a wave, all settled back quietly after half an hour.

When those leaving for work or school had gone, the tea-drinkers and shadow-boxers began to return. Entering the lane, they were unhurried, their bearing calm and their eyes half-closed as if there were nothing to startle them here. For them the greatest joy was mar-

riage; the greatest sorrow, death; the greatest worry,
fire; and the thing most feared, the sound of guns. They
had experienced it all, and nothing confounded them.
Research these people's lives and you would go back
a century in time. Some had been famous actors, some
were uniquely skilled, some were topgrade workers
at the Hanyang Arsenal, makers of guns and cannon.
There were others whose histories were by no means
honourable but nevertheless fascinating, though you
would need a movie flashback to recognize that bent,
wizened and white-haired old lady as she who performed in *The Goddess Scatters Flowers*.

Summer is an outdoor time. After nightfall the stars
hang down low above the lanes and a wind comes
pouring in, brushing past the house doors. This wind,
with its powerful attraction, would draw out into the
open all life hidden within the tiny front yards and
receding courtyards. Small stools and rattan chairs
would be placed on either side of the byway and people would sit there to receive the benediction of the
cool breeze. In those houses with entrances off the
lanes, the common brick-floored area would serve for
taking the air. Water would be poured over the bricks
and families would congregate. Even the old and
bedridden would be carried out by sons and grandsons
to be greeted by their neighbours. Then all the secrets
of ordinary life could be ferreted out. Oil, salt,
firewood, rice, new daughters-in-law arriving and
daughters leaving home to get married—all became
topics of conversation.

Only the younger generation were more mobile,
young friends coming and going again in groups.
Perhaps one in a dress would stand apart beneath the
streetlamp, beckoning. A rattan chair would creak as
a boy moved to her side. The young are reluctant to
look back into the past, preferring to make more
demands on the future. Yet those who demanded the

most were not outside at all but facing their books, outlines or blueprints, sweating in their rooms, surrounded by the haze of mosquito coils.

Strangely enough, there are not so many people out this summer. The abominable television is the culprit, its popularity rising daily. Old and young alike are to be found indoors in dimly-lit rooms, everyone silent and staring straight ahead as an electric fan turns around and around. Now you can have cool air and be entertained at the same time, so no one wants to go outside. A more diverting sight now are the keen TV amateurs, youths with dishevelled hair and greasy clothes who carry out TVs lacking frames, set them down on the pavement and show off self-taught technical wizardry, providing free entertainment to those who are not yet able to afford a TV or do not wish to buy one. Their audience sits quietly, just as at an open-air film show in the countryside.

The day's movements in these narrow lanes are wound up by the young. At the quietest time lovers still come and go, their footsteps in close, rhythmic harmony. Then the streetlamps seem so bright, reflecting off the whitewashed walls and turning the moon a dark red shade. The footsteps halt, a key turns, the woman pushes open the door and enters. The man hesitates, turning to look back as he walks away. The closed door opens and the woman leans far out to wave again and again—this couple is filled with love. But that one—the man seems perplexed and stands to one side while the woman, piqued and mortified, leans against the stone pillars. Both seem stubbornly waiting for the moon to go down. Go home, young lady. It is cold and dewy outside and it is unwise to stay out too long. No use leaning on those stones pillars—they are just unfeeling objects....

Before a main thoroughfare you want to hurry; before a mountain you want to climb; before the sea

you want to sail away. And before these deeply
receding lanes? Well, then you stroll along, stroll past
those high walls, stroll over the broken cobblestones,
with your hand against the stone pillars to support you,
looking for art's realm, exploring life's stream, listening for history's echo…. Perhaps I have found
something small which, for the time being at least, is
recorded here. While it may not seem like much, do
not be impatient, but let me continue to stroll along….

1983